A DECEPTIVE APPEARANCE

By the same author

Sheep, Goats and Soap
The Wrong Impression
Mortal Ruin
Gothic Pursuit
Whistler in the Dark
The Gwen John Sculpture
The Godwin Sideboard
A Back Room in Somers Town

A
DECEPTIVE
APPEARANCE

John Malcolm

CHARLES SCRIBNER'S SONS
New York

Maxwell Macmillan International
New York   Oxford   Singapore   Sydney

First United States Edition 1992

Charles Scribner's Sons
Macmillan Publishing Company
866 Third Avenue
New York, NY 10022

Macmillan Publishing Company is part of the
Maxwell Communication Group of Companies.

Library of Congress Cataloging-in-Publication Data
Malcolm, John, 1936–
    A deceptive appearance/John Malcolm.—1st U.S. ed.
        p.   cm.
    ISBN 0-684-19508-9
    I. Title.
    PR6063.A362D45   1992   92-19954   CIP
    823'.914—dc20

Macmillan books are available at special discounts for bulk purchases for sales promotions, premiums, fund-raising, or educational use. For details, contact:

Special Sales Director
Macmillan Publishing Company
866 Third Avenue
New York, NY 10022

10   9   8   7   6   5   4   3   2   1

Printed in the United States of America

The details of Tissot prices on pages 107–8 and 110 are from *The Economics of Taste* by Gerald Reitlinger, published by Barrie and Rockliff (Barrie Books Ltd) London, 1961

CHAPTER 1

It was sometime during 1876, while he was living in England, that Tissot produced the characteristic part-maritime scene he called *A Passing Storm*. The painting is one of his many highly-detailed, almost obsessive portrayals of his mistress, Mrs Kathleen Newton, this time caught half-resting on an armchair in a room overlooking Ramsgate Harbour.

The result is attractive but disturbing. Through big windows, past a tangle of ships' rigging, you can identify jetties and boats under a stormy sky loaded with dark, ragged clouds that scud haphazardly across a patch of white, glaring sunlight. On the balcony outside, through an open French window, a fed-up-looking bloke in a blue jacket and straw boater is staring morosely inwards with his hands shoved into his pockets, well off-centre in a way which makes his exterior presence uncertain, almost incidental. Much closer, from the foreground inside the room, a highlighted Kitty Newton, in a frothy white and yellow gown, reclines alluringly but thoughtfully, her bright, eye-stopping image looking almost at you, the observer, with a distracted expression. Beside her, on a small table, a silver coffee service and cups stand neglected.

A Passing Storm: Tissot specialized in such moody scenes between lovers, juxtaposing the weather or some incidental detail to emphasize the atmosphere, the tone of the thing. The Ramsgate painting is a classic example of his ability to create tension and to set you wondering what the problem is, what the hell is going on; none of his paintings from Kitty Newton's poignantly-brief period is ever as straightforward as it first seems.

A Passing Storm: the comparison came to mind much later, when I thought back about the morning of my departure and the moment Sue emerged from the bedroom.

'So,' she said glancing reprovingly at the breakfast things left on the table, 'you're leaving, then?'

'Yes, I'm leaving,' I said. 'Then.'

She pulled a face at my pedantry and stared at me across the room. My bag was packed and my briefcase was loaded. I had my dark suit on, making me look appropriately sub-fusc. My raincoat was to hand nearby, thrown over the back of the sofa. Outside our long French windows were no ships, no tangled rigging, no harbour—just the trees of Onslow Gardens under a new grey sky—but above the fireplace a big marine painting by Clarkson Stanfield heaved sea-green billows and off-white spume beneath a battered nineteenth-century man-o'-war, clawing into the wind as though to try and inject an analogy of storm-tossed departure to our confrontation.

This superficial impact was misleading. My departure was determinedly calm, deliberately restrained, even though there was an atmosphere to contend with. The man-o'-war, I had recently established, was painted beating its way home into one of the Medway ports, not struggling out of it. There was no boater on my head. Even when you're dealing with the general run of painters, let alone Tissot, you have to watch out for these art-dramatical images; they can be very confusing to the untutored eye.

'Well, have a good trip,' Sue said, coming round the sofa to kiss me gently on the lips. 'Be a good boy, Tim.'

'I always am,' I said, kissing her back. 'I'll be home the weekend after next. You can count on it.'

She pulled a different face this time. 'I hope it doesn't last too long,' she said. 'It sounds as though it's a major project.'

'It is. But Paris is no further away than Manchester by plane. And you be good, too. Several ladies have told me that men in kilts can be very convincing. Not to mention stimulating.'

She raised her eyebrows, as though the notion of her, my wife, a curator at the Tate Gallery, could even contemplate not being good while visiting Edinburgh, to work on a reciprocal exhibition collaboration. As though the earnest, humorous members of the Scots Mafia, as the mob behind much of Britain's art museum establishment are known, would not appreciate and be attracted to her excellent figure, her blue eyes and wide mouth, the vivacity behind her professional exterior.

'I,' she said, looking at me full in the eyes, 'am not the one, on past record, who needs gentle advice on steering clear of trouble. Trouble of any kind. I'm sure you know what I mean.'

I gave her a tolerant smile. 'Sue, there is no need, absolutely no need, to start bringing up any of that. What I am dealing with is a straightforward business matter. A matter of commerce and trade. Banking and investment. Nothing more this time.'

She nodded thoughtfully. 'That's true. So I suppose I shouldn't be worried.'

'No, you shouldn't.'

She sighed. 'I'll miss you, Tim. Phone often, won't you?'

'Of course I will. I always do.'

She nodded again. 'All the same.'

'I still think you should come over to Paris for a weekend,' I said hopefully. 'It would be a good break. We could do a lot of things together.'

This was what might be considered the immediate source of passing, ragged clouds. It was unreasonable of me; Sue was undoubtedly busy. But I hadn't been to France for a while and I wanted her to come with me for at least part of the time so that we could enjoy a break together. Now that my departure was inevitable I hoped to make the best of it and a weekend away, at the least, surely wouldn't upset her work?

She shook her head briskly. 'No chance, I'm afraid. I'm much too busy. Much too busy. The exhibition season is absolutely packed this year. We're trying to get back on terms with the Royal Academy and the National. Later on, perhaps. It would be great to visit the Jeu de Paume again; I'd love that. If you do have to go back from time to time we'll go together, later. But I've much too much to do right now.'

'All right.' I said resignedly. 'I'm sorry, though.'

'So am I.'

'Don't say I didn't invite you.'

'Now, Tim. Let's not start that again.'

I pulled a face this time, but it was while I was picking up my raincoat and bags. I gave her a quick grin and went downstairs to have a sniff of Onslow Gardens' version of damp London air before heading in the direction of Heathrow.

It gave me a pang to leave Sue but business is business; at that moment thousands and thousands of men all over Europe were doing exactly the same thing and, in a way, it was good for me to have a new challenge. After all, a business in which a new manager could describe a prestige shop in the Rue Saint-Honoré as *une sorte de crypte lugubre* where its rare clients were said to enter feeling the respect and the vague fear that one evinces *en visitant un mausolée* had the smack of a promising business. A business, that is, promising much amusement to a man like me.

I started to brighten up, shaking off the dank greyness induced by another of life's departures as I accelerated out towards the airport. *Cryptes lugubres* are getting fewer and further between these days; you have to get inside them while you can.

CHAPTER 2

Sometimes the feeling that economic existence proceeds in circles becomes overpowering. Years ago, before I joined White's Bank, I worked in business consultancy, sorting out the tortuous tangles that are endemic, like loops in garden hosepipes, to life's commercial and industrial activities. It was as a result of this consulting work that Jeremy White originally asked me to help him, but that aspect had sort of slipped away, as the past so often does, into half-forgotten events at the outset of things, part of the frozen memory-stills of yesteryear. When, one morning a couple of days before my departure, he rang to ask me to pop up for a coffee, that past could not have been further from my mind. Indeed, when I saw that he had another visitor—Peter Lewis, the board vice-chairman—with him, my curiosity contained no element of past thinking about it. I didn't imagine that they were looking at me from an old angle.

'Things are looking bloody awful,' Jeremy said to me, after we'd done the greetings all round in what appeared to be a perfectly normal, sociable sort of way. 'Absolutely dreadful. The government have managed to do everything wrong. We're back to a high pound and high interest rates again. The country's into a terrible slump.'

'True, Jeremy.' I nodded sagely. Peter Lewis, who is a balding, shiny sort of man, nodded as well, looking at me gravely, as though seeking some sort of confirmation of these passing platitudes.

Jeremy waved an arm at the window. 'The art market's a shambles,' he said, as though it were seething about in Gracechurch Street outside. 'Everybody's cutting back. Rotten season, rotten. I'm awfully glad you and Geoffrey are agreed about the Fund.'

In this Jeremy was referring to White's Art Fund and to Geoffrey Price, our accountant, a man who regards the Art Fund with deep suspicion, believing that it is a sort of recreation set up by Jeremy and me to amuse ourselves with, rather than a sound investment activity. In this his suspicions have a measure of truth, but the Art Fund had been doing rather well until the slump in Impressionists knocked the hell out of everyone's confidence. There was nothing anyone could do but keep costs down and ride out the storm. Geoffrey and I were quite agreed on that.

I shrugged slightly, unsure of the reason Jeremy chose to discuss the Art Fund in front of Peter Lewis. 'It could be argued, Jeremy, that this should be a good time to buy. With the market so depressed, I mean.'

He snorted. 'Ha! You don't sound very convincing. We haven't seen the bottom yet. It's going to be some time before the signals go back to green again. Mark my words.'

I nodded cautiously. I didn't really agree but it wasn't the time to start arguing with Jeremy about the state of the art market. The art market, like everything else, is a question of opportunities, of playing against the run of things. The Fund had cash in hand which was earning good interest and a strike could be made if occasion arose. For the moment the art market needed watching, that was all. Besides, with Peter Lewis present, I wasn't going to go into detail; internal politics dictated caution.

'No, no, Tim, now is not the time for you to go coursing off after some muscular art hare, not at all.' Jeremy made a dismissive gesture which was somehow uncharacteristic. The chasing of muscular hares is something he often enjoys but then, in front of the board vice-chairman, his rhetoric was bound to be orthodox. 'We have much else to occupy our time. And our brain power.'

'Yes, Jeremy.' I didn't say that very convincingly either. With the Art Fund quiescent and my overseas activities circumscribed for various reasons internal to the Bank— decentralization was the current vogue and much more responsibility had been devolved on overseas branches or local correspondent banks—I didn't feel that I had all that much else to occupy my brain power but I wasn't going to admit it. Sue and I were at the end of our first year of marriage and I had no tearing desire to take on extra loads, even though Sue herself appeared to be getting deeper involved in her career at the Tate, positively revelling in it, and often worked late or went away, to hoolies like this forthcoming affair in Edinburgh.

'Have some more coffee?' Jeremy was in superficially genial form. 'At least we haven't had to go in for the powdered stuff yet.'

'Thanks.'

He gestured at the silver pot in front of him and I helped myself, keeping a cautious eye on him. Jeremy and I have worked together well for some years. Not everyone can take his tall, blond, Old-Etonian autocratic manner easily, nor his great swooping laughter, his intense ambition and his other arrogant habits. Jeremy is an acquired taste, a City-and–shooting taste or, if you're nautical, a yachtsman's taste. Oddly enough, I am none of these things, so it's perhaps an attraction of opposites. For Peter Lewis I have never felt any great emotion. He served the Bank well in Singapore for some time before being brought back in the wake of a nasty revolution when some older directors—there are still a number about, which indicates the longevity and tenacity of the White family—got the old heave-ho, including Jeremy's uncle, Sir Richard, who was then chair-man. Peter Lewis is a White by marriage and pretty com-petent, dedicated to efficiency, money-making and action in that moralizing way which people with Far Eastern experience seem to adopt and which Jeremy so deplores. Jeremy is not enamoured of a humourless, puritan approach to profits; Jeremy likes profits to be a source of fun.

'Bloody awful,' he repeated, watching me ply the coffee-pot. 'I've no doubt you've come to the same conclusion, Tim.'

'Mmm. Not too good.' Something of a suspicion began to dawn in my mind. Jeremy's expression was not quite right; a hesitation betrayed itself in his manner. I have developed a nose that scents impending danger from his direction. It came to me, as I poured the best Brazilian, with just a percentage of Colombian to add aroma to strength, that he hadn't invited me in for coffee just to chat about how bloody awful the economic climate had become. Peter Lewis's presence was unusual. I mean, Jeremy and I often chatted socially before or after one business matter or another but business usually came into it and it was now, after all, mid-morning on a busy day at the Bank. Peter Lewis was no idle chatterer; he wouldn't be here just to pass the time of day. He sat, shiny and expectant, looking rather pointedly at an empty cup. There'd been a main board meeting the day before; it had been still in progress when I went home, but the Art Fund would not have concerned it very much; I doubted if Jeremy's preoccupation was anything to do with that. No, it was more likely that there was a new political danger within the ever-shifting balance of power between individual directors and Jeremy wanted to chat it over, use me as a sounding-board or, perhaps, as a mole of some sort to glean other departmental secrets. It had happened before, but usually he kept it between us, strictly confidential. I wondered what sort of alliance he was forming with Lewis.

'Tim—' Jeremy suddenly cleared his throat and cocked an eye at me as I drank my coffee, rather like a tall, blond parrot ogling a tea-party—, 'do you remember your visit to Brazil that time, a few years back?'

I put my coffee down sharply in surprise before recovering my composure. To introduce a subject like that in front of Lewis, who had been in Brazil, was disconcerting. 'Graphically, Jeremy,' I said drily. 'I'm hardly likely to forget it, am I?'

'No, no,' he said, with a little too much haste, 'of course not. Of course not. I'm sure you wouldn't. Peter remembers it well. That time you sorted out old Blanco so efficiently. Frightfully top marks and all that. Lots of kudos or whatever.'

'Oh yes?'

'Yes, yes, of course. Old James has never forgotten it. Always sings your praises.'

'Does he?'

'Of course he does. Tim, I'm not referring to all the, er, the *unpleasantness* that occurred at the time. Not at all. No, no. I'm speaking entirely of your professional abilities as an executive of the Bank. Your business acumen. The assessment you carried out. Entirely of that.'

'Oh, are you?'

'Yes, of course I am. Entirely. Of course. The other matters were, well, something that just hampered the real objectives.'

I frowned. My visit to Brazil had been at the behest of Jeremy's uncle, Sir Richard White, in an attempt to sort out the affairs of a perfume company that White's Bank in São Paulo had got themselves entangled with.* Old James White, a distant but dynamic cousin who ran White's over there, had never shown me much admiration that I could remember. I stared at Jeremy suspiciously as I noted the way that Peter Lewis was watching me: rather too intently for my liking.

'Tim,' Jeremy said, leaning forward earnestly, 'the Bank is in dire need of your services once again. In a similar capacity.'

'In Brazil?'

'No, no, no! I'm sorry, I'm not making myself clear. Not in Brazil. In France this time. France.'

My jaw must have dropped visibly at this. 'France?' I queried, when I got it working again. 'My services? Are you sure? You don't want me to go to France, do you?' I was completely unprepared for this: not long after the Brazilian trip I had worked for the Bank in France with, if anything, even more unpleasant results. The departure of Sir Richard White had been a consequence of them.†

Jeremy blinked. 'Tim, really! Of course I mean France!' He put on a hurt expression. 'Please would you listen carefully to what I am saying? This is an important matter. Peter and I are both busy men.'

I sighed. When Jeremy is in reproachful mood or exhibits injured patronage, it usually means he has committed himself, which always includes me, to something irretrievably sticky. My suspicions about his manner were coming unpleasantly true.

'Jeremy.' I said, perhaps a little warily, 'I must apologize for a surprised initial reaction. The mention of France, and

---

* *A Back Room in Somers Town*
† *The Gwen John Sculpture*

a need for my services there, makes me feel that something
terribly drastic must have happened. France? *France?* We
don't look after France! Surely your famous deal with Maucourt Frères puts paid to any involvement in France for us,
doesn't it?'

His parrot-eye turned fishy. There had long been an
arrangement between White's and Maucourt Frères, an
old-established Paris investment bank, which made them
our correspondent bank in France. This arrangement had
been substantially altered in a recent series of share
crossholdings and swaps of the kind only French and Continental banks seem to love, enabling White's to have a holding
in Maucourt Frères and vice-versa. Eugène Maucourt, a big
family cheese on the Paris side, had become a main board
member of White's and Peter Lewis was on the board at
Maucourt's. It was one of those new, European-oriented
moves that aimed eventually to create a pan-Continental
entity into which, many members of White's believed, our
own identity would be subsumed in much the same way as
they believed Britain's would be subsumed into the EEC.
Controversial was the mildest word used to describe this
development, which had been passed only very narrowly at
.a rowdy board meeting in which most of the older Whites
had voted solidly against but outside interests and the
younger Whites, including Jeremy, had voted for.

Jeremy, of course, had the ambitious illusion that
White's, and he in particular, would experience an aggran-
disement of power and influence as a result of this move into
Europe whereas the opponents, pointing to the example of
most Anglo-French ventures, predicted disaster. It was still
a difficult subject to deal with unemotionally. It did, however, start to explain Peter Lewis's presence at our coffee-
seance this morning.

'My dear Tim!' Jeremy's fish-eye reddened upon me.
'It certainly does not! *Puts paid* indeed! What a negative
approach! The whole point of the joint stockholding is to
increase collaboration, provide new opportunities, open up
new markets and to expand our horizons. It is as a direct

result of this exciting development that I am talking to you now about the exciting and original role we want to take in what is potentially a—a—tremendous—'

'Problem?' I queried.

Why else would I be needed in France?

'Tim! Please! Really!' He put on another hurt expression, rolling his eye at me in an expression that indicated I'd let him down in front of strangers. 'I expected better of you. Really I did. There is no question of any problem in the sense your tone implies. While things are in recession here we must look further afield. I hope you're not going to approach this matter in a spirit of truculent Francophobia, because there is no question of calling it off. Peter and I are setting great store by White's participation in a new, Continental venture.'

I shook my head. 'I am not a Francophobe, Jeremy, as well you know. I have always enjoyed visiting France for recreational purposes. I enjoyed myself far more playing rugger in France than I ever did in Scotland or Wales or, come to think of it, even in Ireland, and that's saying something. Doing business in France is another matter. I have no doubt that if you are seriously proposing that I cross the Channel in an executive capacity to do some work for the Bank in France, then not only will I be up to my ears in difficulties but various Frogs will be trying to ensure that success does not crown my efforts.' I gave him a winning smile. 'Going, that is, on any previous form that one has experienced.'

He gaped at me. Peter Lewis does not gape but he, too, got a peculiar cast to his eye. His expression conveyed not only deep disapproval but a sort of moral distress. It was all very well for them: whatever they planned certainly wouldn't involve either of their presences in the firing line. I could be sure of that. They would be warm and safe at head office, playing commercial war games with the rest of the board. I drank some more coffee, thinking about the old days when I went on rugby football tours in France, then later ones, working for the Bank while it was chaired

by Sir Richard. When I looked up Jeremy and Peter Lewis
were still both eyeballing me in their very different ways,
so I sighed and relented.

'All right, gentlemen: I'm sorry. I withdraw my remarks
and apologize for any offence caused. You had better tell
me all about it. What *merde* are the Frogs trying to land us
in now?'

CHAPTER 3

I settled down for a brief re-read of Bellevie's business plan
as the plane took off for Paris. It was all quite simple, really.
Simple if you like complicated business, which is what the
French always seem to like. Eugène Maucourt had raised
it at the board meeting. Maucourt Frères, like many French
and German investment banks, did not just lend money to
industrial enterprises as we do in Britain; they took
shareholdings in the said enterprises. There is a school of
argument which holds that the relative success and stability
of Continental industrial companies is due to these bank
shareholdings, which act as a sort of ballast, or perhaps a
sheet anchor, to the companies' condition. Rather than
being at the mercy of a casino-like Stock Exchange, which
can devalue the worth of a company at the first breath of
a stupid rumour, or deliver its ownership to a megalo-
maniac who breaks up companies as a child breaks a
piggy-bank to extract a five p. piece, these shareholdings
protect their clients from speculation of the worst sort. It
sounds attractive and it is, as long as you know what you
are doing. That is where the complicated part comes in:
knowing what you are doing.

Eugène Maucourt, with the disarming ease of a patrician
Frenchman of gallant manners and polished style, had
given the board a brief *tour d'horizon* to illuminate the way
things were going *chez* Maucourt Frères, rather in the way
that the late General De Gaulle used to perform at press

conferences. Perhaps, on old television newsreels, you may have seen the sort of thing: Algeria might be in turmoil, farmers might be rioting, Usines Renault might be on strike, but the performance was always grave, confident, measured, intellectual and possessed of a long-term philosophical view of an inevitable progression upwards and onwards to better things. On the whole one had to admit that it was admirable stuff and so was Eugène Maucourt's; the board had listened politely and Peter Lewis, as the point of liaison from White's side, had nodded encouragingly from time to time to show that he was *au fait* with what was being said. On the principle that one never wants any nasty surprises at board meetings this was all exactly as it should be.

And then, unusually, Eugène Maucourt had raised the subject of his bank's involvement in the Bellevie business. Unusually, because it was an individual example of the sort eschewed by the De Gaullian—if that is the right adjective —manner. Individual examples usually disrupt the measured flow of that oratorical style. A descent to the particular so often fouls up the generalization. In retrospect he probably raised it partly because there had been some publicity in the business pages of the papers about the move taken to protect the company from an American bid and partly because it was well-known, at least to the directors' wives, as an up-market perfume and cosmetics house of long-standing French lineage. Nip into Harrods or any swish department store and you'll see the Bellevie counter, rather old-fashioned perhaps, with its decoratively packaged promises of glowing skin and irresistible allure.

Maucourt Frères had taken over the shareholding held in Bellevie by the Delattre family who, in straitened circumstances due to unlucky speculation and continuous extravagance, were flirting with an offer from one of the big Americans in the same field. It was felt that since Maucourt were already involved in part of Bellevie's financing, their participation in yet further share ownership made sense, at least, made sense in the French view of sense. It also preserved an old, admired French business house from yet another incursion by *les Anglo-Saxons*. Or something along those lines.

There it might have rested had not Eugène Maucourt gone just a little further and mentioned, almost *en passant*, that discussions were in hand to examine the Bellevie business with a view to future development, indeed perhaps to a substantial expansion because, after all, if *les Américains* had got their hands on it, it was an ill-kept secret they intended to promote the brand extensively, enlarge the business, flood the markets of the world with this excellent, high-quality *marque* and so on. Maucourt's could not be seen to be too conservative in this regard, too cautious; it would be bad for their image. Bellevie was said to be of a size and at a stage where it had to go forward in some way; it could not be allowed to stagnate. Raising his eyebrows and spreading his hands in an inviting gesture, Eugène Maucourt said to the listening board of White's directors that he understood from Peter Lewis they had some experience in these matters, that the nature of the problem would not be foreign to them?

There was a puzzled silence at this. The board of directors of White's Bank are not famous for their industrial or international memories or perceptions. Internal politics, monetary rewards and personal slights, real or imagined, yes, of these they remember every nuance and shift within the last hundred years. But for that in which they once invested and how it performed their subsequent memories are short. The City is about immediate gains and losses, what's happening today or just possibly tomorrow; on the markets, as with Henry Ford, history is bunk.

Except, of course, for Jeremy: Jeremy, like a great long blond setter dog, tail thrashing, teeth agleam, would have started barking excitedly as soon as the thought hit him. Of course, he must have hollered at Eugène Maucourt, of course the problem is not foreign to us. Peter Lewis would have received a knowing wink. Brazil! Think of Brazil! The perfume business we still control there. Indeed—I could imagine him, confidently braying forth—we had almost the same problem a few years back: which way to go, what product to develop and so on. The way Jeremy would speak, you'd think we'd been doing nothing else for years. If we could help in any way, Maucourt had only to say the word.

Eugène Maucourt's excellent manners permitted him a courteous smile and polite thanks. Brazil, after all, is hardly to be compared with France, with the very core and centre of the beauty business. Rio de Janeiro is not Paris, no matter how exotic. Nevertheless, in the spirit of the new collaboration, he would be glad to avail himself of any advice White's might have or care to offer as a result of their undoubted experience before his own experts or perhaps outside consultants made their recommendations. After all, it was a substantial investment and, if expansion were to be undertaken, perhaps White's might underwrite part of the sum involved or participate in some mutually agreeable way?

And that was where Peter Lewis and Jeremy White, like a pair of Lord Raglans out of sight of the guns, promised to send the Light Brigade, in the form of Tim Simpson—me—thundering off in an ill-defined direction with orders to carry out an equally ill-defined reconnaissance while receiving certain fire from unknown numbers of undoubtedly opposing forces.

I didn't want to go. I don't know why, but my immediate reaction was negative. I knew there'd be trouble. They wouldn't have sent for me otherwise.

'I just don't understand you,' Jeremy snapped petulantly in response to my expostulations in his office. 'Really I don't. Here's a wonderful chance to shine. It's right up your street to have a sniff at a thing like this. It's not as though your brain's over-employed at present, is it?'

'Er, well, Jeremy, I've got a few—'

'I thought not. Nothing important at all. You've got time on your hands. Things here in London are as dead as the Dodo.'

That was it; that was the reason he had fired off those opening remarks about the art market being dead. I began to understand it all now. A quick summary of the situation, a résumé for Peter Lewis's benefit, to evidence my acceptance that there was nothing to do for the Art Fund, then whoops, off you go, young Tim, it's a fair wind for France, the brig leaves on the morning tide.

'Jeremy—'

'You're absolutely the man for the job. Horses for courses.'

'Eh?'

'You speak French.'

'So do head waiters.'

'Worked in France before.'

'I'd rather you didn't go into that.'

'Fluently. French fluently.'

'Look here—'

'Perfume and powder puffs. Stinks and pinks. Detailed work in Brazil.'

'Exactly, Jeremy. Brazil. Not France.'

'Fiddlesticks. Business is business the world over.' He began to tick points off on his fingers. 'One available. Two: French-speaking. Three: knows all about perfume. Four:—'

'Jeremy, I do not know all about the Bellevie business!'

'Four: you soon will. Maucourt is delivering the new manager's proposed business plan to you today.'

'You mean Maucourt really was keen on this idea? Be honest, now. What enthusiasm did he show?'

'Oh, he's obviously very pleased. Fits in with new policy of interbank collaboration. Pooling of skills. Perfect example. What's that word they always use? Synergy, that's it. Synergy.'

At this point he cocked his blond brow at Peter Lewis, who nodded his glistening head in a series of emphatic nods. Synergy, I thought: synergy. The generation of energy in excess of the energies put in. Like Chernobyl: they didn't know what they were doing, those two.

I wasn't giving in yet, not to a set-up of this sort. 'I don't believe it. Not a word. Are you telling me that Maucourt showed enthusiasm at the idea of my coming over to sort out ideas for Bellevie instead of one of his own bright sparks? Or instead of some pet consultancy that Maucourt Frères keep on a string? Eh? Instead of using one of those young French technological business whizzkids form the Ecole Whatsitsname, you're saying he's agreed to an English stringer from White's Bank in London coming over to prise the woodwork off the walls in a prestige French name like Bellevie? I can't believe it. How enthusiastic was he? Be honest if you can.'

'Really, Tim, you are so negative! You're also too modest. Of course he was enthusiastic. Of course he wanted to use our expert services.'

Jeremy paused; he never really goes too far if he can help it because it wouldn't be English, and the idea of an enthusiastic Eugène Maucourt obviously didn't quite fit. He toned down his bravura a little. 'Well, you know what those sort of Frenchmen are like: they never actually show much enthusiasm at something like a board meeting, it wouldn't suit, but you could see he was happy about it. It was a ready-made solution for him. After all, Peter and I were two of his supporters on the share-swap thing and he must be keen to show that our new relationship must forge closer links. The sums involved are considerable and they're bound to need support. I know that Peter—' here he gave a sycophantic smile in Lewis's direction—'is very keen that the new relationship should develop mutually. And if we are to participate successfully then we need our own source of information. What have we or Maucourt's got to lose?'

'I just can't believe it. Who's paying for all this?'

'My dear Tim! Using our own resources will save tens of thousands of outsiders' fees! You know that as well as I do. It's the whole reason for the new arrangements. Peter and I are frightfully keen about it.' He gave me another reproachful glare. 'I've never known anything so *insular*. You really must try to think in broader terms, you know. Widen your horizons. I must say I've never thought of you as a Little Englander until now. It's quite extraordinary; you've obviously spent much too much time back here at HQ instead of getting out into the field. You used to be so enterprising and enthusiastic about this sort of thing! It's probably the Art Fund that's done it. Taken your eye right off the ball as far as we, an international merchant bank, with international links, are concerned.'

'International is international. France is French.'

'Really! Do try to pull yourself together! This is your project now. We are relying on you. Peter, who is of course our main contact with Maucourt's, has agreed to go over for a weekend to meet Eugène at his country place, after you've had some time to make an initial assessment. You're to join him there. Please try to show a little enthusiasm when you arrive, will you? Try to snap out of this extraordinarily xenophobic mood!'

'I am not avoiding the sun, Jeremy.'

'Don't be so pedantic! You know precisely what I mean.'

At that point I shut up. There was no sense in protesting further. At the end of the day Jeremy is the boss and I have to do what he says. There was no margin in upsetting him any more, particularly with Peter Lewis in front of us. I'd done quite enough already. Subordinates, in British companies of our sort, are supposed to be enthusiastic about battle plans, like subalterns in trench warfare. It occurred to me that maybe I was being just a little too anti because I didn't want to leave Sue and that maybe the whole thing was not nearly as fishy as I thought it was. Perhaps I really was getting too insular. Or too married. I went back to my office, made the necessary arrangements, received the business plan, read it with some amusement and arranged to depart for Paris.

I hadn't circled back to this sort of consulting work for quite a while. I had to admit that after I'd got used to the idea I felt a bit like an old gun dog being given an airing in a field smelling of pheasants.

It was quite a stirring feeling.

The plane angled its way downwards and we landed.

The name of the airport is of course, De Gaulle; Charles De Gaulle. It made me think about my forthcoming meeting with the statesmanlike Eugène Maucourt as my taxi swished its way to the traffic-laden *boulevard périphérique*, and it made me think also of the resonant business plan in the briefcase beside me.

I wondered, as the familiar outline of Paris approached under a whitish-grey spring sky, whether the plan bore any relation to reality or whether it was just another inspiring picture, an art-dramatical image, painted this time for the delusion of financiers.

CHAPTER 4

I don't use cosmetics much, myself. No, don't laugh: men are not supposed to paint themselves but they do not have to be limited to a splash of after-shave and a puff of talc. They can use deodorants and shampoos of a dozen types, pomades, hair oils, shower gels, bath foams and soaps far removed from the painful carbolic of my boarding-school youth. They can apply an infinite number of creams to every surface and pleat they may care to tend or hope to restore. They can shave with a myriad of scented foams named to flatter their view of themselves, just as their aromatic after-shaves are supposed to induce female compliance. The days when a man used a block of gritty green soap, stropped a lethal cut-throat razor, and bullied a badger-brush into a china soap-pot before risking his Adam's apple are long gone.

It's an enormous business. In South America, where lavender scents are strictly a Latin man's fragrance, I had found myself fascinated by the sheer extent of it, the massive amounts of money involved.

It's also an illusionist's paradise. Selling art is the business of selling expensive illusions to a small number of people, but selling cosmetics is the business of selling illusions to everyone.

Perhaps Jeremy White and Peter Lewis were very perceptive. If a man can understand one illusionist's world, there's a good chance he can understand another. And I did have some prior knowledge, a little learning in the field. But then, as the famous saying goes, a little learning is a dangerous thing. *Drink deep, or taste not the Pierian spring*: a favourite of mine, courtesy of Alexander Pope. *Shallow draughts intoxicate the brain and drinking largely sobers us again.* A motto rugby players are only too happy to adopt.

I had taken a few shallow draughts before leaving England. There are five big international players in the cosmetics world and they are L'Oréal of France; Procter & Gamble and Revlon in the United States; the Anglo-Dutch Unilever; and Shisheido of Japan. Inside these huge concerns is a vast array of brands and names and businesses. Each of these probably specializes in certain sectors of the market, like haircare or skincare, deodorants or fragrances, oralcare or colour cosmetics. Each tries to establish a position in a certain field, in a certain market. New people keep trying to break in. Despite failures and losses, it's an attractive prospect, if you'll forgive the pun. The industry's growth rates are excellent, and gross margins are high: production costs are about forty per cent of retail value compared with sixty per cent for most fast-moving consumer goods. It's quite a scramble.

Apart from the big five there are, of course, dozens, if not hundreds, of smaller and medium-sized players. How they are going to survive is an interesting question and one to which I had to address myself, like the author of the plan in my briefcase. The market is very fragmented and there are niche brands being bought and sold as going concerns almost every day of the week. Joint ventures abound. The advent of satellite television for supranational branding may have helped the big battalions on whose side God is always said to be, but that's no reason for the others to chuck in the towel. Environmentalism has twisted the big boys'— and the girls'— tails. Anita Roddick of the Body Shop has accused them of selling packaging, garbage and waste. All sorts of issues like recycling have been introduced, along with vegetarianism and ecobotanism. Legislators keep interfering in an attempt to catch up.

The plan in my briefcase didn't necessarily deal with all these things because it was assumed that some of them were known to the reader. The author, now the general manager of Bellevie, one Monsieur Thierry Vauchamps, was clearly an experienced hand. The plan read well. It had the plausible logic and the confidence of a professional. Certain aspects, in detail, were very carefully covered by sub-plans, especially the marketing. Since selling the illusion is what the business is all about, this marketing emphasis was not surprising. Production was dealt with in a much lower key; in fact it was hardly mentioned. The creation of a much bigger business was considered, quite rightly, to be a strategic marketing problem. Although Mr Thierry Vauchamps was entitled General Manager, he was clearly the head of marketing rather than anything else. Bellevie had recently taken him on for that reason and I was carrying, in my briefcase, his first, carefully-considered, midnight-oil-burnished proposal to expand and re-establish the Bellevie business in the forefront of its field.

I scratched my jaw thoughtfully as I read and re-read his plan, with its separate sections on the market, the *consommatrice*, the products, packaging, distribution, advertising and promotion, point-of-sale material, beauty consultants, market research and company organization, all accompanied by detailed figures and statistics. Vauchamps exhibited a talent for this type of proposal, which is as much part of a marketing man's repertoire as actually moving the goods. Bellevie was, more than anything, a women's skincare and beauty business with a minor contribution from perfume. Nothing to do with men; it was all about women. Nothing like the Brazilian perfume business at all. In fact, very, very different from it. Skincare is a market quite apart from that of perfume; the way in which ladies consider their skins has nothing to do with their fragrant personal aroma. The market for skincare products is mostly to do with moisturizers, cleansers, hand creams and things which are supposed to repair the damage of time. Skin gets important as you get older and, in case you hadn't noticed, half the women in England are over the age of forty-five.

There's a shallow draught to consider: it's no wonder that the basic ingredients of creams and cleansers, which are mainly things like lanolin, oils, waxes, fats and stearates, can be dollied up with emulsifiers, alcohol and perfume to persuade the ladies that it's worth paying a lot more just in case the unknown factor might put back the wrinkle clock.

A quarter of the dear ladies are over sixty-five. There's a deeper draught. One to sober you up again.

Women; I might have to bone up a lot about women, all of them, but particularly French ones, if I was going to get the hang of this thing at all. And like it or not, it seemed that I would have to get the hang of it.

Now that I was irrevocably committed, it didn't seem too bad a prospect.

CHAPTER 5

Up to the point of my arrival in France you will have detected that things had all been much too smug. Much, much too self-satisfied. Superficially, these things always are. The whole thing stank of an all-too-familiar approach:

'*Bit of a problem in Paris—send Tim—sort it out—quite a mêlée—problem dealt with—jolly good—end of problem—where were we?*'

A type of thinking, so typically British, that encapsulates much of the view of the Continent, particularly the French-speaking part of it, traditionally held in London. A place for sorties, the Continent, a place for a bit of a bash, military or sporting, followed by a bottle of the *vin de pays*, a visit to a *boîte*, then a spot of slap-and-tickle, preferably on a brass bedstead. Then the withdrawal, self-satisfied smirk in place, back to the island fortress. I'd been guilty of it myself. My attitude to Jeremy, you will have observed, contained more than a little of it. The insular view of the French, the stand-offish isolation, Them and Us, nine hundred years of enmity, Agincourt, Crécy, Calais written on my heart, you fire first, all that sort of tosh.

It wouldn't do. This was the nineteen-hundred-and-nineties, not fourteen-fifty-three. Or eighteen-fifteen. It simply wouldn't do. Here we were, supposedly about to become fully homogenized, completely-blended European performers, part of some sort of Continental identity, yet one's first reaction to the Continental mass was one of isolationist suspicion. From the land mass itself, things were bound to look different.

Maucourt Frères brought it home to me with a thump. Maucourt Frères was located in one of those elegant side-streets near the Elysée Palace, a street that actually crossed the Faubourg Saint-Honoré further up from the Bellevie shop. It was a fine, late-eighteenth-century building with imposing arched double doors to the street, a courtyard where carriages once stopped, and long Directoire-style windows in three-storeyed tiers. Paris is a magnificent city and this was an excellent example of its character. The floors creaked discreetly as you crossed upstairs, creaking the creaks of old, fine, seasoned timber. The reception secretary sat at a sort of *bureau plat* with ormolu mounts, beside which she had a tasteful console of modern telecommunication and computer equipment. Light fell across her ante-chamber from the long, formal, curtained windows in great wide swathes under livid, chalky-grey Paris skies. Somewhere outside traffic might hurtle across cobbles, pedestrians might scurry between brasseries and *Les Cafés des Sports* fragrant with coffee, La Défense might be a series of technological skyscrapers, suburb-slabs of terrifyingly monolithic apartment blocks might threaten the edge of the city with dreadful totalitarianism, but here were *l'ordre*, grace and garlic, manners and mansard roofs.

'Mr Maucourt is expecting you,' the secretary said approvingly. She was middle-aged, neat, smart, impassive but very slightly bending to be pleasant, as though she felt sorry for me, or had been instructed to soften an impending impact. Her gaze flicked over me without finding too much of which to object. I smiled pleasantly and she softened her formality a fraction more before asking me to be seated. I was not, evidently, *un hooligan football*, a black-patched pirate or an ash-stained, baggy-suited British *commerçant* of the lower order. The two of us imperceptibly stiffened our spines, elevated our heads, as though on parade. I felt that I was under observation.

She disappeared through a huge, moulded armoire-style walnut door which closed with a soft but solid click. I sat down on a modern reproduction of a Louis XV fauteuil, putting my briefcase to one side. The secretary had taken my raincoat to a stand where my suitcase also now reposed. I was suitably prepared for presentation.

The secretary reappeared and held the door open, indicating that I should go through. I gave her a slight bow, stretched to my feet, marched briskly through the door into the well-furnished office beyond, and stopped dead in my tracks.

Eugène Maucourt was not present. A much older johnny, impeccably suited and silver-haired, pink of complexion and brilliant white of shirt, sat behind the desk facing me.

On my side, in another Louis XV chair, turned slightly towards me and regarding me with the mixture of infuriating scepticism and senior condescension for which I always remembered him, was the unmistakably charcoal-clad figure of Sir Richard White.

Sir Richard White!

What the *hell* was he doing here?

Did Jeremy know about this?

The shock stopped me, as I have said, dead in my tracks. I probably gaped at him rudely. It had been three years since I'd seen Jeremy's Uncle Richard, as he actually is, and that was when we had shoved him off the board of directors, out of his position as Chairman. Jeremy's wife Mary had been his secretary; it was a difficult and incestuous time. Sir Richard had been about to involve White's in a disastrous industrial scheme and Jeremy used the events to force his resignation. Since then, to my knowledge, he had retired, partly to his house in London and partly to his place in the Dordogne, from which he had long pursued a hobby of visiting the sites of the battlefields of The Hundred Years' War, a hobby one might summarize as History with Gastronomic Perks. He was still a shareholder in the Bank, of course, from family inheritance, and frequently attended meetings. Deference was always shown to him on that account. But for Jeremy he had no love.

'Sir Richard?' I warbled, somewhat uncertainly. 'This is indeed a surprise.'

He smiled tolerantly as he stood up, showing his long thin figure to have altered not an inch. 'Mr Simpson,' he said, as though stating a fact. 'How are you?' And he stretched a hand towards me for a Continental-style shake, not too familiar, not too formal, and certainly not warm.

'Well, thank you, Sir Richard,' I said, grasping his hand as briefly as possible. It was like clasping a waxwork. 'Yourself?'

His smile turned slightly mocking. 'I am well,' he said. 'May I introduce you to Mr Charles Maucourt, head of Maucourt Frères?' He gestured towards the desk. 'Mr Maucourt, Mr Simpson. Mr Simpson, Mr Maucourt.'

The silver-haired old johnny came out of his corner with some nifty footwork and a beam of welcome. 'Monsieur Simpson! This is indeed a pleasure. A great pleasure. You were expecting, I think, my son Eugène? I must convey his apologies. He has been summoned to a meeting at the Ministry of Finance. I took the opportunity, while my old friend Sir Richard was here, of receiving you myself and substituting for my son. You know Sir Richard well, of course, and it was an occasion of which I wished to take

advantage, so I asked him kindly to introduce you. I have
long wanted to meet you.'

'Meet me, Monsieur Maucourt?'

For all that he must have been in his seventies, Charles
Maucourt looked in glowing health. He was thick with the
thickness of age but still looked powerful and stocky, as
though capable of strong physical effort. His brown eyes
shone. His thick speckled hair was cut *en brosse* in a rather
dated, Mediterranean manner reminiscent of Jean Gabin
in a Simenon film. He spoke English very well indeed, with
hardly any trace of accent. There were just the occasional
Gallicisms in his grammatical construction but otherwise
he was exceptional. I wondered where he got all his practice; the accent was English, not American, and must have
come from long association.

'But of course!' He smiled at me, revealing a gold tooth.
'The celebrated Tim Simpson! Of the Art Fund.'

'Oh. The Art Fund?'

'Come, come, my dear sir! We are not chauvinistic here,
in matters of art! Not at Maucourt Frères, anyway. I consider your acquisitions for White's Art Fund to be not only
a model of careful and tasteful investment but also, some
of them, very, very exciting. The Whistler of the Thames!
And the Monet of the same river; exceptional! I have been
an admirer of yours for some time.'

'Well!' I was still feeling flummoxed. 'That's very kind
of you, I'm sure.'

'Not at all. You are here for other reasons, of course, but
I could not pass by the opportunity to meet you. It has long
been a matter of regret to me that we did not form a similar
Fund here. Perhaps we still should. But tell me: I have a
question I have long wanted to ask you. Please, please do
sit down.'

He gesticulated at another chair nearby and returned to
his own more imposing seat behind the desk. Sir Richard
White draped his long, wiry, grey-haired figure back on to
his. Old Charles Maucourt placed his fingertips together
and fixed a fervent, bright-eyed gaze upon me.

'Mr Simpson—'

He was interrupted by the entry of his secretary and a young Frenchman of rather dark features but soft, friendly manner, a tall lad of about twenty-odd I would reckon, who smiled cheerfully at us all and looked expectantly at me.

'Hallo,' he said, and waved a thick file he was holding. 'I've got it all here.'

'Christian!' A look of sheer pleasure over old Maucourt's face. 'My dear boy. May I introduce Mr Simpson, from White's Bank in London? Sir Richard you have already seen this morning, I think. Mr Simpson, may I introduce you to my grandson, Christian? He is joining us, at my request, with all the necessary documents for the Bellevie business. I should explain that Christian is currently working with his uncle, Eugène. His father, Roland, my other son, is at the moment in the United States on business and Christian will be going over there soon to complete an advanced business diploma. But, while we have him with us, I thought it would be a good idea if he acted as your point of contact here.'

'That will be great,' I said, shaking the youngster's hand. 'It's very kind of you.'

'Not at all! Not at all!' Old Maucourt expostulated vehemently. *Au contraire!* It is the least we can do! It is very kind of you to come over at such short notice to help us!'

Christian Maucourt nodded emphatically at his grandfather's outburst. 'That's true. I'm sorry, I'm not going to be of too much help to you, but I'll do my best. You just tell me how I can help and I'll see what I can do. I'm afraid you'll be pretty much on your own; I haven't had time to read this up, you see, having only just received the file. It's been somehing of a crisis in view of the circumstances.'

I sat up, sharp. 'Crisis? Circumstances?'

Sir Richard White turned to me with one of his wintry expressions, in which an element of triumph at my ignorance might faintly be detected. 'Haven't you been told?'

I stared back at him with a similar lack of warmth. Anxiety made me congeal in my seat. I might have known there'd be something Jeremy had ignored, or didn't want to tell me. 'Told? Told what?'

Young Christian blinked at me earnestly. The boy looked disconcerted, as though he'd said something wrong. 'It was Michel's project, you see. Michel Bonnet.'

'Michel Bonnet?'

Old Charles Maucourt waved a hand. 'It was most unfortunate, Mr Simpson. Bonnet was one of our brightest younger executives. A superb business graduate. This was a project in which he had an intense personal interest. Intense. Tragic, tragic.'

'Tragic?' My voice had gone a shade hoarse.

'A car accident. En route back from Bellevie's factory. Dreadful. He was killed instantly. The roads of France are very dangerous, Mr Simpson. In your own country you are much safer; half the deaths we have here. But that is why we are so grateful for your quick response.'

'Oh dear.' I somehow managed to contain my natural reaction, which was to shout a great obscene shout, hit someone violently or to run like hell, and make a polite noise instead. 'Oh dear, oh dear.'

So there it was: their own man, Michel Bonnet, 'superb business graduate,' had been first choice, as I had rightly guessed, and was now dead, violently dead. Someone had sold us a dummy. Heat came to my face. Words that I would say to Jeremy came to mind. Words that, more politely, I would put to Eugène Maucourt, when I met him, also came to mind.

'Nevertheless,' old Charles Maucourt brightened as he waved his hand again, 'let me offer you all some coffee. These tragedies have to be surmounted. Life must go on. As we learnt during the war. We are very lucky to obtain your services, Mr Simpson. Things could not have worked out better for us once one sadly accepts the situation. On behalf of Maucourt Frères I must welcome and thank you for your quick response. It is, for me, an extraordinary bonus to have you here.' He leant forward towards me, his kindly face lightening. 'I hope you will not mind if I perhaps take advantage of it to impose upon you?'

His countenance expressed such an intense and demanding query that I, still stifling my true feelings, could only make a gesture of assent, as though I had a choice in the matter.

He smiled at me again and went on. 'Tell me; while we are waiting for the coffee and before we start to go into the situation with Bellevie, there is one question; a question I was about to ask you before Christian came in. Do you mind delaying the discussion just one minute? It is a question I have long wanted to put to you. For once, pleasure before business. Do you agree?'

I opened my mouth, trying to blot out a mental image of a smashed car on a French highway that had suddenly come to mind, swallowed, then nodded at him.

What else could I do?

'Of course, Mr Maucourt.' I said, as gracefully as I could. 'Please ask away.'

Out of the corner of my eye I saw Sir Richard cross and recross his long legs. What the hell was that old bastard doing here? Knowing, presumably, that I was en route? And why had he met young Christian earlier?

'Tell me,' Charles Maucourt asked, his bright eyes twinkling, his silver hair shining as he fixed his eyes compellingly on mine,' in your successful management of your Art Fund, have you ever come across or considered the paintings of Jacques-Joseph Tissot?'

CHAPTER 6

Take a lot of highly-dressed young women of the late nineteenth century, when dresses were really dresses, flounced, frilled and piped like icing on a Christmas cake. Give the young women the prettiest faces you can imagine. Provide them with expensively fashionable hair arrangements and bonnets of extraordinarily lacy complication. Set them in gardens replete with flowers or at public fêtes decked with bunting, accompanied by escorts who appear distracted or aloof, or with children who somehow do not quite fit. Make some of them widows, demure and wistful in black. Put them beside a river or among dockside jetties and tea clippers or even steamships. Express a popular sentimental emotion such as *The Emigrant's Farewell* or *A Lover's Tiff*. Alternatively, paint a ballroom scene in the Orchardson manner, but much brighter, with an amusing theme like a flustered old buffer surrounded by beauties. Or depict a musical recital with fashionable society listening to a diva standing by a piano. Make sure that there is a lot of work in the painting, that the finish is bright and hard and that the details are as crisp as a photograph. Then you have what came to my mind as soon as Tissot's name was mentioned.

I was quite wrong.

Or rather, I was quite right as far as the superficial, art-dramatic image I have mentioned is concerned and which I have described as misleading, confusing, to be treated with caution and reserve, but this was the first image which came into my brain.

Tissot? For the Art Fund?

'You call him James Tissot,' old Maucourt said, enjoying my discomfiture. 'Not Jacques-Joseph. James. It is what he called himself after a certain degree of Anglomania, in his early days in Paris. When he became a friend of Whistler and the Trilby gang of Du Maurier's. Curious, is it not? Mind you, there was Anglomania all over France during the Second Empire. Tissot almost has two personalities; always a Frenchman but also an Anglo-Frenchman. In England you think of him as a pretty Victorian narrative painter, fond of women. Here he is known as a religious artist. A *coureur de dames* and a spiritualist. Almost like two different men. What do you think?'

I was recovering. Despite the presence of Sir Richard White and Christian Maucourt, I found, as the secretary

served us coffee, that I was content to give old Charles
Maucourt his head. It's always obvious when a man hits
stride in describing an enthusiasm. Maucourt was staring
at me intently. His skin was slightly flushed. Give him a
chance, I thought, and he'll spout Tissot-knowledge like a
one-armed bandit hitting a dime jackpot. He's been waiting
for this opportunity for some time.

'Tissot,' I said, smiling a little. 'Tissot. He's never been
a poor man's painter, has he?'

'Aha!' Old Maucourt stuck a finger to his nose and
smiled knowingly but sympathetically. 'You are a young
man, Mr Simpson. A young man. To you, yes, the name
Tissot has the ring of money. But you are aware, without
doubt, of Reitlinger?'

He almost pronounced that like a French name—Rite-
lange-aire—but not enough for me to miss it. I grinned
back at him, at his sympathetic smile, to show that we, he
and I, were starting to hit it off in a way that almost
excluded the other two. Young Christian was watching def-
erentially; Sir Richard had started to sip his coffee, tolerant
condescension containing his normal desire to intrude and
get on with the business in hand.

'Reitlinger.' As I responded I had a mental vision, an
image of the long high bookcase down one wall of our flat
in Onslow Gardens. Books line almost the entire wall from
floor to ceiling. The image, for a fleeting second, had an
element of homesickness to it; Sue and I often prowled
together about that bookcase, digging up art-historical and
other, biographical records. 'Yes, Mr Maucourt. I am well
aware of Gerald Reitlinger's book. You are referring to *The
Economics of Taste*, aren't you?'

'Bravo! Absolutely. You do not disappoint me, Mr Simpson. Do you find it, as I do, an exceptional book?'

'Outstanding.' For someone interested in the value of art
over a long period, like me, it is quite a volume. There are
those who find that sort of analysis vulgar, even sordid, but
they don't run an Art Fund.

'*Voilà!* Reitlinger traces, for James Tissot, an inverted

parabola of price that goes from a fee of one thousand pounds per painting—a fortune—while he was alive, down to twenty pounds or so in the nineteen-twenties. His work, then, was hardly worth the price of the frames in which it was contained. Then what? Just about or before the outbreak of the Second War, The Chantrey Bequest—for your Tate Gallery—buys the remarkable *Ball on Shipboard*, the *Party on Board a Man of War*. Superb! *Franchement magnifique.* Since then, Tissot, I think you will agree, has been reinstated, at least economically?'

'He's certainly not cheap.'

Maucourt smiled. 'Not cheap now, no. Although it depends. It depends on the painting, the subject-matter. Incidental work of his is not so expensive but his major subjects are very sought-after. Art, like life, is an economic lottery.' His smile widened. 'As investment bankers, we all have our ideas about that, do we not?'

'Indeed we have.'

'You have never felt that a Tissot would make a good addition to your remarkable collection? There are, after all, canvases by him which are so parallel to your Whistler of Wapping, that were undoubtedly inspired by Whistler, that I wondered whether you had considered him, had the intention, eventually, of including him in your assembly?'

I smiled back apologetically. I was not quite so disconcerted now. Certainly I could not remember when a Tissot had been available at a price which made its purchase a bargain, nor had I had cause to plead with Jeremy that the acquisition of a Tissot was an imperative necessity for the Fund. Tissot was an artist on the edge of my vision, the border of my art-consciousness. Pretty girls and social gatherings; not an English artist, but that was no drawback because, although the Fund tended to concentrate on major British exponents, we had acquired foreign work with a British angle, like the Rodin of Gwen John or the Monet of the Thames. Tissot fell into this category; why had I ignored him?

'I—to be honest, I hadn't thought about it very much.

The art market is a thing of opportunity as much as a matter of deliberate policy. Like investment of many sorts. I think perhaps I may have missed my chance somewhere.'

Maucourt chuckled. 'I see, however, that I have made you think about it?'

'Indeed you have.'

'In that case—' old Maucourt made a gesture dismissing the subject—'when you have thought about it a little more, perhaps we might have an entertaining discussion between ourselves? One that will not waste the time of our distinguished confrères here today?'

'Of course. I shall look forward to that.'

'Splendid. We can discuss, among many things, the disadvantage of being considered French while in England and English while in France.' He grinned broadly. '*Eh bien!* To work! Sir Richard, I must apologize for my little diversion. Forgive me, *cher ami*; I think that I should now pass the ball, as our rugby-playing friend here might put it, to you?'

Sir Richard White smiled one of his less wintry smiles at old Maucourt and turned his pale blue eyes on me as young Christian watched guardedly. 'I think,' the charcoal-grey-clad old misanthrope said, giving me a look which gave away nothing and made me sit to close attention, 'that by now you will have gathered that our proposed investment in Bellevie is a matter of great interest to me? An investment I would like to discuss with you here, however briefly, before you start your new assignment and before you make any reports or commitments. You see, the late Michel Bonnet was reporting to us here on the matter, not of course to London. For that reason, our discussion must be in complete confidence.' He paused, looked at me again in that condescending way which had always been so typical of him and repeated himself, as though speaking to someone slightly deaf, or perhaps a bit dim. 'Absolutely complete confidence. We do not want any more unfortunate accidents. Fatally unfortunate accidents. Do you understand?'

CHAPTER 7

I'd never been quite sure what Sir Richard White thought of me. His attitude had always been condescending, as though he were dealing with an underling, a Bank servant, who might be worthy but who lacked intelligence. Mind you, he was the same towards everyone. I think that he had reached such a rarified upper atmosphere in his days at the Bank that those of us who were not family were far below his ken, like beaters at a privileged pheasant-shoot: out of sight, coarse, primitive, liable (especially in my case) by reputation to get involved in unnecessary violence.

I stood outside the shop in the Rue Saint-Honoré and stared at the window for a moment before entering. The remarks in the plan, which had amused me more than a little, ran by memory through my mind:

La boutique de la Rue Saint-Honoré, qui devrait être un centre actif et prestigieux améliorant l'image de la Marque et assurant des profits substantiels, est actuellement une sorte de crypte lugubre où les rares clients entrent avec le respect et la crainte vague qu'on éprouve en visitant un mausolée, et dont, en conséquence, le chiffre est beaucoup trop bas.

Which, translated for those of you whose French masters or mistresses did not urge them to concentrate on the subject, by whatever method, means that the shop, instead of being an image-building, active and prestigious centre, was said to be a sort of lugubrious crypt, into which rare clients entered with the vague fear and respect that one evinces when visiting a mausoleum. As a result, sales were low and profits insubstantial. Thierry Vauchamps, the author of the plan and the new general manager, intended, if his plan were to be accepted, to liven the whole place up, re-decorate, sell other beauty products including jewellery, and to hold product launches, special promotions and other media hoolies in order to use this wasted asset profitably as part of his marketing plan.

All perfectly businesslike stuff.

The Rue Saint-Honoré is a continuation of the Rue du Faubourg Saint-Honoré from the point where the Rue Royale crosses it. The Rue Royale, in its short, wide course between the open glory of the Place de la Concorde and the columns of the Madeleine, currently provides a divide, a rift in more senses than one. The Faubourg Saint-Honoré side is all glossy, expensive, conspicuous-consumer snob-shops up to the British and American Embassies and the Elysée Palace. The plain Saint-Honoré side starts well but gradually descends down market until, by the time it angles past the Palais Royale, it is a seedy clutter of tobacconists and café-bars that come to an end at the noisy Boulevard Sebastopol. The Bellevie shop was at least located towards the better Rue Royale end.

Sir Richard White had made it clear that he regarded Vauchamps' plan as an excellent one. He felt that my running the ruler over it was a matter of form, a gesture of management rather than anything bearing on a decision— in Sir Richard's view of life's landscape, decisions were made by people like him, despite gestures of management —and he also made it clear that he hoped I wouldn't waste any time in arriving at my own suitably accommodating conclusion.

On the other hand, there was an element of worry about the scene Sir Richard—and his old friend Charles Maucourt—were contemplating. The late Michel Bonnet had been an excellent chap, excellent, if a little inclined to be headstrong, impatient. He dashed about a lot. Such dashing was perfectly right, was indeed what he was paid for. But there were limits to dashing. The car crash that had killed the man was evidence of that. Deeply regrettable but not altogether surprising. Bonnet always drove very fast. The impact must have been severe, for the car was burnt out. Sir Richard cleared his throat at that point of his address to me. It had been said by Bonnet, just before he left the factory, that he had some important information that he was bringing back to Paris. No one knew, now, what that was. But I, Tim Simpson, was to understand quite clearly that in taking over Bonnet's assignment I was to proceed carefully, not to tread on toes, not to repeat the distressing tendency I had shown in previous circumstances to attract unfortunate controversy.

On the other hand yet again, I was surely a man who could look after himself and it was up to me to clear up what the important information was, if indeed it was important. Sir Richard looked at me significantly when he said this.

A nod's as good as a wink to a blind horse.

I braced myself, seizing the shop's rather large brass Art Nouveau door handle with its decoration of weepy leafwork and wispy tendrils, and felt its cold unused surface beneath my hot palm. Then I shoved the door open, activating the clang of a bell that reverberated round the still interior until well after the door had closed behind me. There was no escaping the timbrous announcement that a person or persons had entered, no slipping quietly aside to look at the stock. One stood exposed in the doorway, receiving the unrelieved gaze of several sets of curious female eyes embarassingly concentrated upon one.

It was a high room, almost vaulted, lined with great long brown cupboards going right up to the ceiling. Some of these cupboards had glass doors behind which, on shelves, rows of jars and perhaps small bottles ranked themselves along like chemist's medicaments or pimple creams. Other cupboards simply had solid doors, as though to contain dangerous drugs in security. All the woodwork was hand-grained in a mid-brown varnish which had darkened, but the lighter graining painted by the varnisher provided twisted yellow streaks in imitation of the figure of an unidentified wood such as light oak before fuming. In front of these high cupboards, glassed or solid, stood the shop counters which ran along either side of the premises. These in turn were glass-topped but not all were glass-fronted.

Some were, revealing arrangements of bottles and jars inside the counter-cabinets; others were panelled in front in the same hand-grained imitation wood finish. On top of the counters were more cosmetic jars and display racks or samplers with lipsticks and other cosmetics in them. The shop assistants, all naturally female, were in white coats. It was so like a chemist's shop of considerable vintage that I almost felt I ought to have a prescription with me or to be sidling furtively to the counter where contraceptives might be discreetly hidden; one of the solid-fronted ones, perhaps?

I certainly felt that I had no business to be there.

Sir Richard had made it quite clear that he wished White's Bank in London to participate in Maucourt's financing of the expansion of the Bellevie business. It was high time White's became more committed to a pan-Continental approach. He, Sir Richard, had supported the new cross-shareholding with Maucourt's enthusiastically, unlike other, older members of the family. He had thrown in his considerable vote on the side of this development.

Well, he would, wouldn't he? What had he got to lose?

A solid, darkish-grey dame of some sixty years or more came out from behind a counter at the far end and advanced briskly towards me in the same way that one walks towards a largeish dog of uncertain temper which one artificially wants to impress with one's lack of fear. She might have been once attractive, but was not now in the slightest. She was well-kept rather than well-groomed, healthy in a consciously medical sense rather than an alluring one, and, from the way her head projected forward, accustomed to giving orders.

Giving orders; Sir Richard obviously had much experience of that. Now that I was over in Paris, he said, I was to report to him, Eugène and Charles Maucourt directly, with Peter Lewis acting as liaison with London. He actually said, to make it crystal clear, as though to someone who might otherwise not understand, that as far as this assignment went, I was completely detached from Jeremy. I was on secondment to Paris and Paris was where my loyalty had to go. This was nothing to do with Jeremy's department nor—he paused fractionally—the Art Fund. So from now on I should consider myself under orders emanating from the Maucourt building. He wished me to understand that very clearly. In Sir Richard's view of underlings, of course, an order coming from so high an authority as himself would countermand all other orders, especially from family members as low as Jeremy, who came from a mere cadet branch. On the other hand, I reasoned to myself, even Sir Richard must surely have absorbed the lesson of our last disastrous involvement with him, after which he had lost his Chairmanship? Or was he, in clearly making an attempt at a powerful come-back, ignoring previous events?

Perhaps, like the Bourbons, Sir Richard had learnt nothing and forgotten nothing.

'Monsieur?' The darkish dame was addressing me strongly, from dead in front, adopting a stance which suggested that surely a man of my age and appearance could have no business in such a place, except perhaps as a messenger, a delivery-boy sent to collect a jar of expensive cream for an elderly female relative and hence of no importance. It was implied, somehow, that the idea of me as a customer was not to be taken seriously.

I smiled upon her. She came to nowhere even near my chin.

'I have,' I said pleasantly,' a rendezvous with Mr Vauchamps. My name is Simpson.'

A look of displeasure chased briefly across her face. With an effort she eradicated it and regarded me calmly, as one would a fool who had lost his way and needed patient treatment.

'You have come to the wrong place, monsieur,' she said. 'The offices are next door, above the courtyard passage.'

'Oh dear. Excuse me.' I gave her an undeserved smile and looked about me. Behind the counter an attractive brunette was fiddling with some lipsticks and blushers, watching me amusedly. Her white coat had a coloured piping round the edges as though she were a sergeant of some sort; the others were plain white and their wearers were the sad-eyed females whom I had noted on entering. My impression was that the staff were all expectant, waiting for something or someone, but then the lack of customers might simply have accounted for that. I smiled again at the matron-like figure before me and withdrew to find my way to the office entrance next door.

Phew! *Crypte lugubre* was putting it mildly. Mr Thierry Vauchamps had, if anything, pulled his punches where his description of the shop was concerned. It was preserved in aspic, it was in a time-warp, it was a throwback. In the late 'thirties it might have been considered sort of modern-Teutonic in style, one severely holding out against the jazzy zigzags of Art Deco but still Modern, in a Bauhaus style gone medical, a ladies' cosmetics shop attached to a Swiss sanatorium. It hadn't altered since, well, certainly not since the 'fifties. Quite remarkable, and very gloomy.

I paused before entering the office passage.

Sir Richard White hadn't actually said that he thought that Michel Bonnet's death had anything fishy about it. Sir Richard, like a very senior and old-fashioned Civil Service Head of Department, possibly a Foreign Office man, was being distinguished for what he did not say rather than for what he spelt out. We were all being very subtle, weren't we, about this. So subtle that my hackles started to rise. It was beginning to fall into place now. Here were Maucourt Frères, with Sir Richard egging them on, examining Bellevie, using their bright boy, Michel Bonnet. No need, at that stage, for any coarse clods from London to be involved; Sir Richard, via Eugène Maucourt and Peter Lewis, could invite White's to participate at the right moment, when all the facts were in place, when Bonnet had produced a suitably doctored report. Then the hitch: the car crash. How very unfortunate. No reason to change policy, of course, but it did seem that there might be something to clear up, something which was probably quite straight-forward but just might have an element of danger in it. Better check it out. And how better to do that than to lure

White's in London into thinking that they themselves had
had the bright idea of sending their own man, the expend-
able roughneck whatsisname, that fellow Simpson, been
involved in perfume in Brazil, Sir Richard had only too
good a memory, forgot nothing, remembered only too well.
And, at the end of the day, no change in decision really
likely; read Simpson the Riot Act when he arrives over here,
make sure he's quite clear who he's working for, tell him to
get on quickly, check everything carefully and, if there
really is anything ugly about, who better to cop it than him?
Certainly don't want another French bright boy to get it in
the neck, nor a member of the family. Simpson has a reputation for that sort of thing; tell him to go lightly, not to
tread on toes, but to investigate thoroughly within the
time-scale dictated.

In the meantime Sir Richard could carry on with his
comeback, work his strings from Paris, keep Peter Lewis in
line presumably, and plan to have his response all set up
when Jeremy undoubtedly found out. The accident had
perhaps forced Sir Richard to show his hand a bit early,
but in drawing me to France he was losing nothing along
whatever route he had chosen for his re-entry to the world
of White's and Maucourt's.

And provided the report by me was suitably tailored,
there could be no comeback if, after White's participated
in the investment, anything went wrong. Sir Richard would
have the perfect way out: London's own man, Jeremy's
lackey, would have rubber-stamped the whole thing.

'Can I help you?'

She was blonde, small, rather smart. Her wide, intelligent
eyes looked straight into mine. I found that my thoughts
had occupied me all the way through a courtyard and up
some stairs into a reception area without a receptionist. I
must have been standing uncertainly on the marble floor.

'Thank you,' I said. 'I'm looking for Mr Thierry Vauchamps.'

She smiled and pointed down a corridor. 'His office

is that way. His secretary is outside. Have you an appointment?'

'Oh yes.'

Her smile widened. 'You're English. You must be Tim Simpson, from White's Bank.'

'That's right. How did you know?'

She chuckled. 'I'm Berthe Cauvinière, the market research manager here. It's my business to know such things.'

'Really? I didn't think market research included clairvoyance as well.'

She put a finger to her nose. 'Call it company intelligence, then. The intelligence of the grapevine.'

I grinned and shook hands with her. 'I'm glad I met you first. I'll be needing some market research, I'm sure, very soon. I used to be in market research myself, years ago. May I call on you at a convenient time?'

She dimpled. 'May you call on me? How very Edwardian! Of course you may, kind sir. My office is that way. I'm not always here so check with my secretary. OK?'

'OK.'

She smiled again and swished off. I admired the retreating form, and bet myself she knew I was doing just that, before ploughing on down the passage to meet the man whose sense of humour surmounted the gloom in the shop below. I had known, of course, that the office entrance was not via the shop but had been unable to resist going in to see the place. The word lugubrious, both in English and in French, means doleful, dismal or mournful. Vauchamps had got it pretty well right. It seemed extraordinary that their flagship outlet in Paris was in such a retarded condition: I had taken a quick look at Bellevie's stand at Harrod's and at other department stores in London without getting anything like the aged impression that the premises below conveyed. A *marque* for the mature lady, perhaps; a rather *soignée*, groomed, respectable image, a bit dull, one that avoided hype or sexual fire. But it was still a very highly-regarded brand, with products that were said to be excellent; nothing like the fusty, old-aunt, clinical prescription adhered to by the place in the Rue Saint-Honoré. It amazed me that it remained as it was.

Throughout Sir Richard's grey, oblique address to me, Charles Maucourt had said nothing. He sat behind his splendid desk, nodding gravely from time to time, looking from Sir Richard to me and back again thoughtfully. His manner was confirmatory, supportive of Sir Richard. Young Christian, holding his file, waited obediently in a quiet posture. I was in new territory. Considerations in London went to the side of my mind. You can deal with overseas, with that sort of strange ambience, in different ways. You can remain resolutely English, totally foreign, retaining a national isolation, secure in the knowledge that very shortly you will return to your natural habitat like a fish plunged back into its pond; the Channel-sortie approach I've already mentioned. Or you can try to absorb things a bit, merge, grow a few local tendrils, use your foreignness for leverage rather than impact. The more I listened, the more it seemed that Sir Richard wanted me to adopt the former mode, the mode that would keep me separate, available as a brief extra resource untuned to local transmissions, to be returned to its pond in short order. That was the public impression he gave so I made up my mind, then and there, in Charles Maucourt's office, to take the second route.

'Monsieur?'

This time the challenge came from a rather pretty dyed redhead, neatly clad in grey, outside Vauchamps' office. I had reached my destination. She brightened at my identification, asked me to wait for a moment, and in no time I was ushered into the presence. From behind a rather grand rosewood desk, in a traditional room decorated in totally modern style, jumped a grey-suited, smart Frenchman of my age, with an impish grin on his face, hand outstretched.

'Well, well! Mr Simpson! You've wasted no time at all, I hear! Straight into the tigress's den. You're a brave man.'

I blinked, for a moment unsure of his reference, then

realized that in a place like this local intelligence travelled rapidly. In about two or three minutes, I quickly calculated. I gave Mr Thierry Vauchamps a smile in return for his grin; I felt I was going to like this man.

'Of course,' I said cheerfully. 'I read your instructions before starting out. I must say I admire them. In assignments of this sort one starts at the bottom and works one's way up.' I gesticulated downwards and then towards him. 'I'm not sure, though, if one should pass through the crypt before reaching the nave?'

CHAPTER 8

'I am impressed.' Thierry Vauchamps sat back in his large chair, behind his large desk, chuckled, and nodded emphatically. 'First, you have obviously read my plan, and second I, like all Frenchmen, love *jeux de mots*—it is good, from crypt to nave. Or knave, eh? Pretty good. I refuse to take offence; better to be a knave than a fool. Third, you obviously know something—how much I'm not sure, but something—about this business. Which is more than can be said for the late Michel Bonnet, rest his soul, who was too fast for himself. Fourth, much more important, you have the ear of these financial fellows, who—no disrespect —are a pain in the posterior for a marketing man like me. And fifth, less important but *impressionnant*, you are not afraid to rush in where mere men are terrified to tread. The shop, eh? You agree with my diagnosis?'

'It's incredible.'

'Incredible. For so long the place has been allowed to stay like that. All due to Madame Delattre, of course. The tigress you met as you came in.'

'Delattre? Hang on; isn't Delattre the family who owned the company until Maucourt bought them out?'

Vauchamps eyes widened. 'You didn't know? You didn't

know that she—that old tigress-witch—went along with the deal?'

'Deal?'

'Of course! The purchase of the shares. It was a condition. Madame Delattre is the widow of one of the original Delattre brothers who owned the place after the war. She has run the shop since the 'fifties. Didn't you know that?'

'It's not in your plan.'

He gave a great hoot of laughter. 'Of course it's not! My plan has upset enough people as it is! I didn't need to remind them of that; I just had to put forward management plans to use the shop properly. We are a little more tactful over here, you know.'

'Tactful? Surely Maucourt's must have dealt with this when they took over the shares? Did they really agree that she could stay on ad infinitum? I can't believe any competent firm would let that slip by.'

His mouth opened a little. He gave me a long pitying look. '*Mon pauvre Anglais.* Has no one briefed you properly on this business? Do you not know about Madame Delattre?'

'Know what?'

He closed his eyes, opened them, looked quickly round the room, at the door, then at me. His voice dropped. 'France is said to be a complicated country for an outsider, but it is not really all that complicated. We are, however, very discreet. Perhaps too discreet for you. Anyway, it is a fact that Mr Charles Maucourt and Madame Delattre are, shall we say, very old friends? They were, for example, in the Resistance together during the war. When they were still both teenagers, like many of the Maquis. Indeed, no one is quite sure why they did not marry. They were both in the Franche-Comté, operating with a group in the mountains. Some tiff or another, perhaps, may have separated them. But it is certain that soon after Madame Delattre married Jean Delattre, Maucourt's became the financiers of Bellevie. Eventually—now—the part-owners. The two ex-Resistance lovers never lost touch, if you'll excuse my pun. In view of their long, er, friendship, it is hardly likely that Maucourt would put Madame Delattre through the door as part of the package, the package of baling out her family debts, now is it?'

'Jesus.'

'He cannot help us. But you, I think, can help me, so I am glad to help you. I believe, naturally, that my plan is a good one. This is a good business which has been neglected. The products are good products and the factory can produce more. Bastoni, the works manager, is an excellent chemist and manufacturer. It needs finance and good control but this is a good market—I cut my teeth in this industry and I know what I am doing—so I see nothing but a splendid future.' He leant forward confidentially. 'I will fill in all the background information you need. The sort of personal stuff no one else is going to pass to you, for obvious reasons. Naturally you will have to do your own cross-checking in the market and so on, but I know you will come to agree with me. It is in the interest of us both. And if, *après tout*, it all goes well as I know it will, there will be a place for you in this too. We will need help all over the world. Quite apart from an Engish company, with directors and so on. Think of that.'

I sat still for a moment. Appeals to naked ambition or greed are not always put so plainly, but then, in England, some of us tend to be naïve. A simple succession of nods was enough to satisfy his querying look at me and he pressed on, still confidential in tone.

'Frankly I need you, apart from getting the finance organized, to push for the change in that *sacré* shop below. It's essential to our entire image. My friends in the business are laughing themselves sick. If we are to revitalize the brand and produce the profit results which are lacking right now there has to be a real explosion in that place. It should generate activity and confidence, even excitement. You've seen my new product schedule; no way can I launch those new skincare products and cosmetics down there as it is. Somehow old Maucourt has to be taken aside and convinced of the need to retire that old battleaxe. Damn it all, she's had a hell of a good run; the only women who come in there on a regular basis now are the crones she grew up with, her *salon de thé* companions. I've made the point in my plan but so far there's been a deafening silence; not a word. The death of Bonnet accounts for part of it, of course. Everyone's a bit thrown by that. He was entirely on my side, by the way, about the shop. He thought it was dreadful. Dreadful.'

'I'm sure he did. Of course I do, too. It's obvious. But I only met Charles Maucourt for the first time today so I'll have to tread a little carefully. I haven't quite got his confidence yet. No one told me anything about Madame Delattre. And I'm not a member of the family.'

'That's a good thing! You're not family. They'd be too terrified to try and force his hand. I can't tell you how pleased I was when I heard that someone was coming over from London so quickly. It needs an outsider to sort it out. A hatchet man. The old hag has read my plan, you see, I'm sure of that. I didn't give it to her; I expect old Maucourt slipped her a copy. She hasn't spoken to me since I sent if off. Just black looks and icy silence. I bet she's trying to scupper me. Can you credit it? I am the general manager here and I have to pussyfoot around the old bag who runs the shop attached to my offices just because she and Maucourt screwed each other silly for years. It's incredible. She should have been fired—no, not fired, pushed under a bus —years ago. She's awful.'

He pulled a cigarette out of an open packet in front of him on his desk, gestured at me, got a negative shake of my head, and lit up from a Bic lighter. Strong blue vapour gushed from him moodily. Madame Delattre, quite obviously, had a bad effect on his nerves.

'Well,' I said, when the smoke had eddied a bit and I could see him clearly again, 'I need to start tomorrow. Is there an office I can use here?'

'Sure. It's small, but there's one across the passage. Ask my secretary for anything you like.'

'I need introductions to all the heads of your departments. You don't mind my talking to them?'

'Of course not! It's essential. Most of them are mad keen to get going, especially Madame Cauvinière, our market research manager. She has a lot of the data you'll need, of course.'

'Oh.' I didn't know why, but a faint pang of disappointment went through me when I heard the married title. 'And the factory; I'll need to visit that, too.'

A perplexed look crossed his face. 'The factory? Do you need to do that at this stage?'

'Indeed I do. If the expansion shown in your plan takes place, then factory capacity will be massively affected.'

'Oh. Of course; forgive me. I see everything in marketing terms and Bastoni runs such an efficient unit I only visit once a month. Telephone and fax are quite enough otherwise. He comes up here too, of course.'

'Is it far away?'

'Nantes. On the outskirts of Nantes.'

'That's quite far!'

Vauchamps shrugged. 'Does it matter where the factory is? Not really. Paris would be too expensive, that's all. We got very good incentives for setting up in Nantes, apparently. It was before my time, of course; I would have gone south, but the west needs industry, and it's modern and clean. You can fly if you want; Bonnet was mad keen on his sports car so he drove. Unluckily for him. I'll tell Bastoni to expect you when you've fixed your programme. Anything else?'

'It was said that Bonnet found something important when he visited the factory. Just before he was—before his accident. Any idea what it was?'

He shook his head. 'I can't imagine. Honestly I can't. The manufacturing side of this business is of no real interest to me, I have to admit that. It's the least thing to worry about, provided you haven't got maggots in the face cream or sulphuric acid in the colognes. What's important in this business is packaging, presentation, image, advertising, distribution. I don't have to tell you that. But I understand; you have to visit the factory to complete a professional assessment of the company and to check out Bonnet. So by all means go and talk to Bastoni. He'll show you everything; it's all stainless steel and tiled floors. You could eat crème caramel off the desktops without flinching; really hygienic and impressive. Anything else?'

'No, I don't think so. I'll start first thing tomorrow on the staff. Except for Madame Delattre; I think I need to get up my strength before tackling her.'

He grinned. 'OK. Where are you staying?'

I gave him the name of my modest hotel in the same area and he nodded. 'We must have dinner together. I'm sorry I'm engaged tonight but we'll fix it up, eh, while you're here. Perhaps when you've had a few days to sort yourself out?'

'That would be great.'

He nodded vigorously. 'I think there's a lot of potential to be realized here. We must talk it over in confidence. That crone below may still live in the days of kohl and henna but we must move into the twenty-first century. See you tomorrow.'

'See you tomorrow.'

I shook hands with him and went out, stopping to get his secretary to show me the small office I could use during my stay. It was quite adequate, with two spare chairs and a window overlooking the street, which is more view than I've ever had at White's Bank. I sat down and made some notes, conscious of the noise of traffic and the buzz of being in the shopping sector of a city rather than the dull financial districts where money lies flat or remains hidden instead of rolling round the counters, in and out of pockets. Here I was, alone, with enough to think about already, a mass of facts to digest and the tip of some sort of iceberg warning me of dangers down below.

It was impossible to concentrate. I had to talk to someone. I got up and went towards the obvious attraction.

Berthe Cauvinière was coming out of her office door as

I reached it and her eyes widened, then crinkled mischievously as I approached.

'Already? So soon? Goodness, this is unexpected. To what do I owe the pleasure? Just impatience?'

I grinned at her; natural flirts always have that effect. 'Call it thirst. A thirst for knowledge. As one market researcher to another.'

She made a funny disbelieving noise, then led the way back into her office, her small blonde figure looking just as good as it had at first sight. She sat behind her desk and made herself look professional, bolt upright, alert, a sharp gaze on me as I sat down in front of her. Her eyes were very blue.

'Madame Cauvinière—'

'Berthe. I prefer to be called Berthe. Here we are normally informal.' She gave me a frank stare. 'It is a habit we have picked up from the Americans in this business.'

'Oh. Good. I'm Tim, then.'

'Tim. What can I do for you?'

I held up the file I was holding. 'The plan Thierry Vauchamps has put forward. I'm having a look at it.'

'I know. And clairvoyance has nothing to do with that either. He said you'd want to talk to me.'

'Would you like to comment on the factual part of it? The statistical basis, I mean.'

'Oh.' She looked puzzled. 'Do you mean do I agree with it? Because I do; it's a good plan. The logic is incontestable. But—'

'No, sorry. I didn't mean that. I wasn't asking you to comment on the validity of you boss's plan. I'm sorry I didn't make myself clear. I was asking about the data he's used. The sources and so on. I assume you are responsible for them?'

'Oh.' Her face, which had been closing, cleared. 'I see. Well, actually, I fed Thierry a lot of the information, but he is a bit independent. He likes some of his input to come direct. There's quite a lot down at Nantes, you know. I do

mostly test panels, consumer surveys of products and so on;
the qualitative side as well as the quantitative.'

'I thought so. You see, the plan depends quite a lot on
new skincare products. Over the next few years particularly. It makes sense because Bellevie has the right image
for that kind of clientele—I smiled at her—'the older
woman, that is, worried about wrinkles and repairing the
ravages of time.'

She smiled back. No one looked less in need of repairing
the ravages of time. '*La femme d'un certain âge? Ou d'un âge
certain?* How true. But, fortunately for Bellevie, this sector
of the population is increasing all the time. Think of Calvin
Klein's 'Eternity' and so on. We should be in a good position to exploit that market if we go for Thierry's plan.' She
pulled some sheets of figures out of a folder in front of
her. 'Older women with money, concentrated in towns and
cities. In France and Germany this is a rich potential. The
strategy is impeccable in that sense.'

'I agree the logic reads well. The strategy then follows
automatically and the practical measures show a lot of
experience. I took to the remarks about the *crypte lugubre*
with great amusement.'

Her face went serious.

'Thierry should not have done that. It was not tactful to
do that. He knew it would cause hurt to Madame Delattre.
And *politiquement* it was not clever. I warned him about
that '

She had gone very professional and upright again. I
sensed that something personal was coming into things.
How well placed was she to warn her boss about his
behaviour? Or were her sympathies so strongly with
Madame Delattre?

'Has Madame Delattre mentioned it to you?'

'Oh no! Certainly not. She would never do that. Madame
Delattre is a very professional woman and a heroine. Really,
I mean a heroine, a remarkable person. It is not right to
print things about her shop without at least discussing them
with her first.'

I had a mental image of Madame Delattre, to whom the informality acquired from Americans evidently did not apply, of discussing the total destruction of the shop décor with her, and shivered, wondering whether Maucourt's financial rescue package had come before the plan or after. 'The shop is pretty awful,' I said.

'It is grim, I agree. But there is a correct way of doing things and an incorrect way. I was cross with Thierry about that.'

I nodded cautiously. 'Well, I hope that the matter can be resolved to the satisfaction of both parties.'

She smiled. 'Now you are talking like a lawyer.'

'Perhaps that's what I'll have to be for a while.'

'Acting for whom?'

'Good question.' I looked at my watch. 'A question I certainly can't answer now. I'm keeping you late.'

'Oh no you aren't. I am often late here. I work as I please, you see. An independent woman.'

'Ah. Aren't all women independent these days?'

She grinned broadly. 'They are. But those who have had a husband and have got rid of him are more independent than the others.'

'I'm sure.' I stood up, feeling a strange sensation of relief. The situation had been defined as clearly as if I had asked her outright. 'In that case, I'm glad I haven't imposed on you. I'd like to continue tomorrow, if I may, when I've had time to think further. May I?'

'Of course.'

'Thanks very much. Until tomorrow, then.'

'*A demain.*' She nodded emphatically, her eyes holding mine for a moment. 'I shall look forward to it.'

'Me too.'

This was encouraging. For the first time I began to feel that I had an ally. Thierry Vauchamps was one too, but in the sense of serving his ambitions, whereas this lady was straightforwardly friendly. And flirtatious. I whistled cheerfully as I packed up my papers and headed out of the building.

I was stopped as I stepped on to the pavement. The stocky, darkish-grey figure of the shop's châtelaine barred my way so purposefully that I almost stepped back a pace in my tracks. She was not wearing her white gown of shop supervision, as she had been when we first confronted each other. This time she was in a dark brown tweedy outfit of the sort Scotswomen use when hunting stags. It made her look older than the first impression had indicated to me. Of course; if she had been in the Resistance, had been a heroine, she must be about seventy at least.

One of the twenty-five per cent, certainly. Deep draughts would be called for.

'Monsieur Simpson?'

'Wha—er—yes, I'm Simpson. Can I help you, madame?'

Her grave, almost aggressive expression did not alter. She stuck out a hand, straight at me. 'I regret I did not know, when you arrived, who you were. I am Madame Delattre.'

'Madame.' I took her hand and shook it, bowing slightly. It was dry and strong, very firm.

'Monsieur Simpson. I would like to speak to you. Are you leaving now?'

'Well, er, yes, I was, madame. I will be back tomorrow morning.' Not now, I was thinking, not now, I don't feel strong enough for this. 'I had it on my agenda, of course, to come and see you.'

This was a lie; I had intended to run through everyone else before facing this daunting obstacle.

'Ah.' Her manner became even more alert. 'So you intend to see me tomorrow?'

'Yes, madame. Certainly. Your area of responsibility is, of course, an important part of my—my work.' This was pure cowardice; sycophantic rubbish.

'Excellent.' She nodded approval. 'Excellent. Tomorrow will fit in perfectly with what I wish to do.'

'Oh? Good.'

'Monsieur Simpson, may I impose upon you to ask if

you would be so good as to see me first thing? First thing tomorrow?'

'Er, well, yes, by all means. If that is what you wish.' Oh Christ.

'It is imperative. I must see you first thing tomorrow. The particular matter will not wait.'

'Very well, Madame Delattre. Nine o'clock?'

'Nine o'clock, monsieur. We will meet in absolute confidence, of course.'

'Of course, madame.' Bloody hell.

She stuck her hand out at me again and I shook it gravely. Her gaze flicked over me as though assessing or measuring me. She seemed to be about to say something more, but her face closed and she detached her hand, nodding briefly to me. Then she turned abruptly and marched off down the pavement.

Office grapevines, I thought. Bloody office grapevines. She knows already what all my work is going to be about and she's aiming to head me off. Meeting in confidence will forestall some action or another she doesn't want put through.

I started to walk slowly towards my hotel, thinking of office grapevines. 'The intelligence of the grapevine,' the delightful Berthe had said.

Thinking of office grapevines, it would be intelligent, as well as friendly, to phone Jeremy.

CHAPTER 9

'My dear Tim!' On the telephone, Jeremy's voice was gratifyingly agitated. He was at home, where I hoped to ruin his evening for him. I was in my hotel room, in an armchair, with my stockinged feet up on a side table. 'What the hell is going on over there?'

'I've just told you, Jeremy. At least, I've told you what's

been happening to me. How long have you known that Sir Richard was making a comeback?'

There was a sort of windy, throttled noise at the other end of the line, rather like the sound you get from a vacuum cleaner that has blown an important pipe connection somewhere.

'I take it,' I said, laying it on fairly thick,' that you didn't know from Peter Lewis or any other source that the chap who they got to do this job in the first place snuffed it in a car accident while on his way back from the Bellevie factory to report something important? A chap called Michel Bonnet? One of Maucourt Frères' blue-eyed, brilliant boys? Their first choice, of course. Or did you?'

The windy, throttled noise deepened in tone.

'I also take it,' I continued, still rather getting my revenge, 'that you didn't know that events are complicated by the presence at Bellevie's dismal shop of one Madame Delattre, for some time mistress of Charles Maucourt, who rules a bunch of woebegone chickens in white coats in a manner and in surroundings certain to discourage the lady punters? Who takes a dim view of one Thierry Vauchamps, a cheerfully mercenary general manager who has virtually promised me all sorts of directorships if she is removed and all goes well?'

'Tim! Stop this! At once!'

'How long have Sir Richard White and Charles Maucourt been old mates? Can you tell me that?'

'For heaven's sake! Donkey's years. They met during the war.'

'Which one? Napoleonic or the Kaiser's?'

'Tim! Pack it up! This is no laughing matter. This is very serious.'

'Well, thank you, Jeremy. I am pleased to hear that I have your undivided attention.'

'My uncle was in SOE, damn it. He worked undercover with Maucourt, who was in the Resistance down south somewhere. That's how Maucourt's became our Paris correspondent bank. They kept their relations going after the armistice. For God's sake, surely you know that?'

'No, Jeremy, I did not know that. No one has ever told me that. And since I wasn't even born at the time, the niceties of your family's wartime affairs are a mystery to me. Especially since no one has ever thought to tell me them. You especially.'

'Damn it, Tim! Can't I send you anywhere without a bloody riot breaking out?'

'Thank you, Jeremy. That is very kind of you. I blew this whole storm up myself, entirely unaided. I insisted on coming here, against your advice, to do just that. All in the first day. Your in-law Peter Lewis had nothing to do with it, of course. Nor Eugène Maucourt. Charles Maucourt is also uninvolved. And Sir Richard is just taking a kindly interest in the Bank's affairs as a philanthropic exercise by a shareholder, not because he aims to get back on the board. I wonder, if he worked with old Maucourt in the Resistance, how intimately he knows Madame Delattre, too?'

'Jesus Christ!'

'What do you do to them at those board meetings, Jeremy? Why do they always try to outflank you?'

There was a silence. Not even the throttled sound.

'Even in making this telephone call I am behaving in a disloyal manner to Sir Richard, Jeremy. He made it quite clear that while I am here I report to him and his cronies, not to you. Although, to be fair, he must have known I'd be on the blower to you fairly sharpish. He does, however, think that orders emanating from him countermand all others and that, therefore, I am his man for the duration. A duration at the end of which I may wish to affirm that attachment. Putting two and two together, I think I am expected to anticipate a *coup d'état* on the White's board and to move my loyalties elsewhere, or perhaps to ride along with Vauchamps and get into the Bellevie business. What do you think?'

'You tell me.' Jeremy's voice was suddenly sharp again. 'You tell me what you think.'

'Oh good, I'm glad you've asked my opinion. I think this is a load of horse shit. I think that Bellevie may or may not be a good investment and that the Vauchamps plan may be a good one or it may not. I think I can sort that part of it out without assistance, threats or diversions. That sort of thing I can do. I also think that Sir Richard is a clumsy idiot. The Frogs, of course, are all too clever by half, Eugène especially, but I rather like old Charles Maucourt. He is cracked on Tissot, by the way; thinks we should buy him.'

'Tim! Will you please forget the damned Art Fund! Just for once!'

'I'll try, Jeremy. I hear you, Jeremy. The part I cannot deal with concerns your board politics. I'm not sure if Peter Lewis is a dupe or a villain, but, knowing his experience, I think he's a villain. I'm not sure why I had to be drawn over here rather than anyone else; perhaps to isolate you in some way? I can't think that's it; after all, Geoffrey can look after you better than me from an accounts point of view. I'm just a spare galloper. And as for isolation, just say the word and I'll chuck this in, come back, and clobber anyone who even breathes on you. You can be sure of that.'

'My dear Tim.' He was recovering fast. The English, after all, enjoy a good crisis. Routine work bores an Englishman stiff. 'Your sentiments are not just admirable, they are much appreciated. There will be, however, no need for you to return here. Not yet. You are much more valuable to me where you are. Geoffrey and I now have work to do over here. We will act with all despatch. It is quite clear that Uncle Richard is back to his old tricks and that Peter Lewis is a dyed-in-the-wool snake in the grass. If that is not a mixed metaphor or something. Mark you, I have always suspected Peter Lewis; the Far East makes 'em all too clever by half. What surprises me is that they have shown their hand at this juncture. It must have been the car accident that forced it on them, which in turn means they are in a hurry for some reason. Maucourt's are, obviously, deeply entrenched with Uncle Richard and Peter Lewis, so you must proceed very circumspectly. By all means let them think that you may transfer your loyalties. In merchant banking and broking such things are regrettably common.'

'Indeed they are, Jeremy.'

'Do look after yourself, Tim. Thank God no art matter is involved, otherwise there'd be bodies all over the place.'

I managed to ignore his second remark. 'Of course I will look after myself, Jeremy. It has been a long day. From an art-dramatic departure to a closing encounter with a French female dragon. I propose to go out and have a large dinner accompanied a bottle of *vin de pays*.'

'*Vin de pays?*' Horror filled the tones in the receiver. *Vin de pays?* 'For heaven's sake! My dear Tim, do you never consider your health? You must not do anything of the sort. Drink nothing other than a good claret. Or, knowing you, a decent burgundy. On me. There will be no querying your expenses, I do assure you, on this affair. Not at all. You must keep yourself in peak condition. Peak condition! Stay away from those awful Midi wines and that stuff from the south. *Vin de pays* indeed! Acid ages a man frightfully, dear boy. You must take care.'

'Thank you, Jeremy.'

'The very least one can do. The very least. Keep in touch, Tim. Close touch.'

'I will. You may depend upon it.'

We rang off. I put on my shoes, preparatory to going out. It would be no good ringing Sue; she would be at a committee meeting, sorting out Edinburgh and transfers of Peploes, or some such Scottish colourists. I sighed.

Not *vin de pays*; a good burgundy. I stopped sighing. This might turn out to be not too bad; even a superior kind of sortie.

Although, as it turned out, most of it had yet to come.

CHAPTER 10

The first person to confront me in the shop the following morning was not the dragon Delattre but the dark attractive beauty with the piping round her white coat.

'I am Tina Buisson,' she said, taking my hand formally in a firm, dry shake. 'I am in charge of the beauticians and their training.'

We were alone in the shop, just before nine. It didn't open until nine-thirty and this was the time that everything was polished up, prepared and arranged for the day's work but, little having apparently moved since yesterday, dusting and de-fluffing seemed to be most of what was required.

'How do you do?' I chimed back, shaking her hand just as formally. I really should have been introduced properly by Thierry Vauchamps, but this was no time to stand on ceremony. 'I had planned to have a talk to you in due course, once I got my bearings, so to speak. Mr Vauchamps has given his full approval. I believe you train the girls outside France as well?'

'Oh yes.' She smiled. 'I go to Harrods and the Kaufhof and all over Europe; the Bahnhofstrasse in Zürich, a lot of German shops, of course—they have the money and the habit of skincare there—but I appoint a local supervisor to run the courses for our girls and for new recruits so I don't have to spread myself too thinly.'

She beamed at me cheerfully and I noticed her focusing on my nose for a brief glance. My nose was broken in an early altercation on the rugger field and has remained somewhat flattened ever since.

'That must be very interesting,' I responded somewhat lamely. 'Travelling around Europe and fixing up all those glamorous girls.'

'Oh.' She pouted just a little. 'It's not so bad, no. A job gets to be a job, you know, like any other. But I like to get out and travel, to get away from here; it's so claustrophobic.'

'Ah.' Conscious of my forthcoming meeting with Madame Delattre and her insistence on its confidential nature, I tried to look sympathetic without getting in breach of professional etiquette. 'Head offices do tend to get a bit introverted, perhaps.'

As I said it I was conscious of a mental image of White's back in Gracechurch Street, with its mahogany panelling and gloomy passages, its publicly earnest dealing rooms full of shouting yuppies, its incestuous gossip about office politics and White family rivalries. I had got away from all the former but none of the latter; White family rivalries had a persistent habit of dogging my footsteps and looked to be a major occupation for a while.

The dark beauty nodded emphatically. 'Introverted? Introverted doesn't even begin to—'

She was interrupted by the bursting open of the back door of the shop, set behind the counters and giving access, presumably, to the rooms where the assistants changed and to the offices above. Framed in the doorway was the attractive blonde presence of Madame Berthe Cauvinière, market research manager of sympathetic and, yesterday, humorously attractive demeanour. She looked far from calm.

'Tina! *C'est terrible!*'

'*Quoi?*'

'What?'

'Oh—Mr Simpson! Oh Tim! Have you heard the terrible news?'

'What? News? What news?' Fear squeezed my heart. What on earth could have happened now?

'Madame Delattre! Dreadful! Poor woman!'

'Madame Delattre? What about Madame Delattre?'

'An accident! Horrible! She has fallen under the Métro on her way to work this morning. Killed instantly. Vile!'

'Jesus!'

'*Berthe! Non! C'est pas vrai!*' Tina Buisson let out a shriek. Her face was ashen. The two women stared at each other in horror. Then, moving swiftly as though impelled by invisible force, they rocketed forward to clutch each other in support, leaving me standing by a counter loaded with jars of foundation creams in beige-tinted hues.

Dead? Madame Delattre? Never to be interviewed by me?

A chill of fear mingled with a guilty sense of faint relief. Why had she been so insistent on an early meeting?

The two women were in full spate.

'Under a train! Horrible! I've always feared it. The sort of thing one reads about in the newspapers, never imagining that it could happen to—to someone—someone—'

'Like Madame Delattre?'

'Exactly! Like Madame Delattre! A heroine. A strong woman. Full of vitality. A horrible accident!'

'*Ah non!*'

They clasped each other again. I pressed my hands, as the implications sank in, to the cold surface of a sheet of gelid plate glass shielding a bank of moisturizing gels.

Why just before my meeting? Why?

'How on earth did it happen?' I heard myself ask trying to use a tone of voice that combined fearful concern with genuine inquiry.

'No one knows. I use the same Métro and saw a crowd gathered on the platform. It was *awful*. It never occurred to me that it might be someone I knew. Then I saw— I saw—Berthe Cauvinière allowed her blonde self to be clutched a bit tighter by the dark Tina Buisson—I saw who it was. They said she just fell off the platform as the train was pulling in. There was a crowd, of course, there always is at that time of the morning. It was packed. Pushing and shoving. Beasts, they are. Frightful. She was all— all—crumpled up—all—'

She stopped dramatically. Another white-coated assistant, rather an older woman, had come in from the back of the shop and was staring at her in expectant dread. I began to feel more than a little *de trop*. Within minutes the whole place would be seething with white-coated wailers, each getting the news in sequence, each reacting individually. It was no place for me, a stranger, a man. I had emotions of my own to contend with. I murmured a quick excuse and slipped off towards the offices to look for Thierry Vauchamps.

It was, after all, he who had said, yesterday, that Madame Delattre ought to be pushed under a bus. I could remember, all too vividly now, his vehemence as he said it, the emotion she obviously induced in him.

Well, developments were swift in this business.

Solving his problems, the Métro had worked just as effectively as the conceptual bus; there was virtually no opposition to his plan to revivify the shop now.

Nothing very much to stand in his way at all.

Just my investigation and approval.

CHAPTER 11

The flat on the fourth floor of the *fin-de-siècle* block in the *huitième* was not as large as I had expected for a wealthy man but it was tasteful, expensively furnished and doubtless worth a fortune.

'Dreadful,' old Charles Maucourt said to me, sitting down rather heavily for his well-kept, still-strong frame. 'It has been a terrible shock, Mr Simpson. Madame Delattre and I were old friends. Very firm old friends in the way that men and women can be when they have shared danger together and trust each other absolutely.' He gave me a quick look and gestured at a chair. 'Please, please sit down. It is most kind of you to come and see me. To take my mind off things and make me feel a little less old. I had hoped that our discussion would take place in happier circumstances, cheerier days. But never mind.' He smiled wanly. 'We will occupy ourselves with a more fruitfall subject, eh? We are fleeting but art is eternal. What?'

'I hope so, Mr Maucourt' I said evenly. 'I am deeply

sorry myself. I had been looking forward to an interesting discussion with Madame Delattre first thing on the very morning of the tragedy. She was keen to have an early talk to me about my work, I think.'

'Really?' He shot me another quick look. 'At your request?'

'No, as a matter of fact. She buttonholed me the evening before. I think she was concerned about the, er, the plans for the business.'

A slight smile came to his lips. 'You are a tactful man, Mr Simpson. Agnès was deeply committed to Bellevie. It was her life. After the war, when everything seemed to be destroyed and everything seemed so drab, it focused her energies and her abilities in a way that was curative, therapeutic, positive. You can say that she lived for Bellevie, after the war, in the same way that she had lived for the Resistance. That shop was set up by her almost unaided many years ago. She supervised the design and execution personally. To have changed it would have been an admission that, for her, the days were numbered.' He shrugged expressively. 'We all have to change and to accept that our days are numbered, but when you have adopted the psychology of survival, of refusing to believe that you are not immortal, that you can harass your enemies for ever, it is difficult to change.'

I nodded in what I hoped was an understanding way. Old Charles Maucourt and I were sitting in what was evidently his living-room, a place furnished in rather heavy fabrics that deadened sounds from outside. A housekeeper had let me in. In a sense I felt slightly at a loose end, so a diversion that might at least be considered kind was no strain. The Bellevie shop was in chaos and Thierry Vauchamps' management team uninterviewable. In fact Vauchamps had closed the shop, as a mark of respect, until the funeral. His eye had avoided mine for the rest of the day I spent, fruitlessly, around the Rue Saint-Honoré. Although the offices were still functioning, Berthe Cauvinière had been sent home suffering from shock, Tina Buisson was calming frayed female nerves and Vauchamps himself was occupied with arrangements, condolences, incoming inquiries from shocked acquaintances and trade calls from all quarters. The best thing I could do was to stay for a day or two and use the time as efficiently as possible in the circumstances. I went off and did some homework. I visited trade associations and talked to a couple of retail audit firms. I sauntered down the major shopping streets and looked at *parfumeries*. I re-read a couple of international market research reports I had picked up in London and thought how much I would enjoy discussing them with Berthe Cauvinière. I ate alone near the hotel and went to bed early after phoning Sue, catching her at home just the once and missing her badly.

'Tim!' Her voice on the telephone was like a shot of adrenalin. 'How are you? How's it going?'

'Slowly,' I responded. No reason to raise anxiety, no need to set her alarm bells ringing, not yet. 'But never mind; that's what I'm paid for. How's things with Edinburgh?'

'Oh Tim! You have no idea. There's so much work. I'd never have believed it took so much organizing. But I'm getting on. When will you be home?'

'The end of next week, as planned.'

'Not before?' Her voice had a disappointed pout to it.

'Sorry, sweetheart. Look after yourself, won't you?'

'And you. Stay away from trouble, Tim.'

'No problem this time.' I already had my fingers crossed.

We gabbled endearments and rang off. I stared at the wall of my hotel room. What was the best thing to do next?

The summons from Sir Richard White which made the decision for me came as something of a shock. I wasn't supposed to know but I assumed that old Charles Maucourt would be numbed with grief, keeping himself immured at home. Sir Richard White, with his flat, calm, Anglo-Saxon delivery, dissolved all my assumptions.

'Monsieur Maucourt,' Sir Richard remarked gravidly to me on the telephone, 'is an old and close friend of Madame Delattre's and is much upset by her death. All of us, from our side, have expressed our sympathies. In view of the circumstances and the way in which you and he, so to speak, to a certain extent hit it off over the art business at our meeting, I thought it might help if you dropped round to see him for a chat. I'm sure he'd appreciate that. And of course it would be good for the future relationships. D'you follow me?'

The tone of the last question was the same he always employed, one that somehow hinted that he was thinking on a plane above one's own, above the affairs of mere employees who might not appreciate the subtleties of what he was saying. I had no objection to being trotted in as the useful squeaker who might divert his betters' cares with his clever prattle, but the implication Sir Richard produced— that a privilege was being conferred, that one was being allowed to mingle with superiors in a way which might be to future advantage—made me smile secretly to myself.

'What about his family, Sir Richard?' I queried. 'Eugène and so on? No doubt they're being supportive. I don't want to get under their feet.'

'Good heavens.' His voice sharpened. 'You are an ingenuous fellow. Has no one briefed you at all? His sons disliked Madame Delattre intensely. They have always, quite correctly, been intensely loyal to their mother, who died a few years ago.' He paused for a moment and the line's silence put a meaningful pause into my expectant ear as he silently debated what he had just said with himself, what servants'-hall gossip might be deduced from it. When he resumed his tone was once again brisk, detached, factual. 'No one is implying that there was in recent years anything, er, anything untoward, in the relationship between Charles Maucourt and Madame Delattre, of course. But their close relationship—of a business nature following their wartime collaboration—was a source of friction. Even though his wife and Madame Delattre had established a reasonable, one might say a working, relationship with each other. After all that time one has to adapt, to accept. But his sons have always viewed Madame Delattre with suspicion.

They felt threatened by her in some senses. I can tell you this because I have known Charles Maucourt for many years and, as a man of the world, I'm sure I can rely on your discretion.'

'Of course, Sir Richard.'

'Good. I dare say you will find as you go on that things which may seem one thing to an outsider are quite different to those who know, who have viewed events over a long period. I met Charles Maucourt and Agnès Damprichard, as she then was, during the war. They were in the Maquis, the French Resistance. She in particular was a fervently active thorn in the side of the enemy. She was exceptionally brave. It is not the time, now, to go into all that history. But there was, I should say, unease about them in his family in later years. She exercised a powerful influence and there were other, er, factors. I can, I hope, trust you not to trespass on the past unless invited to do so. In my view it would be a comfort to Charles Maucourt if you could chat to him about art. You will have gathered that he is keen on Tissot.'

'I have, Sir Richard. Gathered that.'

'A painter of vulgar society.'

'Sir Richard?'

'Nothing. Merely an expression of James Laver's. It is lamentable, Mr Simpson, that despite my hopes there has been another unfortunate accident. A fatally unfortunate accident.'

'I'm afraid so.' Lamentable, indeed; the old bugger was making it sound like my fault.

'Well, I suppose neither of us could have foreseen it.'

'No.'

'I do hope, Mr Simpson, that this will be the last one.'

'Me too.'

There was a slight silence as he took my exclusion of his title. Then he spoke, dry and chilly as ever. 'I will leave you to carry on, then.'

'Fine.'

He rang off.

Very illuminating. Very explicatory. I phoned Charles

Maucourt and made the arrangements; he seemed very pleased, almost grateful for my call. So here we were, he still very smart in a snowy-white shirt but with a handsome tweed sports jacket and grey flannels replacing his suit and polished Italian shoes gleaming below discreet grey socks, talking about the late Madame Delattre, when I was supposed to be diverting his attention with a natter about art instead.

'Did she have any children?' I asked, still half-thinking of the fusty shop, the pharmacy-image, and trying to reconcile that dismal interior with someone who had presumably roamed the wild mountains of Eastern France pursued by the Gestapo while shoving explosives under railway lines or ambushing convoys.

'Alas no,' old Charles Maucourt said sadly. 'It would have been a great blessing for her. But it was not to be; perhaps some of the wartime stress—who knows what effects these things have? The Germans persued her avidly, you know. After her marriage turned out to be childless she doted on her nephews but, as you may have heard, they were—still are—profligate. It was because of them that we at Maucourt Frères stepped in financially.'

'Er, yes, I had gathered something about it.' I cleared my throat, perhaps a little awkwardly. 'You obviously kept in touch with her and the Delattre family after all your experiences in the war?'

His gaze was clear and unblinking as he responded, holding my own stare firmly. 'She was two years older than me, Mr Simpson. When you are my age that is nothing. When you are in your teens it is a great period of time. It is hard to describe, now, what the aftermath of the war was like: chaotic, confused, angry. Communists and crypto-Socialists everywhere. She and I were the only survivors of our little cell. The others were caught in the Vercors, you see.'

'Vercors?'

His gaze turned a little grim. 'Once again you make me feel old. There was a massacre in the Vercors. It is the mountain plateau south-west of Grenoble. Thousands of young maquisards collected there to avoid the forced labour camps. We stayed in the Doubs and the Jura but the others joined them in the spring of 1944. When D-Day was announced they hoisted the tricolour and declared the area free. It was a terrible mistake; guerrillas should never fight fixed battles. The Germans annihilated them and killed everyone—including women, children, farm animals, even dogs and cats—in the place. Agnès and I were left to carry on by ourselves; we had never agreed to the idea of travelling all that way south in the first place; there was too much to do where we were. As it happened, our refusal to go saved our lives.' He sighed and let his gaze slip from me. 'Anyway, what I am saying is that we parted for a while at the end of the war. She was older and was looking for a new life; too much had happened, we had been too much under stress. None of us wanted to be reminded of it. It was time to try and start again. I came back to Paris and and was absorbed into the family business.'

He paused in thought for a moment and I resisted the impulse to pressure him to tell me how they met again, where, and what happened then. We had got far away from art and I felt guilty about that, but he wanted to talk and it was best to let him get it out of his system.

'Cosmetics,' he said slowly, looking slightly bemused. 'Imagine, Mr Simpson, how far that is from the days on the run in the mountains. Imagine. I could hardly believe it, when I met her one day, not so very far from our bank, at a café, purely by chance, in the Rue de Rivoli. Smart, cultured, chic, she seemed. It was the early 'fifties; I stared at her in disbelief. We had not seen each other for over five years. And she told me she had married Delattre—he was no relation, by the way, of our famous General de Lattre, far from it—and was deeply involved in the business. They needed money for expansion then. She laughed as much when I told her I had tamely returned to the family finance house as I did at her new occupation. It was logical that I should capture that account for our bank.'

And her? I nearly asked him. You captured her too, by all accounts, or at least by what Thierry Vauchamps said. Or was it a recapture? But I nodded gravely and said, 'What a fortunate meeting. It must have been a splendid chance that brought you together again.'

He smiled and shrugged. 'I think we would have met again anyway. You know how it is; some old comrades' association, someone with common or mutual background. The world is not so big and there were not so many maquis-ards—or so few—in Paris that we would not, eventually, have met. It is really ironic, though, Mr Simpson, is it not? A woman who went through such experiences, who took so many risks, ends up running a cosmetics business and is pushed to her death by an uncaring crowd in a Paris Métro? Bizarre. Terrible. There is no understanding the Gods, Mr Simpson, no understanding them at all.'

'I'm afraid not, Mr Maucourt.'

He shook his head, shrugged again, and shook himself, as though throwing off a burden that clung to his broad shoulders and must somehow be thrown off by physical rather than emotional effort. '*Enfin!* Enough of these unhappy musings! If we want to talk of more agreeable matters, Mr Simpson, why do we not contemplate the ironic life of Jacques-Joseph Tissot? *Un Parisien de Londres devenu Londinien de Paris.* It is an extraordinary story. One that you should find most interesting. Here—' he sprang to his feet and went to a chest of drawers, from which he extracted a folder containing what looked like some old magazines. '*Voilà, Mr Simpson!* The magazine called *The Graphic* from 1873! One of the only copies, I believe, still in existence! And here—he opened the fading cover carefully to reveal an engraving across two pages, showing a terrace over-looking a huge tangle of shipping, on which two girls and a sailor, next to a table set for a meal, were disporting themselves—'here is one of his greatest views of the Thames. Straight from Whistler's *Wapping*. Absolutely superb. Not unlike the one you captured so brilliantly for your Fund.* Don't you think so?'

I had to nod in agreement. The similarities were remarkable. 'Very like the one with Jo Hiffernan and Alphonse Legros in it,' I said, probably gaping a bit at the sight of it.

'Exactly! Whistler must, at that time, have regarded him as a disciple, one of his own school. And the whereabouts of the painting is completely unknown.' He closed one eye and winked at me. 'Does it not make your young mouth water?'

CHAPTER 12

Christian Maucourt, at about twenty, looked nothing like his grandfather. He was soft and gangly, with a shy, dark look that must have made him very attractive to girls. Thinking of the college friends of my youth, I could imagine a few just like Christian, none of them sportsmen in the brutal sense that most of my closest friends were sporting men. His type would have been boys with tennis racquets or golf clubs, boys whose recreations were not likely to bring them into violent contact with anyone. Boys not even with squash gear or fives gloves; for them there would be no muscular, sweating collisions while gasping in dusty confined spaces or on the open field; no clashes of hockey sticks, no crashing impacts, butted heads, broken fingers, arms, collar-bones, legs; no cracked ribs or split foreheads, flattened noses or missing teeth.

On the other hand, Christian Maucourt almost certainly could ski and ski well. I could imagine him swooping gracefully down the steep, firred slopes of an expensive resort, judging risk to a millimetre even though his long, coltish legs were not yet too set, too structured or muscled hard

* *Whistler in the Dark*

into steely, sprung implements which, later, could easily go stiff. He would be a good swimmer too, and a dancer. Almost certainly he would dance well; there was something about the way he moved, swerving round the corner of his desk, that spoke of body control, judgement, to a rhythm. Christian Maucourt's whole young presence spoke of cared-for upbringing, money, breeding, the cultivation of correct pastimes, education and advantages gratefully absorbed, modestly treated.

I took the file off the desk in front of him and put it on my lap.

'I didn't take it when we first met,' I explained, 'because I wanted to get my own impressions first. I thought that this material might put me off my path, interrupt my stride. Someone else's details often do that; set you off in the wrong direction, I mean.'

He nodded carefully from behind his desk in the office he was using at Maucourt Frères, his young eyes wide and curious in his smooth, unlined face.

'Has your uncle—Eugène—seen all this?' I asked.

'Oh yes.' He nodded again, emphatically. 'He took over all Michel Bonnet's papers after the—the car crash. The papers that were here, that is. Some were with him, of course. We never recovered those; they were all burnt.'

'Mm.' I turned the file papers over, seeing market reports, bank assessments, balance sheets and profit-and-loss accounts that I already possessed in most cases, or could easily obtain. Michel Bonnet had taken, firstly a banker's approach, checking out the profitability of the competition as well as Bellevie. Then there were a couple of retail audits, a thing about retail distribution—the breakdown between traditional *parfumeries*, department stores and so on—and a broker's report on L'Oréal. Here and there were a few jottings in, presumably, Bonnet's own writing—*grands magasins, pharmacies, grands surfaces, coiffeurs-parfumers*—he was, evidently, approaching the thing from the marketing end, like Vauchamps—*échantillons, nuanciers-testers, booklets, pancartes, vitrines*—he must have been assessing the impor-

tance of all that point-of-sale stuff. No, here were a few
product notes: *produits, soins et traitement visage, maquillage,
ongles, lèvres, bain, packaging, éléments, ingrédients*—this was
much too much to deal with at one swallow.

'Can I take the file with me?' I asked.

'Of course.' Christian Maucourt leant forward earnestly.
'Of course. It is available for you. I promised Sir Richard
to pass it on to you. All of it.'

'Sir Richard?'

'Yes. I met him, you know, before our meeting.'

'Oh yes. Of course.' I affected a casual interest. 'Was he
specific about any of it at all?'

Young Christian shook his head. 'No, no. He just wanted
to see what I would be passing on to you.'

'Oh. Did he look through it, too?'

'No. Well—just a bit. A—what do you say?—a quick
ruffle through. A few minutes. Nothing specific.'

'I see. Unusual for him.'

'Oh?'

'Yes. Sir Richard in the past either demanded tedious
detail—the full chapter and verse—or he wouldn't touch a
thing, wouldn't look at it. Not like him to half-pass a file or
half-look at it. All or nothing, that was Sir Richard.'

Christian Maucourt shrugged. 'I do not know this.'

'Did he say nothing?'

'No. Nothing specific. Just that it should be made available to you, that's all, provided you wanted it. And that—
he smiled shyly—'that you could use what you wanted. He
was quite specific about that. He said that you would need
to look at what had been done before in the deceptive way
that you usually, apparently, do.'

'I beg your pardon?'

He blushed a young man's blush and suddenly looked
confused. 'Perhaps I should not have mentioned that. I
should not have repeated it.'

'Deceptive? What an extraordinary adjective to use.'

'Please.' He looked a bit worse. 'I should not have said
it. My father is always reproaching me for being gauche. I

am a fool. It was not meant to be repeated, of course. Please forget I said it. I am sorry.'

'Oh, don't worry. Sir Richard's always been a strange old bird. Never could work him out. He has rather a set opinion in my direction, you see. Due to the past events.'

'Really?'

'Yes.' I got up. The poor boy still looked very embarassed. 'I'll tell you about it some other time. For now, thank you very much.'

'Where are you going? What are you going to do?'

'I think it's time I went to see Nantes. To look at the factory.'

'Oh!' His face brightened. 'The Bellevie factory?'

'Yes. Thought I'd fly down tomorrow.'

'Oh! Please! Can I come with you? It would be most interesting for me. For my experience. I have never been to a cosmetics factory. I am specializing in business studies, you know, and it would be most relevant.'

I hesitated. Had Sir Richard put him up to this? I didn't really want him; I much preferred to work on my own. In an assignment like this I moved much faster solo.

'Please?' His face was quite open, genuine, like a small boy seeking an outing to the zoo or the circus. 'I could help you, perhaps.' He smiled at me shyly in supplication. 'I understand that you once played rugby. I do not follow the game but I do know that the English have beaten us for the last two years, haven't they?'

'Indeed we have. But this year's match—the Grand Slam one—was damned close. If it hadn't been for our pack we'd have had it. Your lot were inspired, especially the backs.'

'There you are! Sir Richard says you were a forward. Perhaps the combination of an English forward and a French back might be a good one? I have never played rugby but could we not go together? I would like to experience an investigation like this. May I back you up? Please?'

'Well—' put like that, it was going to be churlish to refuse the boy. 'Yes—I suppose—if you'd really like to.'

'Great! I'll drive you! It will be much better. You can

see the countryside; we will pass Chartres, Le Mans and Angers. All along the Loire from Angers to Nantes. It's very nice.'

I shook my head emphatically. 'Thank you, but no. This is not a pleasure excursion. If you come with me, you come by plane. There's a flight first thing, early. It will give us a full day at the factory.'

He pulled a face. 'You are not perhaps nervous of driving? After what has happened?' Then he brightened. 'Perhaps you would prefer the TGV? The fast train?'

I gave him an old-fashioned look. 'No, I am not afraid of driving, never have been. This is a pure business visit, not a jaunt. But since you ask, and he is clearly involved, I should tell you that Sir Richard has forbidden the recurrence of any unfortunate accidents. Fatally unfortunate accidents. So we won't take your car, just yet. Or the TGV. I prefer aeroplanes.'

He grimaced. I wasn't quite sure whether this was a simple reaction to what had happened so far or whether it came from my invoking Sir Richard, with whom he had clearly been having conversations. I left him, read the file, and met him as planned the next morning. We flew down to Nantes on a bright, fresh spring day, with strong wind from the south-west, just as you might find in England, only the country below us was bigger, spread wider, and was much much emptier. We hung over the wide estuary of the Loire before landing, with Saint-Nazaire out towards the sea, and I caught a good view of the high bridge and the built-up tangle of the city on either side of the river we dropped over Aerospatiale's factory and landed safely enough at the airport of Nantes Atlantique.

Bastoni was waiting for us in his office. I had told him not to bother meeting us, we'd take a taxi, and on the 'phone his voice seemed to approve of that. It usually helps factory managers if you don't interrupt their day with little chores like meeting people at airports, particularly when those people are foreign consultants or bankers, taking a look at businesses in the way that manufacturing men so resent. He was very neat, very dapper, certainly Italian looking, with dark hair very carefully waved and a waist-coated coarse-woven suit of a type that only very thin men can wear and still look thin.

Bastoni looked thin.

He greeted us very politely, raising his eyebrows at Christian Maucourt, whom he'd never met before, and offering us coffee, which we accepted. We passed the usual preliminaries about what we were there for and exchanged regrets at the tragic turn of events with Bonnet and Madame Delattre. Bastoni had been in the business much longer, of course, than Vauchamps, and had that detached, rather sardonic way of looking at the marketing hype which attends the retail cosmetics world that a manufacturing chemist, concerned with processes and laboratory testing, precise measurements and not emotional fervour or image-targeting, tends to get.

On the other hand he seemed genuinely shocked at the death of Madame Delattre; his thin gloomy face lengthened and puckered at the mention of her. He shook his head sadly over the accident to Bonnet, making some comment or another about the rash haste of youth and the danger of France's roads. We discussed the concentration of the industry and the changes in ownership that were occurring; Revlon had recently sold a chunk of their business to Procter & Gamble, it had just been announced in the papers, and we went through all the implications of that. Then, as the conversation hovered on the broad, macro-economic aspects of business, be looked at me curiously.

'How unusual— he smiled just too politely, his thin dark face taking on a condescending look—'I must say, to find an Englishman undertaking this kind of inquiry for a French bank. We have got so used to you staying away from our affairs that it is a pleasant surprise to come across this kind of potential collaboration. After all, you still seem a little hesitant about Europe, don't you? In fact, the nearer the completion of the Channel Tunnel gets, the more the doubts appear to multiply. If you'll excuse my saying so?'

Young Christian blinked and shuffled his feet without speaking, embarassed. I managed to resist retorting what I wanted to retort.

'Not at all.' I smiled. 'With Mrs Thatcher gone I'm sure that everything will proceed steadily. We simply want to make sure that all the implications are thought through.'

What I would have liked to have pointed out with considerable force was not simply that Britain has put through about ten times more EEC measures than his native Italy, where the plundering of central funds is considered a normal business pastime; it was that Italy of all countries is the last place from which criticisms of EEC partners should be launched. Italy, to Italians, is an economic bad joke. None of them support it. Speak of Rome, or Naples, or Piedmont, or Tuscany, and the ranks can scarce forbear to cheer, but Italy, that symbol of ice-creams and operas, is something remote, something that regionally-minded Italians plunder, a place whose taxes they never pay. For the Italians the EEC is a wonderful, new, enormous central source of fraudulent opportunity which Italy, with its limited national resources, cannot match. To be lectured on the acceptance of the EEC by an Italian is more than English flesh and blood can stand; a belief in abiding by the rules of the game has never caught on in Italy.

'Perhaps we can see the factory?' Christian Maucourt inquired earnestly, catching the edge to my smile at Bastoni, the set tension of my legs as I braced them under my chair.

'Of course.' Bastoni got up and took off his jacket, replacing it with a long white coat. We were handed similar white garments, freshly laundered. 'You must excuse me if I ask you to wear these. We have strict regulations on hygiene, all over the premises.'

'That's understood.'

We set off, passing into high, clean, laboratory-like working bays where sterilizers and vacuum driers mingled with homogenizers, agitator vessels, and granulators. Storage vessels for exotic oils, fatty compounds, emollients, resins and other mixtures shone; emulsifiers glistened in stainless steel. Drums of waxes, starch and acid derivatives were carefully inventoried along with enzymatically-produced bio esters. Bastoni talked volubly and my irritation towards him began to abate. Christian Maucourt was looking more and more confused; manufacturing plants are not easy for new young bankers. I didn't understand much of it, but Bastoni seemed to know what he was doing; the white-coated staff greeted him respectfully as we passed from department to department. It was hard, though, at first, to see how the products in the jars and bottles in the Rue Saint-Honoré came into being.

'Any questions so far?' Bastoni stopped outside a laboratory door and raised his eyebrows at me almost in challenge.

I had one ready, thinking of Thierry Vauchamps and Berthe Cauvinière, although not in equal measure.

'Skincare,' I said. 'The essential core of Bellevie's business. How much has the ecological thing affected the ingredients? The use of plants and so on.'

'Oh.' Bastoni smiled condescendingly. 'It is the fashion to push that type of thing now, I suppose. There's one we're testing in here.' He opened the door and we went into a typical laboratory room with benches down each side and test equipment, analytical balances, that sort of gear, set out neatly. 'A skincare product based on a Far Eastern plant, a tropical thing. Depending on whether you want a cream, a lotion or a fluid from it, you process the aqueous or alcoholic extract from the plant together with other elements. For a cream you use diglycerin diolate, wax, stearate, squalane, crystallized ozokerite, that sort of thing, with antioxidant and perfume. For a fluid type of product then lanolin, stearic acid, various polymers, glycol and so on. It's supposed to have a moisturizing, decongesting and wrinkle-eliminating effect, but you have to be very careful these days about what you claim for such products.'

Christian Maucourt blinked at him. 'What are kohl and henna?' he asked.

Bastoni stopped, blinked back, then laughed. 'Kohl, my dear young friend, is one of the most ancient forms of cosmetics, probably from Egyptian times. It's made from powdered antimony or lead sulphide to produce a smoke-black colour. The earliest mascara, you might say. Henna is a browny-yellow hair dye. Kohl, henna and rouge—to redden the skin—are the earliest forms of cosmetics. Why do you ask?'

Christian Maucourt blushed. 'I just heard of them recently, that's all. I wondered what they were.'

Bastoni grinned. 'You won't find them here. We are rather more advanced.'

I picked up a jar. 'Cream relaxer,' I read off the label. 'What's that?'

Bastoni smiled. 'It is for hair styling. Quite a product. You mix first waxes, cetyl alcohol, mineral oil and petrolatum. Separately you mix propylene glycol, water and alkalis. The two compounds are heated separately at seventy-five degrees Celsius and mixed at twelve point seven pH value, stirring them together. You then add sodium hydroxide pellets and water at fifty-five degrees. When it's ready you fill your bottles or jars with it.'

'What on earth does it do?'

Bastoni's smile widened back to a grin. 'It straightens kinky hair. Shall we go on to the packaging department?'

Oh dear, I thought as we moved off, oh dear. This Bastoni was no simple production chief. He was a quintessential technical man, replaceable probably, but in a very much more powerful position than Thierry Vauchamps' strategic plan revealed. The secret of the business might lie in creating images, in capturing market share, manipulating advertising and promotional spend, but here was another dimension to be carefully considered. The factory was not likely to generate any art-dramatical images; it was too dense, too difficult to visualize for that. Raw materials poured in; mysterious processes took place; products came out. What control did the marketing man in Paris have over all this?

After the raw material and formulation departments, after the mixing, blending and chemical processes, the filling of jars and bottles seemed a very simple, comprehensible affair. Not that the machinery was not complex and sophisticated; it was, but it was easy to understand what it was doing, what was going on. We finished our tour and Bastoni treated us to lunch in an immaculate canteen-dining-room where the food was very good and everyone mixed without rank or favour. He seemed more cheerful, more forthcoming in this setting and made no more cracks about the EEC, although we discussed the new directive on positive listing for materials and how few it covered compared with the thousands actually used. Afterwards we returned to his office and, avoiding chemistry and ingredients, I made notes about capacity and production flows so that I could get an idea of what Vauchamps' plan would entail by way of manufacturing investment and increased inventory. Bastoni was helpful on this and gave me various documents which set out what was needed; he seemed to be in favour of the plan.

'Thierry is a professional,' he stated. 'I respect him. I am sure he has thought it out very carefully. We need those new products, of course, all of them, as well as the selling and promotional spend he is asking for. I will be even busier if the plan comes off, but I am happy about that.' He smiled modestly. 'It will mean that we here in Nantes will have a bigger rôle to play.'

'Of course.'

'When do you expect to complete your—your assessment? To make your report?'

I smiled. 'As quickly as possible, is what I have been asked for. Which in reality means about two or three weeks.'

'Oh! Pretty soon! That's good, because we need it. I'm glad it won't be a few months, like so many of these consultancy things.'

'No. The bank are after a quick decison. Tell me, have you any idea what it was that Michel Bonnet was after?

Why he telephoned the office in Paris, just before the accident, to say he had some important information?'

Bastoni pulled another long face. 'No. I am really sorry
but I haven't. I have racked my brains without success.
Everyone has discussed this. His visit was almost identical
to yours today. We talked of company strategy, of products,
then I gave him a tour of the factory, just as you saw it. He
made a lot of notes. Alas, they were destroyed in the crash.
No one can think of what it was about. Some afterthought,
but what? It's a mystery.'

He was looking intently at me as he spoke, eyes widening,
brow furrowing, as though dredging the cells of his memory
for clues. A tic jerked the corner of his mouth. 'I was the
last person he talked to, here. I have ransacked my mind.
Everyone in the Rue Saint-Honoré knows what happens
here. It's an open book. Products are made as a result of
marketing decisions.' He spread his hands. 'We simply
serve the marketing organization. We do not even design
the packaging. There is much liaison with us, of course; this
is normal procedure, laid down by systems and planning in
Paris.'

I nodded slowly. 'So I understand. Well, if you do think
of anything please let me know, won't you?'

'Of course!'

'In the meantime I must get on.'

'And what is your feeling?' Bastoni's manner was still
preoccupied. He looked anxious. 'So far, I mean; I realize
it's still an early stage.'

'So far, so good. I haven't come up with anything wildly
negative yet.'

'Good! Good! I'm sure you won't, though.' His face lightened. 'This is a good business. Really it is.'

For the first time he displayed warmth towards me. An
enthusiasm surfaced. The charm I have always associated
with Italians broke the gloom of his thin face into an attractive smile.

'Right.' I smiled back. 'Well, thank you very much for
being so open with us and for the very interesting tour. If

you can call us a taxi, we'll let you get on with your work.'

'Not at all! I wouldn't hear of it. I'll run you to the airport myself.'

He sprang to his feet and issued instructions to his secretary while I stared at Christian Maucourt in front of me. An English pack and French wingers; how far could I trust him?

Bastoni drove us with a great flourish to the airport in a 3-litre Alfa-Romeo and assured me of his support if I thought of any further questions. He pumped our hands briskly in farewell. We bade him a cordial goodbye and he turned his charm on us both with the polished ease of an Italian professional, making me feel guilt at my initial irritation with him and his remarks about the Common Market. After all, we deserved much of the publicity we were getting and it wasn't a matter to be avoided in conversation, to be flinched away from; it had to be faced up to, to be discussed. My thoughts about Italy had been unworthy; not all Italian business is conducted by the Mafia or by fraudsters and felons. Watching him drive away, I silently reproved myself for the very sortie-approach I'd so deplored on my arrival; it was disgraceful to be dropping back into it this way.

I found myself, after we had checked in, staring at Christian Maucourt again. He licked his lips nervously under my gaze but stared back with a puzzled expression.

'What is ozokerite?' he demanded, almost aggressively. He'd kept pretty quiet on our tour and I guessed things were perplexing him.

I grinned. 'Ozokerite,' I said, 'otherwise known as ceresin, is a waxlike natural mineral mixture of hydrocarbons. It is used as an emulsifier and thickening agent. It smells absolutely foul.'

He frowned at the idea of using something foul-smelling as a skin moisturizer. 'What about stearic acid?'

'That occurs naturally. In butter acids, tallow, animal fats and wools. Like lanolin. Lanolin is a refined derivative of the secretion of a sheep's oil glands. The thing it keeps its wool waterproof with. Natural wool is greasy.'

He shuddered slightly. 'Does everything come from boiled animals or petrol hydrocarbons in this industry?'

'Dear me, no. The great thing now is to be all vegetarian about your face creams. I tell you what,' I said, getting all avuncular as we walked out to the plane, 'how would you like to do a bit of sprinting, out on the wing you might say, for me?'

'Sprinting?'

'Running around. Getting me some information.'

'Oh!' His face lightened and a flush of pleasure spread across it. 'I would really like that. Really I would. Can I do that?'

'Sure. Providing, as Sir Richard would say, you take care not to have any unfortunate accidents.'

'Why? What do you want me to do?'

'Firstly,' I said 'you can leave Thierry Vauchamps to me. I take it that that is where you heard of kohl and henna?'

He flushed. 'Er, yes. When I got the plan from him.'

'That's OK. I'm more interested in what you can tell me about Michel Bonnet. Did you know him well?'

'No.' We were approaching the entrance ladder; his legs were longer than mine and he had to slow down. 'Not really. He worked for my Uncle Eugène, you see, and I have only just started to help there.'

'Can you please make some inquiries about him? What you can tactfully find from his family? It will be much easier for you to do that than me. See if you can find where he was digging, what information sources he visited. Try the secretaries at the bank. Find out what he actually said. Go gently, though. OK?'

'OK.' He smiled cheerfully. 'Anything else?'

'Just one more thing. Ingredients. The last word in Michel Bonnet's notes. I want you to find out all you can about ingredients. I'll tell you how to start. But have a look into what it is that Bellevie use, mostly. Talk to Berthe

Cauvinière. She'll help you. Tell her I sent you, but make an appointment first. OK?'

'Fine.' He looked delighted. 'But what are you going to do? In the meantime?'

'In the meantime— I paused with my foot on the stairway up to the aircraft—'I am going to chase after a hare. A strong, muscular hare.'

CHAPTER 13

The basement of the Tate Gallery is not unlike the bowels of a ship. Once you are down there you have to pass through big security doors, several of them like steel watertight jobs in the bulkheads of a powerful vessel which risks being torpedoed or struck by rocks. The fact is that they are watertight, have been ever since the Thames once rose far more than anticipated and flooded the lower levels of the place with muddy river and ooze. Since there are far more paintings stacked in the basements of the Tate Gallery than there are out on display to the public up top, at the time this was a disaster of remarkable proportions.

As I followed her through the third set of such doors, Sue turned and looked back at me worriedly for the umpteenth time.

'I wasn't expecting you for *days*,' she almost wailed. 'I'm so busy, Tim! What are you doing here?'

'Playing hookey. Why haven't you said you're pleased to see me?'

'I am! I am! But it's so—so—'

'What?'

'So alarming. I don't like sudden descents like this, you know that. I like to be advised in advance. To dash back from Paris like this! And why do you want to see the Tissots?'

'I've told you: I'll explain when we're there. I'm very disappointed that they're not on display. It's quite disgraceful; I wouldn't have had to bother you if they were out up top, in the galleries. I might just have nipped over and gone back without telling you.'

She pulled a face at me. 'I've told you; the Tissots were out last year. We have to rotate these paintings; we've far too many.'

'Yes, there is a lot of art about, isn't there?'

She didn't deign to reply to that; she coded one more security door's electronic panel and we pushed through into a cavernous, cool basement in high painted cement, with great steel mesh racks in rows going up to the ceiling. These racks are mounted on rails, with castor-type wheels, so that they can be pulled in and out. Each high vertical mesh rack, like a great sliding door, has paintings hung on both sides and there are rows and rows of racks. I began to catch sight of familiar pictures: a Gilbert Spencer of a farmyard; one of his unmistakable brother Stanley's; a Morland; something by Luke Fildes, oh yes, *Applicants for Admission to a Casual Ward*—that was it, surprisingly small, really. Sue stopped and gestured to a young, blue-jeaned assistant.

'Here we are,' she said. 'Can you pull this one out, please?'

The lad nodded and heaved on one of the racks, actually, I now realized, pulling it out of the way so that we could get at the rack behind, and see it clearly. He brought two chairs over and planked them down.

'There you are,' Sue said. '*The Ball on Shipboard*. Now what is all this about, Tim? Why have you dashed back so soon?'

I didn't reply. I was staring at the painting. After a few moments I had to sit down.

'Jesus Christ,' I said.

It is spectacularly colourful. The deck is overhung with bunting made from the most gaudy flags in the world. White Ensigns and Union Jacks vie with the Stars and Stripes, Russian Imperial Eagles, the German Imperial ensign, something with a red and yellow Scottish lion in it, even a blue and white striped Uruguayan flag with a smiling gamboge sun. Under this fantastic canopy, ladies in flounced, frilled and bustled dresses of every colour parade themselves. Away to the left, through rigging, can be seen land beyond a river estuary in which boats are sailing and a cutter is being rowed by a crew of matelots. Beyond the well-deck of the ship an orchestra plays, couples dance, and rows of sailors look on. The perspective of these different levels jumps at you; the spatial construction is exceptional. Men, whiskered or clean-shaven, old and young, converse with the ladies, striking various attitudes in various clothes. There is an area of open deck right in front you that creates an extraordinary clearing. Across it, slightly right of centre but very prominent, are two young ladies in flounced black-and-white dresses, facing away from a white-whiskered old man who stares blankly into space. Nearby, on the left, a girl in a green and black striped dress stares back over her shoulder at something or someone behind and above you, while an old gaffer in naval togs looks, in turn, over her head at something else, something invisible. It is like a brilliant photograph which catches a frozen moment at a social event: afterwards, looking at it, the context becomes impenetrable, full of misunderstandings and questions. What was she saying? Why is he doing that? Who the blazes is the officer in uniform?

'Mere coloured photographs of vulgar society,' I murmured.

'Tim? What did you say?'

'I was quoting Ruskin. Miserable sod.'

It is quite a large painting, about four feet long by three deep, in wonderful condition, so intensely coloured that it hits the eye abruptly, like dashing a sharp eyewash on to the pupil and causing, for a moment, the shining dresses and the calculated poses to hit the retina with a cold brilliance, a magnificent concentration, that betrays an exceptional but chilly masterpiece.

It is the most important painting of Tissot's time in England.

'It's supposed to be a ball given on the Royal yacht at

Cowes, for Cowes Regatta, in eighteen seventy-three,' I said.

'I know that,' Sue said crossly. 'I do know this painting, Tim. Why are you here and not at work?'

'Sacheverell Sitwell speculated that one of the two prominent young ladies in black and white dresses, the one with the straw hat tipped up on her head, is Alexandra, the Princess of Wales. Sitwell suggests that the old gent to the left of her may be the Tsar Alexander the Second—the ball was given in honour of the Tsar—or, he says, perhaps Lord Londonderry. I'm not sure if he means the Lord Londonderry who never spoke to his wife after her affair with Harry Cust or his father. From his age it must be the father. But I don't think it is. Or the Tsar, either.'

'Tim! I have read *Narrative Paintings* by Sacheverell Sitwell, damn it! It's *my* copy at home, you know!'

'He's talking through his hat. That's the problem with Tissot's paintings. They're never quite what they seem. It wasn't given—the ball—on the Royal yacht. It was on HMS *Ariadne*. On the twelfth of August eighteen seventy-three. In honour of the Tsarevitch and Tsarevna of Russia. Not the Tsar.'

'What?'

'That's not Alexandra either; she wouldn't be wearing the same dress as another woman. When I was researching Moreton Frewen's life I found a book by Frewen's biographer, Allen Andrews, about Edward the Seventh's love-life. A pot-boiler really, but there's an illustration of this painting in it. Funny old world, isn't it? You never know where things will pop up next. Andrews points out that the Jerome sisters often wore identical dresses, usually by Worth of Paris. After all, like Tissot, they'd recently fled the Paris of the Prussian War and the Commune. Those two dresses in the painting are by Worth of Paris, who was the Jerome couturier. So those two ladies in black and white, Andrews says, are the Jerome sisters of New York.'

'*Tim?*'

'If they are the Jerome sisters—and we know that they

attended the ball dressed in identical dresses because Princess Alexandra herself commented on it—and it is the ball in question, then it is the one at which Lord Randolph Churchill met Jennie and fell in love with her, instantly, as a result of which they married and Winston came about. If that really is Jennie Jerome there, this must be one of the most important paintings in British social history.'

She didn't say anything. She was looking at the two black and white creations with wide eyes. She didn't look happy.

'If those are the Jerome sisters then one of them is Jennie and the other is her older sister Clara. Clara Jerome. You remember Clara Jerome? She married Moreton Frewen. Dear old Mortal Ruin himself, the one Donald White, Jeremy's cousin, got into such a—*'

She stood up abruptly, marched over to the young blue-jeaned lad and peremptorily asked him if he would mind leaving us. He hesitated for just a moment, saw her expression, and was gone through the watertight bulkhead doors like a ship's rat from a flooding hold. She came back and smacked the spare chair beside me round so that she could sit on it akimbo, bang between me and the painting.

I peered round her to get a proper view as I went on. 'Funny, isn't it? How life goes round in circles. I mean, after all that business when Sir Richard and Donald White were forcibly retired, that violence, and the Moreton Frewen thing, here we are, miles from anywhere, sitting in the basement of the Tate and images are facing us, echoes are reverberating all around us of those days when, if you recall—'

'Tim! Stop that now! Stop! Tell me—*now*—what the *hell* this is all about. And don't babble like that!'

I told her. I told her carefully, keeping to the major events. When I finished she blew out her breath, through the nose, letting it blow loudly and long.

'Just the two deaths so far?' she inquired sarcastically.

'Just the two.'

'Both accidents?'

* *Mortal Ruin*

'Of course. A car and a train. France seems to be danger-ous, transport-wise.'

'Dear God. I really thought you'd be out of trouble this once.'

'I still could be. Apart from Bank politics, of course.'

'Of course.' It wasn't said sincerely. 'And Sir Richard is back on the scene?'

'It might just be coincidence.'

'It might.' She didn't sound convinced. There was a long silence while she thought, still facing me. Then she bright-ened faintly, half-turning towards the painting. Her voice picked up in certainty, in confidence, as she started to speak. 'The Jerome sisters theory is almost certainly hog-wash, Tim.' Her tone became more cheerful. 'Thank heaven for that; it helps to calm me a bit. I don't want Moreton Frewen back from the past to haunt us. Not all that nastiness and White family skeletons. There, fortu-nately, you are wrong.' She turned back to me trium-phantly. 'For good reasons, but wrong.'

'Oh?' I looked at her, then round her, at the painting, where the two pretty black and white ladies still stood frozen in their elegant stances, enveloped in black-ribboned, snowy-white flounces like iced figures on a boarded cake.

Sue stood up and pointed to the painting like a teacher for the enlightenment of a class. 'You haven't looked closely enough yet, Tim. Or perhaps you should have read the Tate's little booklet by Malcolm Warner. Look at the group up to the left here, of four girls sitting talking to a man. See them?'

'I see them.'

'See the two pairs of identical dresses?'

'I see them.'

'See that girl there and that one? Same dresses. There are no less than four pairs of identical girls in this painting, in identical dresses, I mean.'

'Damn. Damn, damn, damn.'

She smiled for the first time, relief flooding into her face.

'Bad luck, Tim. Just when you thought you had something clever coming on. Tissot had a habit of using the same model in the same dress twice in the same picture, in different poses. I think your premonitions are all wrong this time. There's *The Rivals* of eighteen seventy-eight in which he does it with two pretty girls in a sitting-room, for instance. He had a wardrobe of dresses for his models. You often see the same dress in different paintings.'

'Ah.' I made an attempt to clear my mind. 'But the pairing technique was probably used after this painting, wasn't it? Which comes first, the chicken or the egg? Did he paint identically-dressed ladies before this one or only after? In other words did he see the Jerome sisters at the Cowes Ball first and subsequently use the idea of identically-dressed models, getting it from them, or had he done it before?'

Sue bit her lip, frowning. 'I don't know. I think there's an earlier one—appropriately called *Too Early*—an empty ballroom thing like Orchardson, that had identical dresses in it, but I'm not sure.' Her face lightened. 'Ah! I've got it! Andrews must be wrong; that black and white dress was used by Tissot in a painting called *Reading the News*. The identical dress, painted after this picture. So it can't have belonged to the Jerome sisters.' She gave a triumphant wave at the painting. 'End of the Jerome connection, Tim. End of Mortal Ruin. Maybe coincidence ruled those accidents after all.'

'Blast. But good. Very good, Sue. Thanks.'

She was grinning, the relief relaxing her face completely. 'You are a superstitious old twerp, Tim. Really you are.' Coming away from the painting, she kissed me on the cheek. 'You had me terribly worried for a while. There's something else I've remembered too; I did a lot of research at the time of the Frewen thing, remember? I read Ralph Martin's book on Jennie from cover to cover. *Lady Randolph Churchill*. Two volumes. Jennie's dress for that ball was very décolletée; completely bare shoulders and very revealing of bosom. Poor Randolph could hardly take his eyes off her.

I remember thinking no wonder she caught him at once.'
She gestured at the painting. 'Look at them; like most of
Tissot's, these are quite circumspect. They cover the body,
shoulders, arms, the lot. So they can't look like the Jerome
sisters did on that occasion.'

'Hell. I really was away there, for a while. I thought that
Sir Richard and/or Charles Maucourt were up to something
vengeful of real sophistication.'

I stared at the painting in irritation. Was Andrews really
so wrong? Tissot would hardly have dared to show the
Jerome sisters in racy outfits. He already incurred the wrath
of critics about raciness: when the painting was shown at
the Royal Academy one critic said that there was 'not a
lady in a score of female figures' and the reception was
hostile. Miserable British critics had to find fault with him.
Tissot could not, presumably, make the figures recognizable for fear of retribution from aristocratic, indeed royal,
sources. The sisters could, all the same, have been the inspi-
ration for him; where else would he have seen or heard of
an identically-dressed pair of pretty ladies at a Royal ball
on a ship? From what other source could the idea have
come to him?

Sue squeezed my arm. 'Never mind, Tim. It was a good
theory, but you're not resurrecting that old business again.
These different versions of women are a bit like those ship
portraits where you see the same vessel from different
angles. Tissot did that with his models. *The Rivals* is a classic
example; they're not really rivals at all, just the same girl
in different poses. Perhaps he got it from ships' portraits;
he was a considerable ship painter, after all. All that rigging, always accurate. It came from his youth in Nantes.'

'Where?'

'Nantes. He came from Nantes.' She raised her eyebrows
at me in mock surprise. 'Surely you knew that? His father
was a linen-draper and his mother made hats, both of them
successfully. That's why he painted dresses and hats so
accurately too. All that fashionable clothing. And ships.

Nantes was a major port then—what's the matter? Why are you frowning like that?'

'It's a bit odd; Charles Maucourt never mentioned it.'

'Mentioned what?'

'Nantes. Damn it, he and I went through quite a few of Tissot's Thames paintings and etchings, full of ships and rigging, at his flat, but he never mentioned Nantes. I know I didn't go there until after I'd had my session with him, but all the same; it's a bit creepy, that.'

'Oh, Tim. Now please don't start that again, I beg you. Please. I was just starting to feel happy once more.'

I nodded. 'Sorry. It could just be that he thinks of Bellevie as a Paris company and relegates the factory out of his thinking. A lot of city people tend to do that. There's probably nothing in it. How could there be? After all this time. The factory was built in Nantes to get regional development grants; it was EEC money, I think. A few years back. Pure coincidence, I'm sure.'

She frowned, now. 'Why is he drawing your attention to Tissot like this?'

I shrugged. 'I was suspicious, but now I think it's just an enthusiasm of his. He seems to have a thing about him. He has a lot of information on Tissot but it's in old magazines and engravings, not in actual paintings he's trying to flog to me or anything. He says he's always admired the Art Fund and likes to follow its progress. He's even boned up on his Reitlinger, which is a bit old hat but still very useful. I've never really bothered about Tissot before because he's a special case. Between the Impressionists and the narrative boys. A Frenchman in England and an "English" painter in France. I'll have to mug up on him, I guess.'

She shook her head ruefully. 'I thought you'd be completely tied up with the cosmetics business.'

'Well, I am, really. Tell me, sweetheart, how did you come to know so much about Tissot?'

She gave me a prim look.

'Sorry,' I muttered.

'Do credit your poor wife with a little knowledge, Tim!

Please! I am a serious member of the senior staff here, not just your back-room assistant! We do possess his finest English painting; I could hardly ignore that, could I? And you know my thing about Impressionists; Tissot was actually invited to join them at one time; he was a close friend of Degas until the Commune and of Manet and Whistler and Sargent and so on. He practised etching with Seymour Haden, Whistler's brother-in-law, and mastered it quickly. There's no challenging his technical skill.' She gestured at the gaudy canvas. 'Staying over here retarded him, though. Cut him off from the main stream of French art development. He's a very interesting figure, even if he's an oddball.'

'Oddball? Why?'

'His paintings are enigmatic. Ambiguous. Tense.' She shivered a little. 'They're often very cold. A sort of non-committal but very intelligent, very observant coldness. Look at that—' she gestured at the striped colours again. 'He saw, as Moreton Frewen clearly did, that this society was empty, purposeless. There is no interplay between the people you are looking at, is there? And his private life affected his work. Come on; I haven't time to give you a lecture on Tissot. We must go. I must get you out of here.'

'Oh, great.' I put an arm around her. 'Shall we pop home?'

'Tim! I have to work!' Her eyes flashed indignantly. 'You've interrupted me enough already. Really!'

My arm still held her. 'I was going to say for a bite of lunch. But if you're so occupied I'll see you later, after I've called in at the Bank. Yes?'

She smiled disbelievingly. 'Bite of lunch, I'll be bound! But yes, I'll see you later, Tim. I'm so pleased you're home. Is it just for tonight?'

'Just for tonight.'

'Pity.'

I released her and she turned to go. A mischievous look came into her eyes. 'I tell you what,' she said, gesturing at another painting, also a Tissot, on the rack. 'There's one

over there with a little story—a *jeu de mots* I think you'd
call it—HMS *Calcutta*.'

'Really?'

It was a smaller painting. A slice of tight deck carried
round the stern quarter-lights of a ship, its railed gallery
overlooking a dockyard. Two girls, flouncily dressed yet
again, leant on the rail watched by a young naval officer.
One, hiding her face behind a fan, was half-raised out of her
chair, so that her expensively-clad, beribboned posterior
pointed towards you, the viewer.

'*The Gallery of HMS Calcutta*,' Sue said. 'Calcutta? The
old French pun? *Quel cul tu as*. What a bottom you've got.
The classic *jeu de mots*. Look at her. Pushing it at you.'

'Good heavens.' I really was quite surprised. 'How saucy.
I'd no idea Tissot was flippant like that.'

'Ah—' she smiled—'there's no knowing when you're
looking at a Tissot. He may not have intended it that way
at all, it may be just some joker's pun, but the English
always suspected he was laughing at them while he was
here. He had a very detached eye for the English society he
knew so well. They thought he was judging them. That was
one of the difficulties he had. Jealousy was another. Come
on, Tim.' The mischievous look was still in her eyes. 'Save
the frisky stuff for later. I've got work to do.'

'Very good, madame. But this is work for me, you know.'

She grinned. 'No one at White's Bank has ever believed
that, except you and Jeremy. Come on; let's go.'

She snapped off a light and we left the gaudy painting,
the ships, the flags, the pretty dresses, and frozen stares
from Tissot's glassy masterpiece, entombed with the other
canvases in the steel-racked, high-ceilinged silence of art's
most expensive cellar.

CHAPTER 14

He wasn't pleased to see me. He strode up and down a bit, muttering. He glared in my direction. He relented, sat down behind his desk, changed his mind, stood up again, glared at me a bit more, relented once more, and sat down again.

'Calm yourself, Jeremy,' I said. I was comfortably slumped in one of his spare chairs, my legs stuck straight out. 'There's nothing you can do now. I'm here. Accept it. I'll leave you shortly and I'll be back in France tomorrow, I promise you. But for the moment I'm here.'

'Why? Damn it, why? I specifically told you to stay there!'

'That was before the death of Madame Delattre.'

'What the hell has that got to do with it?' he nearly shouted.

I raised my eyebrows and gave him an old-fashioned stare without replying. He glared back at me, wilted, groaned, then put his head in his hands. A picture of despair, he was.

'Dear God,' he moaned. 'Dear God. Why did I agree to send you? Why? It wasn't as though you wanted to go.'

'Come, come Jeremy. *Courage, mon vieux.* You must be brave. You would have to have faced up to much of it anyway. Especially Sir Richard. Let me summarize the situation from my angle. I get sent to France to do a new shining job for the combined forces of that famous Anglo-French alliance, White's and Maucourt Frères. *Les Blanches Maucourts* one might call it. The trouble is that I find it is not only not a new job, it does not shine, and the previous incumbent has been killed in a car crash. His papers have been conveniently cremated. I find, to my astonishment, the presence of that *éminence grise* Sir Richard White, hand in glove with old Charles Maucourt. I am slipped, willy-nilly, the assistance of young Christian Maucourt, who has been nobbled, previously and cunningly, by Sir Richard, who refers to me, for some extraordinary reason, as deceptive. Deceptive! Me, deceptive! I ask you, in all this throng, who is the least deceptive man you can perceive? I find a fast-thinking marketer presiding over a dismal shop inhabited by a resistant dragon-lady he hates, whose heroic past is bound up, in addition to past ownership, with that not only of Charles Maucourt but also of Sir Richard. A past no one has thought useful to acquaint me with. The dragon-lady having indicated that she has things to say to me, yet a further accident conveniently removes her from the running. This time it is the prosaic Paris version of the Tube which obliges. The factory in Nantes is presided over by a sinister Italian who, I suspect, knows more about cosmetics than anyone else in the company—ah! I've just thought of something.'

'What?' Jeremy almost lunged forward at me.

'We know nothing about that Italian.' I scribbled a note in my pocket diary. 'I must look into his past career, check where he's been. To resume: in the meantime, behind the scenes and back at the ranch, there is obviously a rare old upheaval going on. The stately Eugène Maucourt, who one could perhaps credit with starting my end of things, has been conspicuous by his absence. You must excuse me therefore if I feel a desire to touch base, as the baseball players say, by seeing you personally. It is good to see you personally, Jeremy. I was beginning to wonder if you'd still be here.'

'Tim! Really! Surely you could credit me with greater durability than that?'

'I was joking, Jeremy. Humorously over-dramatizing. May I know, before I return to the skirmish, what the headquarters dispositions are and how many staff officers and generals we can count on? Could we start, for instance, with Peter Lewis?'

He flushed. 'Peter Lewis is on the other side,' he snarled. 'I shan't forgive Peter Lewis for this.'

'On the other side? Is this spiritualist imagery? Has he

left us? Or are there, definitely, battle lines drawn up?'

A deeper red suffused him. 'Peter Lewis claims that Uncle Richard's return to business affairs is very recent. He says that Richard got bored with life in the Dordogne and that with his knowledge of French he feels he can add experience and weight to the board in some capacity or another. The Maucourt share swap is what sparked it off, apparently. If I'd known that this was going to be one of the results, I'd never have supported the bloody deal. Anyway, according to Peter Lewis, Maucourt's have offered Sir Richard a non-executive directorship on their side already!'

'What?'

'You may well shout what! He's going to be a director of Maucourt's. In an advisory capacity. That links him back to us already. Old Charles Maucourt had no hesitation. Bent Eugène's ear to compliance straight away, apparently, on the strength of their old association.'

'You mean that Peter Lewis *and* Sir Richard are now both on Maucourt's board?'

'Precisely, my dear Tim! They are. And while they may not have much clout there now, who knows what they'll be up to next? Come nineteen ninety-two, we'll have Maucourt's entire board landing at Hastings to emulate Duke William of Normandy. In this bank's direction anyway.'

'But look here, Jeremy, surely Peter Lewis must have known all this? He never said a dicky-bird at our meeting. How the hell does he explain that?'

Jeremy glanced moodily at his desktop. 'He claims he's acted entirely in good faith. That Uncle Richard sprang it on him suddenly and swore him to silence until it was announced officially. If you had been in France, Tim, doing as I told you instead of swanning about here asking useless questions, you'd have received the news today. It'll be in the *Financial Times* tomorrow.'

'Good God! Sir Richard must be seventy if he's a day.'

'It's only a non-executive post, Tim. Advisory capacity.

And he's a fit man, you know. Mind you, he's paid dearly for it, I reckon.'

'Paid? How has he paid?'

'Lewis has confided to me—and this is in the strictest confidence—that Uncle Richard has agreed to take over a slice of the Bellevie shares from Maucourt's.'

'Eh?'

'You may well shout eh as well as what! Maucourt's needed to offload a bit of the risk. Uncle Richard has obliged for them. In his personal capacity, of course; he's a wealthy man, you know. So what better way to show their gratitude? "Claw thou my elbow and I'll scratch thy breech." What? He takes a block of Bellevie shares, which brings in cash to Maucourt's and dilutes their risk, and they bung him a directorship. A distinguished English banker, or even ex-banker, of Francophile turn of mind, is a perfectly legitimate appointment. Especially with nineteen ninety-two on the agenda.'

'No wonder he's taking an interest. The cunning old stoat must know something we don't. I don't suppose he gives a damn what I come up with. He'll push for expansion willy-nilly.'

'Ah.' Jeremy held up a finger. 'Now there I think you're wrong. He needs a good report from someone seen to be uninvolved. At present White's have not participated, but we've been invited to. If our independent assessment is favourable and we pitch in, then the steamroller will be rolling. Other shareholders can be found, more money can be generated. He could probably turn a profit before more cash has to be pumped in. But I don't think he'll do that. I think he really does want to stay with this project for a while because he's bored. Remember, Tim, before we uprooted him he was a very busy man. He's done virtually nothing for three years. Now he has a chance to play the game again, both at Bellevie as a shareholder and at Maucourt as an adviser. Today Paris—'

'Tomorrow London.'

'Precisely. And after that Brussels or Frankfurt. Why not?'

'For heaven's sake, Sir Richard isn't in that league. You used to say that he was barmy. Off his chump.'

Jeremy grinned. 'You mustn't resurrect old family feelings, Tim. I did, it's true. But I never doubted his cunning. He's never been stupid. He had tremendous experience and I think his enforced rest may have done him good. Perhaps a sabbatical is a good idea, after all. I remember you telling me that the architect, Richard Norman Shaw, took six months off in Aix-les-Bains or somewhere when he was feeling clapped out in his late fifties and then he came back and designed some of his best work. Whatever the case, we mustn't underestimate Richard.'

'I certainly won't do that. No wonder he's watching me. He has a lot hingeing on Bellevie.'

'Yes, he has.'

'I still don't understand why they didn't get another French squeaker like Michel Bonnet to do the job. If they really believe there is a danger of some sort and that someone else is likely to be eliminated in transport they should call in the police.'

Jeremy bridled in mock horror. 'The police? Gendarmerie? My dear Tim! Think of the scandal! The plod? Maucourt's would never do that. There is no evidence on which to draw in the police, surely?'

'I suppose not. But what are they all after? What politics are affecting these moves?'

A furtive look came into Jeremy's face. His eye avoided mine. For the first time I was conscious of a suppression of information in his mind, of an unwillingness to explain.

'Jeremy?'

He blew out a long sigh, then squeezed his nose between finger and thumb. 'My dear Tim, you know how things are at present. The last thing we want is to have to cut staff, announce redundancies like they're doing all over the City. We need to link up with Maucourt's and possibly even another European partner if we are to stay in business. It's creating all sorts of new alignments and groupings within the board. People like Richard and Peter Lewis have all sorts of connections.'

'So have you.'

'Indeed I have. But mostly with the big insurance boys and the pension funds here. I blame myself: I've never been much of a European. I like James in Brazil and our mutual friend Andy Casey in Chicago.'

'We're still going to need them.'

'Indeed we are. But nineteen ninety-two is upon us, Tim, and we're caught a bit on the hop, like the railways with the Channel Tunnel. We're going to have to get a shift on. That's what's causing ructions.'

He stared at me and I waited for him to throw out his usual expostulations, his coloured explicatory phrases as to the nature of the ructions. But he didn't; he sat behind his desk in an upright posture which contrasted, perhaps deliberately, with my own slump into his spare chair. A silence fell which emphasized the space between us and I realized, now, that he wasn't going to elucidate any more; I'd heard all he was going to say.

I stood up. 'In that case I'll leave you to do some shifting while I get back to the Bellevie grindstone. You will let me know what's happening, won't you? It seems that nineteen ninety-two is bringing all sorts of insect life out of the wood-work. Old and young.'

His eyes rested on me thoughtfully. 'Have they offered you a job yet?'

'Who?'

'Maucourt's.'

I shook my head. 'No, they haven't.'

'They will.' He nodded grimly to himself. 'They will. Where are you going now if you're not back in Paris until tomorrow?'

'Home,' I lied, thinking of muscular hares and frilly dresses. 'Why?'

He scowled at me. 'I have a suspicious mind,' he said.

'So have I. Think of the trouble it has caused. Tell me

something, Jeremy: apart from Donald White, about whom I need not remind you, have there been any other members of your family who invested in ruinous schemes of Moreton Frewen's and who have cause to hate old Mortal Ruin and his memory?'

He stared at me. 'Not that I know of. Good God, what on earth is making you bring up that horrid old subject again?'

'Oh, nothing. Well, you brought up Brazil, remember, and I wondered if there were any other family skeletons in the closet. Sir Richard wasn't a victim of Frewen's investments by any chance?'

He scowled. 'Richard is not of that generation. His father, to my knowledge, certainly would not have speculated on a Frewen scheme. In fact his father was very successful, which is one of the reasons why Richard is wealthy, though he must be given credit for increasing his inherited capital. Uncle Richard can be very shrewd. Why do you ask?'

'Oh nothing. Just a train of thought.' A vision of the two pretty girls on the deck of the ship still persisted in my head.

'This will be something to do with Tissot,' he ground out. 'I feel it in my bones.'

'Really, Jeremy. We have better things with which to occupy our minds. You said so yourself.'

'I meant it, too. Tim, will you please understand that the Art Fund is somewhat *non grata* right now. The board think it's a flippancy of ours and they're in a serious mood. Just keep the Fund in low profile, will you?'

He glared at me expectantly, so I made a mollifying noise and left quickly. It was not the time to point out how well the Fund had done, nor how it tied in with our investments in Christerby's, of which many were jealous, nor what good publicity it had brought us. I wasn't supposed to be taking that line. The Fund was obviously out of favour and there were new lines to toe.

I've never been very good at toeing lines. Jeremy knows that.

That's the trouble with working for Jeremy; we've got to know each other far too well.

CHAPTER 15

The tiny office Charles Massenaux occupies above the premises of Christerby's, international fine art auctioneers, is lined with shelves which sag under the weight of the catalogues he keeps for reference purposes. The room is filled with a scratched oak desk, behind which Charles Massenaux sat in a well-padded arm chair, and a small hard uncomfortable mock-Hepplewhite, on which I perched uncomfortably.

'Tissot,' Charles Massenaux said. 'Good God, whatever next?'

Charles Massenaux is normally attired in dark pinstripes and snowy white shirts against which flashy red ties tend to gleam. Today he was in a waistcoat and Bengal-striped shirtsleeves on which a thick layer of dust had settled. A cobweb clung to one trouser leg. He looked slightly dishevelled. Catching him like this, *en deshabille* so to speak, made me feel that White's Bank had invested wisely when it bought thirty per cent of Christerby's shares. Charles, as the director in charge of fine paintings and as an expert on the Impressionists, was obviously earning his keep. He had emerged from the bowels of the auction rooms, dusty like this, obviously in mid-catalogue of an unkempt collection of canvases, at my bidding.

'It is not often,' he had snarled at me, 'that I allow an interruption while I am cataloguing. Indeed it is rare. My cataloguing time is sacrosanct. I need absolute concentration while cataloguing.' A lock of his flowing dark hair had fallen over one eye. 'If it were not for the fact that you are on the board as a non-executive director, I might have told them to send you packing.'

'I thought that we were friends. Directorships, especially non-executive ones, are as nothing in the face of genuine friendships, Charles.'

'What do you want?'

'Charles, really! I come, cap in hand, to consult the oracle. As an ancient Greek to Mount Whatsit. Talking of Mount Whatsit, can we go up to your office to read the runes?'

So there we were, up in his office, reading them. In front of me, open at the relevant page, was Reitlinger's *The Economics of Taste*. The relevant page, between Tintoretto, Jacopo Robusti, and Titian, Tiziano Vecellio, contained the entry for Tissot, James. The entry read as follows:

JAMES TISSOT, 1836-1902

A Frenchman who came to England in 1871 and who painted anecdotal pictures, but charmingly in a manner deriving from Whistler and Manet. He had a modest vogue in his lifetime and was even reputed to have made a £1000 fee on occasions. But it was decided at his death that he had not created High Art. Furthermore, his own admirers were antagonized by the religious paintings of his last years. By the 1920's Tissot's poetic and evocative paintings were hardly worth the price of their frames. A revival began in the 'thirties and today the better sort of Tissot should make over a thousand pounds.

		£
1873	Murietta C. *On the Thames*, bought in (see 1833)	598 10s.
1874	Lord Powerscourt C. *Avant le départ*	945
1875	Barlow C. *The World and the Cloister*	367 10s.
1876	*The Railway Station*	388 10s.
1881	Houldsworth C. *The reply*, bought in	787 10s.
1883	Murietta C. *On the Thames* (see 1873)	273
1888	Charles Waring C. *Les Adieux*	231 10s.
	William Lee C. *Visitors to the National Gallery* (see 1929)	157 10s.

1903	Branch and Lees. *The Captain's Daughter*	183	15s.
1913	Lord Holden C. *Waiting for the Fourth*	44	2s.
1928	Tate Gallery buys *The Visit*	40	
1929	C. *Visitors to the National Gallery* (see 1888)	21	
	Tate Gallery buys *The Picnic*	200	
1937	Chantrey Bequest buys *The Ball on Shipboard*	600	
1940	C. *In Kew Gardens*	73	10s.
1945	Chantrey bequest buys *The Party on Board a Man-of-War*	2500	
1947	C. *Reading the News*	304	10s.
1951	C. *Henley Regatta*	945	
1954	C. *Waiting for the ferry*	1627	10s.
1957	C. *Amateur circus*	1207	
	Hide and Seek	892	10s.

'Over a thousand pounds,' I read out from the text, still perching uncomfortably, and then checked the date of publication of Reitlinger's book: 1961, Barrie and Rockliff, London. These figures were getting towards the 'inverted parabola' referred to by Charles Maucourt, but not anywhere near the exponential shape to be expected in recent years. I had my reluctant but curious companion working on that.

'Tissot,' Charles Massenaux repeated. 'What in God's name are you up to now, Tim?'

'Just carry on checking. Charles. The last few volumes of the Art Sales Index. Although Reitlinger said over a thousand pounds, the better ones obviously fetched a lot more than that, even when he was writing.'

He bared his teeth at me and scribbled down figures from the open books in front of him. The lock of hair fell back over one eye. 'I take it,' he said, without looking up, 'that Sue knows all about this?'

'Indeed she does. She opened the vaults of the Tate to

me only a few hours ago so that I could look at the very
acquisitions and Chantrey Bequests referred to in the
Reitlinger list.'

'Did she just?' He scribbled again. 'And how many dead
bodies have you told her about so far?'

'Just the two, Charles.'

He stopped. His eyebrows shot up. He put down his
pen and shoved the lock of hair out of his eye. 'Are you
serious?'

'You asked, and I answered. They were accidents,
actually.'

'Accidents? With you in the offing?'

I gave him a prim look. 'There is no need to be offensive,
Charles. No need at all. I take it that you are not an admirer
of Tissot's?'

'Not really, no. It's a bit like I told you when you were
after the Pre-Raphaelites. I've been brainwashed to believe
that the Impressionists beat all that lot hollow and I tend
to believe my brain. In his early days Tissot was very Pre-
Raphaelite. All those mediæval paintings after Leys, that
Flemish-Breton gothic approach. Chaps in red tights or
armour and ladies in wimples or whatever. The pretty girls
came afterwards. He could paint, I grant you, he couldn't
half paint, but it was all a bit photographic. Ruskin had a
point.' He chewed thoughtfully for a moment at something
imaginary in his mouth and then went back to looking at
the figures in front of him. 'There was a lack of aerial
perspective, too,' he said.

'What does that mean?'

He frowned. 'I'd have to have a painting in front of me
to explain.'

'Oh. What else?'

Charles shrugged. 'He's good, Tim. And he's got a
following. Just that there's something—something—' he
paused.

'What?'

He shook his head. 'Something difficult to explain. Something cold. De Goncourt said that Tissot had an eye like

poached mackerel, yet somehow he's laughing at you while you look. Those frozen narratives of picnics and socializing are never quite what they seem.' He shivered slightly. 'On the other hand, portraits like Colonel Burnaby and those soldiers in the Tuileries are good, really very good. He's hard to place. Between Impressionism and narration, geographically. The ultimate technician and yet a psychologist at the same time. Every scene he did makes you wonder what the hell is going on, who's looking at whom and why. Then a pug dog or a child or something, always incidental but intrusive, significant somehow, but of what? Something you can't put your finger on.'

I grinned. 'He seems to have got to you, Charles.'

'He has. He's not my cuppa tea but I can't ignore him.'

'So how much is he getting to?'

He slapped the last volume shut on the desk in front of him, scribbled one more figure on a sheet of lined paper and handed it to me. 'The major figures,' he said.

The list was straightforward. It made me whistle softly. It read:

82/3	*A Widow*	£122,000
	Reading the News	£170,000
	The Garden Bench	£520,000
85/6	*The Rubens Hat*	£280,000
87/88	*Fête day at Brighton*	£473,000
88/89	*Kathleen Newton*	£388,000
	Tryst at Riverside café	£228,000
	K. Newton at the piano	£230,000
	K. Newton in an armchair	£170,000
	Reading the News	£790,000
89/90	Pastel-*Princesse de Broglie*	£600,000

I finished re-reading and whistled again. *Reading the News* was the one Sue had mentioned, with the 'Jerome' dress by Worth's in it. A hell of a price, having sold for £304 10s. in 1947, for £170,000 in 1982/3 and £790,000 in 1988/9. The 'inverted parabola' was rocketing into orbit at this near end.

'It looks to me,' I said, my eyes meeting those of Charles Massenaux, 'as though something's working itself up towards a million quid.'

He smiled the smile of an oily auctioneer. 'I shouldn't be surprised.'

'You look knowing. Is something coming up soon?'

He shook his head. 'Not that I know of. Not here, anyway. But there'll be one as the market recovers. Tissots come up quite frequently, although not always the celebrated ones.'

'Here? Paris? New York?'

He shrugged. 'It would normally be here. London is where he'd get the price. The French aren't all that keen.' His lips pursed. 'The Americans might push him up, though. There's quite a few in galleries and collections over there.'

'Would you know?'

He cocked an eye at me. 'If it came to us, yes of course, whether in London, Paris or New York. But not if another auctioneer got it, not necessarily. I can't keep up with everything.'

'Could you keep an eye out for me?'

'For a Tissot? For investment by the Fund?'

'Yes. If you got wind of a good one, could you let me know?'

He pulled his mouth down at the corners. 'For you, yes. Only for you, though. And it'll cost you.'

'The best lunch you've ever had.'

'Done. You and Jeremy know your lunches. How is Jeremy by the way? Does he know about this?'

'Only in a manner of speaking.' I stood up. My meeting with Jeremy had been disturbingly inconclusive. Evasion was not one of his characteristics in normal circumstances; Jeremy is usually only too frank. 'I'd rather not bother Jeremy with this, Charles. We'll leave him out of it for the moment.' I shook my head sadly. 'Jeremy's got other things on his mind just now.'

CHAPTER 16

She came out of the bedroom wrapped in my large towelling bathrobe, and picked up the gin and tonic I'd put by the settee. Her hair was tousled and her skin glowed from the friction of a hot shower.

'You should put some clothes on,' she said.

I put my tongue out at her and swilled the remains of my own drink and ice around in my glass. 'You pinched my robe,' I said. 'And you took over the shower. Your dressing-gown doesn't fit me. These pyjama trousers are a temporary measure of decency. Until I can shower myself.'

'You could catch cold. It isn't warm enough yet.'

'May is not out, that's true. You're quite right. But then my inner fire has been restored.'

She sipped the gin and tonic and regarded me steadily. 'Why did you come back?' she asked.

'I was missing you.'

She tossed her head slightly, as though to throw off my avowal, and repeated herself. 'Why did you come back? You could have seen those Tissots next week.'

'Imagery,' I said.

A slight frown creased the space between her large blue eyes. 'What does that mean?'

'Images. They were disturbing me. They always have. There were lots of them. Tangled rigging and pretty dresses. A smashed car. Jars of moisturizing cream. A blue-eyed blonde. Elegant bank chambers. The Paris Métro with a body under it. Boards of directors. Moreton Frewen. Jennie Jerome. Gerald Reitlinger. Did you know, by the way, that Reitlinger lived in the village next to Frewen's? That came to me from Anthony Powell's memoirs. Reitlinger died because he couldn't be bothered to have the chimney swept.' I crossed to the sideboard and poured myself another drink. 'I think my mind is carrying too much knowledge. It weighs on me like a suspicious win in an endlessly sinister game of criminal Trivial Pursuit.'

'Who is the blonde?'

'Berthe Cauvinière. The market research manager. Quite a girl. Much more knowledgeable than she volunteers.'

'Why does her image disturb you?'

I put some more ice in my glass. 'Oh, that. Well, just sex, I suppose. Or something like that.'

'Tim.' The tone was dangerous.

'Sorry. I'm being flippant. I didn't rush back here just to work off a disturbing image in that sense. In there just now. That was another disturbing image. Set of images. You, in my mind. Entirely you in my mind. I needed you.'

Her face softened into a humorous cast. 'You should not,' she said, in mock severity, 'let such things interfere with your work. With the professional demands of your calling.'

'Oh yes I should.' I left the sideboard and went back to slump in the armchair facing her. 'If I can't work without the tender passion of my wife, let alone her professional artistic judgement, I am fully justified in ensuring its availability.'

'Oh really? So you're going to follow me to Edinburgh, are you? I might find that embarassing.'

'You aren't going to be in Edinburgh for more than two or three days, are you?'

'No, I'm not. You think you can last for two or three days?'

'Every now and then. But I shan't let it become a habit.'

'Oh Tim!' She laughed richly. 'You are impossible. Absolutely impossible. You've been away for much longer spells in the past.'

'So I have. But I wasn't married then.'

'Good heavens, I hope you're not going to become all possessive and jealous and madly randy simply because we're married, are you?'

'Why not? It's as good a reason as any.'

Her face broadened into a wide smile. 'Not bad, Tim. Not bad at all. You're doing quite well. It isn't that I'm

not pleased to see you. For whatever reason. But quite apart
from looking at Tissots and rushing me to bed, there must
have been something else.'

'Well—to be honest, among all the other things I wanted
to see Jeremy.'

'Why? You could have phoned him, surely?'

I shook my head. 'I'm not sure. I wanted to see him, to
see his face while I talked to him. And the other things—
the Tissots, seeing you, wanting to get a bit of distance
between me and the Maucourts, all of them, Sir Richard,
Nantes, the Rue Saint-Honoré, the lot—it all added up to
a need to get back. To see things objectively.'

'So are you pleased with the result?'

I shook my head more vigorously. 'No. Apart—' I gave
her a grin—'from the last hour or so. My meeting with
Jeremy was very inconclusive and you exploded my Tissot-
Jerome-Frewen theory. That was all less important,
though, than my intention to get more background from
Jeremy and he didn't give it to me. He's holding back, for
some reason.'

'Why? What do you think it is?'

'I don't know. Changes at the Bank, I suppose. I haven't
been over-occupied lately. If there are any big upheavals
we might find ourselves losing out in some way. I think
that Jeremy has a fight on his hands and, for some reason,
needs me out of the way while it's going on.'

'That's very unusual.'

'Yes, it is. Which means it's probably serious. I wonder,
if you see Mary sometime, if you can tap her gently for
info?'

I looked up at her expectantly. She and Jeremy's wife
Mary have always been close friends but Mary, once a
secretary at the bank—to Sir Richard himself—is nothing
if not discreet. Sue stood up, drink in hand, and came across
to to stand in front of me, putting her hand through my
hair to tousle it.

'Making me a spy, are you?' she chided. 'If a spy is what
you ask, then a spy I'll be. But don't worry about things,

Tim. You've dealt with much worse before. And if the Bank goes sour you can always live off my moral earnings. Would you like that?'

I put my arm round her, not round her towelled waist, which is where you're supposed to hold a woman, but round her hips, which is much more stimulating, and pulled her on to my lap.

'I promised you dinner,' I murmured, sliding a hand under the towelling as she bent to kiss me. 'I'd better get showered, too.'

'Afterwards,' she said firmly, pushing me back into the armchair and letting the towelling fall open all around us.

CHAPTER 17

'Speaking French as you do—' Eugène Maucourt's eyebrows raised themselves a little and his mouth eased into what might pass as a complimentary expression—'I expect that you must have conceived, among other things, the possibility of transferring your abilities on to a wider stage, to the expression of a greater potential?'

I blinked. In London, the stage is considered to be the widest possible. The potential is to deal with not just the European continent but the open sea, the gorgeous East, the whole world. From the City of London, Paris and its Bourse are seen as parochial. Ridiculous, perhaps, but London accounts for the major percentage of Europe's cross-border share trading and regularly captures half the domestic market in German, French and Italian shares. This encourages us to ignore the internationalism present elsewhere and most often we ignore that of France. They, on the other hand, think of us as an insular little lot.

Here I was, back in the finest plot of land in Europe, richer in history than we like to concede, with its three sea-coastlines, its colossal variety of terrain, produce and rivers, and Eugène Maucourt was opening, as Jeremy had predicted, with a siren song.

'I have often thought of working abroad,' I said truthfully. 'And offers have been made. Up to now, however, I have not considered the possibility in any great depth. For both personal and professional reasons.'

Eugène Maucourt was a greyish man in his forties, spare and slim but rather lined for his age. He wore a quiet suit with a faintly tweedy pattern in it, a twill or a semi-herringbone, and he sat bolt upright behind a very modern desk which was superficially empty, its hard bare top gleaming coldly in no relevation of anything about the man, his habits or his method of working. The lack of clutter, of papers, of even an ashtray, provided a psychological sterility which was presumably intentional, like the rigorously unornamented premises of a Jesuit whose thinking, whose pure intellect, needed monastically sparse surroundings. We faced each other across this void in an office which was almost as bare as the desk, an office carpeted in a dun brown, walled in heavy cream colour, with one graphic photograph behind glass depicting a moustachioed Maucourt of the Belle Epoque who was perhaps a founder, a great-grandfather, or a success story of some sort.

'You also,' Eugène Maucourt remarked, as though establishing something I had deliberately concealed, 'speak Spanish, from your youth in South America.'

'Yes.'

Spoken in these surroundings, a reference to a youth in South America sounded wilfully prodigal, extravagantly dissipated, as though one had spent one's early years doing the tango with sultry partners in night clubs from Mar del Plata up to the Copacabana. The fact that I had been far too young for dissipation and had been mainly incarcerated in St George's School, Buenos Aires, did not emerge.

'You have,' Eugène Maucourt remarked, as though now reading from a charge sheet of a prison record, 'a degree from the celebrated and ancient university at Cambridge, where you played rugby with distinction. Sporting achievements are, of course, of little interest to our professional consideration except as evidence of a healthy, disciplined attitude. But subsequently your character as a *conseil de direction* and your remarkable experience in investment banking with White's must, as I am sure you are aware, provide you with powerful credentials as far as an establishment like ours is concerned.'

'Possibly, but—'

He held up his hand to stop me, to show that he had not yet finished. 'Mr Simpson, I know that your loyalty is not in question and that your integrity has always been of the highest order. I admire that. It is, however, likely that there will be changes, drastic changes in the structure of merchant banks such as ours and White's very soon. There will be a more European emphasis to share trading and so on. We can not logically survive as we are. The integration of our financial identities has already commenced. We will combine more and more. It is also, I must tell you in absolute confidence, likely that we will combine with a third partner, one who will ensure our presence in the most powerful market of the European future. I am referring, of course, to Germany.'

'Er, well, I'm not sure—'

'Mr Simpson, I am not asking you to make any hasty or ill-considered decisions. Nothing could be further from my mind. But what I am indicating to you is that the structural changes which are envisaged will impose the necessity of forming here a powerful professional group, a central *corps d'élite* whose present remuneration and influence will be impressive and whose future will be of limitless possibility.'

I blinked again. At the words *corps d'élite* his right arm, which had been resting, like his left, on the bare surface before him, rose sharply into the air in a gesture, palm open, forearm at forty-five degrees to the horizontal. His voice mounted a mini-crescendo. It was irresistibly reminiscent of *Le Grand Charles's* performances at the Elysée Palace. Performances which pandered to that strange Continental love of the dictatorial posture, the platform of the supremo in full oratory, which we find both pompous and comic. Eugène Maucourt, quite clearly, was an ardent admirer of this didactic approach; his voice now acquired a richer tone.

'Reflect, Mr Simpson! Reflect on what I have indicated! We are highly discriminating here about whom we choose. People have to be not only of the most superlative qualifications but they have to *fit*. My father is certain of your ability to fit, of your discretion. I have received excellent reports of you. When you have had time to think about the future, please let us meet again and discuss what arrangements would persuade you to transfer your talents to our cause. I am sure that White's will not stand in your way. They know where the future lies for young men such as you.'

'That's very kind,' I said courteously. 'And I am very flattered. I assure you that I will give the matter very serious consideration.'

'Excellent. Excellent.' He stood up and held out his hand, stiffly open at the end of his long, stiff arm. He was very tall and the arm came out like a cast-iron handle on a high village water-pump. 'In the meantime we await your report on Bellevie, a business we all wish to progress rapidly, with the most intense anticipation.'

'I'm sure you do,' I said, taking his hand to shake it carefully. 'I'm sure you do.'

'How is it coming along?' He released my hand and raised his eyebrows in query. 'We have to discuss it soon you know, with Peter Lewis at my house in the country.'

'Oh, it's coming along. I am giving it the utmost priority.' I crossed his dun carpet to reach the door. 'The utmost priority.'

'What is the next step on your programme?'

I paused at the door. The question hadn't been an expression of kindly interest. It was said in the commanding tones of a man in authority.

He wasn't in authority. Not over me, not yet. Slight prickles started on the back of my neck, but I tried to ignore them. You never know, in any business, who'll be above you next week.

'I am assembling the neccessary data,' I said, keeping it cool and courteous still. 'I propose to complete an interview in the Rue Saint-Honoré this afternoon, now that things have quietened down a bit.'

He frowned. 'An interview? At the Rue Saint-Honoré? With whom?'

The prickles hackled. I gritted my teeth, loosened my jaw again, and spoke carefully. 'With the market research manager. She and her files must have much of what I need. Her name is Berthe Cauvinière. Madame Berthe Cauvinière.'

The change in his expression stopped my intended departure dead in the doorway. His face set, white, his old-forty lines drawing deep like railway tracks etched into an early map. A dreadful fear gripped me, seizing my limbs.

'My dear Mr Simpson.' The voice was no longer formal. 'I am most terribly sorry. I thought you knew. During your absence, Madame Cauvinière was killed in an accident. A most tragic accident. Evidently I must apologize for the fact that no one in my organization has contacted you?'

CHAPTER 18

'She fell,' Christian Maucourt said wretchedly. 'She fell from her apartment window.'

'When? For Christ's sake, when?'

'Last night. It was quite late.' His young face creased. 'It has been suggested that she'd had a bit to drink.'

'Who by? Who the hell suggested that?'

'The police.' His expression made me feel like a bully. It wasn't fair to half-shout at him like this. It wasn't his fault. Although he was technically working for Eugène Maucourt, and was thus close to hand when I left his uncle's office in a state of mental turmoil, he was still only a student, an

apprentice trying to cope with things that most lifetimes
leave out. I was filling his little office with my threatening,
angry presence as he looked at me apologetically. 'I—I
hadn't even had time to see her,' he said.

He looked almost tearful. I sat down heavily. I knew
there'd been something wrong with that blonde image I'd
had. Guilt suffused me. I could have seen her the day
before, easily, if I hadn't gone chasing after strong, muscular Tissot-hares and worrying about Bank politics. If I'd
just got on with my job, in other words.

Another accident. It simply wasn't possible.

'I didn't hear until mid-morning,' Christian Maucourt
said. 'They phoned from Bellevie. You hadn't arrived yet.
I went down to the Rue Saint-Honoré immediately. They
said she fell late last night. Into the courtyard. This morning the police say her alcohol level was high.'

'For God's sake! She wasn't a boozer, surely? People
don't just fall out of windows, either. It stinks. It absolutely
stinks.'

'Tim, you must not jump to conclusions. I have no doubt
the police will investigate thoroughly. She seems to have
been alone. There is no suggestion of foul play.'

'Like Madame Delattre? And Michel Bonnet? No, it's
too much!'

'But what do you suggest? Why should these not be accidents? They are unrelated, all different.'

'Oh no they're not! They are all connected with Bellevie.
All three of them. Just because the type of accident is different doesn't mean they're unrelated.'

'But why?' He looked really distressed. 'Why? What
motive could there be?'

Not a bad question for a youngster. The key question,
right out in the open. The purpose of my assignment, if you
considered the reality of the thing, if, like me, you have a
suspicious mind, one which had reacted with suspicion
right from the first moment of that coffee-seance with
Jeremy and Peter Lewis. What motive could there be? Why
did I assume that these were not accidents, that there was

a motive, that Bellevie was not just a straightforward case of a well-known business needing an injection of capital and some marketing oomph after a period of relative neglect? Why did I assume that these accidents were not just accidents? Too much past experience, was it, that weighed upon me?

'I don't know,' I answered lamely. 'I don't know what motive. There could be several. If a big expansion plan goes ahead there is a lot of money involved. People can make or lose a lot. Bellevie shares can go up and down. The key executives can make a lot, either by expanding empires or by bonuses and so on. Bellevie was always a family company but they had a share flotation a few years ago. The family kept control but part of the shares are publicly quoted. You know what stock exchanges are like; the Bourse is no different. We better start work.'

'Start work?'

'Yes. Start work. We need a list of shareholders. All of them. We need biographical details of all the main executives, but especially Vauchamps and Bastoni. I need to check on much wider aspects than the plan I started with.'

'But, Tim, this is terrible. You make me feel suspicious of everyone. Surely it is enough to do the objective business assessment you started with? You must not become so—so personally involved. It is as though you are starting a murder investigation.'

'I am,' I said grimly. 'Think of it like that and you'll have the right idea.'

He gaped at me.

'A murder investigation? You are upset. The police will deal with everything, Tim. You cannot—'

'Oh yes I can! I can do anything I bloody well like, within the law!'

I stopped. If I'd been in England I might have gone further, said more. But I wasn't, and Christian Maucourt was staring at me, with his dark soft eyes, as though witnessing an epileptic in his worst throes. I let a moment pass, to cool off. Stick to the facts, I heard a warning voice inside my head advise, change tack, try something else, keep calm, try to keep calm.

'Did you get on to anything about Michel Bonnet at all? I managed to get the tension out of my voice a bit. 'Did you have any time for that?'

'Not much.' Christian Maucourt's expression went back to apologetic again. 'My uncle has kept me quite busy. But I did manage a few calls.'

'And?'

'And he was a very thorough man. Very clever also, as my grandfather said. He checked into many things.'

I managed to stop myself screaming. 'Things? What things?'

'Well—the financial background. The accounting. He was very strong on that.'

The accounts, I thought bitterly, the bloody accounts. Book-keeping. He would be, wouldn't he? 'What else?'

'I—I don't know. Tim, really, I have had so little time.'

I bit back an answer to that and thought of another question. 'Where was Bonnet killed?'

'What?'

'Where was he killed? I mean in what place did his crash take place?'

'Oh—I see. Near a place called Ancenis, on a curve of the N23 from Nantes to Angers. That I have found out.'

I frowned. 'The N23? Not on the motorway, the A11?'

'No, no. Definitely not. It was on the N23, near Ancenis. Between Ancenis and Varades. There is a bend and a downhill curve where it happened. He went too fast, off the bend. The car went into some bushes by the road. It was late and there was little traffic. The A11 motorway is very straight, very modern. He would not have crashed on that.'

'Then why the hell wasn't he on it?'

'Tim, please! I am not a clairvoyant; I cannot read a dead man's mind!'

I held up my hands in what I hoped was a mollifying gesture. 'Sorry. Sorry, Christian. I didn't mean that as a personal thing on you. I was thinking out loud. Try think-

ing with me. Here we have a man who everybody says is
dead keen on fast motoring. Right? He phones up the office,
says he has found out something important and heads back.
So what does he do? Instead of going straight to the *autoroute*,
to the fastest track he can motor on, he takes the older N23,
the original road which meanders along the north bank of
Loire, through God knows what villages and speed restric-
tions, to arrive in Angers. Why? When there is a perfectly
good motorway which the N23 joins at Angers anyway, and
which goes all the way via Le Mans and Chartres to Paris.
What for?'

'I don't know. It is a good question, but I do not know.'

'Well, we have to know. We have to find out. What did
he say when he phoned? And if, as a matter of fact, it was
late when he crashed, how did he phone anyone before
leaving? Who was working so late when he phoned?'

'Tim, please! He phoned some time after six o'clock. The
call came to the Bellevie offices.'

'Who took it?'

Christian Maucourt stared at me as though I was dense.
'Berthe Cauvinière, of course! I thought you knew that?
She often works late.'

I closed my eyes. Then I opened them again, carefully.
'You spoke to Berthe Cauvinière about this?'

'Yes, I did. You told me to speak to her, remember? At
Nantes airport? I asked to see her and to talk about Michel
Bonnet. She said she'd see me today.'

'Jesus Christ.'

'What?'

'Go on. Just go on. Please.'

'She said he phoned to say he had come up with something important and he wanted to see Thierry Vauchamps
the next day. He said he would not be leaving until he
checked some other things at the Nantes factory and asked
if she knew where he could locate Vauchamps. She said
she'd leave a note on Vauchamps' desk because he'd left
already and she gave Bonnet Vauchamps' home number.
She asked if he wanted to speak to Madame Delattre, who

was still down in the shop with Tina Buisson going over some stock figures, but he said no, it didn't concern the shop. Then he rang off. That was the last time he spoke to anyone in Paris.'

I scratched my head. 'Berthe Cauvinière never said a word about this to me.'

'Did you ask her?'

'No, I didn't. I must say I didn't. I wasn't looking at this sort of thing then. She and Madame Delattre were still alive then. Bonnet's accident might have been an accident then. It isn't now.'

'Tim, you cannot say that!'

'I think I can. Did you tell Berthe Cauvinière that you wanted to talk to her about ingredients?'

'Yes, I did.'

'What did she say?'

'She hesitated. She seemed, I don't know, slightly distrait. Then she said OK, of course, anything I can do to help. Come tomorrow. We'll talk then. It's a touchy subject, ingredients, with cosmetics companies, she said.'

'You bet it is. And if you base a whole expansion plan on the wrong ingredients you can come a horrid cropper in today's markets. I have a feeling that was what Bonnet was after. There's a growing change in attitudes and I'm not sure if the plan takes care of that. It's all about marketing, not production.'

'We can check that.'

'We can and we must. That's what I wanted you to start on. So the minute you contact her to arrange it, she sails out of a window and forgets her parachute. It doesn't bear thinking about. It has to be thought about. I can't stand this; everything's so insubstantial. What the hell is going on?'

'I think you are meaning well, Tim, but you are tormenting yourself, distressing yourself. When you meet the police inspector, Levroux, who is handling the matter, he will reassure you. There appear to be no suspicions. She had had a good dinner, she had quite a high alcohol level, the window has a low sill, she fell. She screamed as she fell, just like anyone in an accident. He will tell you.'

'Oh? He will, will he?'

'Oh yes. I believe he is seeing everyone at the Rue Saint-Honoré. Just as a routine. He will spend a few minutes with you when you go to the offices. To continue your financial assessment.' He blinked at me earnestly. 'You must think of it entirely as that. A financial assessment, Tim, not a wild goose chase for a non-existent criminal.'

'Thank you, Christian. Thank you for your calm advice. Do I take it that you're still willing to help me?'

'Oh yes! Of course! In this financial assessment. If you do not fall into the English trap of seeing everything as a violent excursion, a campaign. Of course I am here to help you.'

'If that is—' I allowed sarcasm to enter my tone—'your uncle will allow you to shove the odd hour in my direction?'

'Of course! You must not get so emotional. You must not see a plot in everything, Tim. My Uncle Eugène is a very busy man. He needs assistance and he has priority over everyone else. I'm sure you must understand that.'

I stood up. 'Indeed. I understand that only too well. He's been a bit conspicuous by his absence, but he's certainly back now, isn't he?'

Christian gaped up at me. 'Conspicuous? Absence?'

'Sure.' I turned to the door. 'He starts this whole thing off, gets me sent over here, is away when I arrive, stays away while I'm here and comes back as soon as I go over to London.'

'But he has seen you now, has he not?'

'Indeed he has.'

Christian Maucourt stared up at me expectantly. I decided to say nothing about his uncle's offer. My mind had now got that to deal with in addition to those images I'd described to Sue. Muscular hares and frilly dresses had been joined by ingredients and the scream of a falling woman. I needed space to think in, but I hadn't got time to make it.

'I'll clear your presence in the Rue Saint-Honoré,' I said. 'I would be glad if your uncle could spare you for a day or two. This week.'

Christian nodded. 'I'm sure he will,' he said. 'Shall I ask him?'

'If you don't mind. Please impress upon him the need for your uninterrupted attention. He wants my report quickly, so he must help. It will be something of an accounts, almost a book-keeping, investigation. I take it that you have some familiarity with the subject?'

For the first time, he scowled back at me.

'I am,' he said, with some hauteur, 'the son and grandson of a banker.'

CHAPTER 19

Thierry Vauchamps did not look very well. It was four in the afternoon and it seemed to me that he would have done better not to have come in at all. Dark, puffy welts were raised under his eyes. His shave was already showing signs of heavy wear. Alcohol is a major ingredient in cosmetics; apart from its useful volatility for after-shaves and colognes, it is used in cold creams, freckle lotions, face packs and skin lotions. It has properties of water retention, as any man with a hangover knows. The shave you give yourself the morning after, when fluid is retained under the skin, is not nearly as close as you think; as the fluid drains away and the puffy skin returns to normal, out come the bristles into a splendid five o'clock shadow. Thierry Vauchamps already had something more like a midnight eclipse.

The rather cocky man I'd liked on my first day at the Rue Saint-Honoré had shrunk into a listless, sallow malingerer. No spark of action or energy could be struck from him. The grand plan hadn't been mentioned, nor the rejuvenation of the shop below. He almost crouched behind his desk in a deep gloom.

'Terrible,' he repeated yet again. 'Terrible. She was a wonderful personality as well as an excellent, a professional market research manager. I cannot think what must have happened.' He raised his heavy eyes to mine. 'A woman alone, without a husband, perhaps a little depressed, or even a little overconfident, who knows? These accidents are a dreadful lesson to us. My wife is shattered. Everyone liked Berthe Cauvinière. I have had to send Tina Buisson home. Coming on top of Madame Delattre's death, it has devastated her. I can tell you that we will have no company left if this goes on. Two appalling accidents within so short a time.'

Three, I nearly said, three, but then I supposed that Michel Bonnet didn't count. He didn't work for Bellevie; he was an outsider, like me.

'Well,' I said instead, 'they were none the less appalling but at least they were not here, on the premises. They were at random, outside.'

He frowned slightly. 'Just so,' he said.

'What I mean is that it's not as though you've had two accidents within the company property. They are quite at random, *par hazard*, they involve two important executives but they are quite unconnected, caused by different circumstances in the outside world.'

His face cleared a little. 'Of course they are. I do not imagine that anyone is suggesting any link of any sort?'

'No. No one that I know of.'

His eyes widened slightly. 'What possible link could there be?'

'I cannot imagine. I gather from Christian Maucourt that the police have ruled out any suspicious circumstances.'

'Yes. There is an inspector, a Levroux, to whom I have spoken. He seems to be quite satisfied. There will be some routine inquiries.' He shivered. 'The report of someone who heard the—the circumstances—is quite horrifying.'

'So I believe.'

His eyes became speculative as they rested upon me. 'I hope this will not delay your own investigation unduly? I understand that you wanted to pursue some inquiries with Berthe; will this dreadful business bring matters to a halt?'

I shook my head slowly. 'I don't think so. It messes things up, but I think we can manage. If I can have cooperation from you?'

'Of course. Of course. What can I do? We must think ahead, try to be positive.' He made an attempt at a brave expression.

'I'd like young Christian Maucourt, who is helping me, to look through some facts and figures. He was going to consult Berthe Cauvinière but that, obviously, will not now be possible. I've asked him for a couple of days.'

Vauchamps nodded carefully, as though motion might damage his head. 'Of course. Anything to speed the process. Is this to do with market statistics?'

'Yes,' I lied. 'Some aspects I wish to consider. And some figures from the supply side. Perhaps your accounts department would be good enough to let him have a look at the purchase ledger.'

'The purchase ledger?'

'Yes. It's a question of compounds, ingredients, that sort of thing.'

'Is this not outside the scope of your assessment?'

'Not really. I need a complete picture.' I gave him a reassuring smile. 'Just tying up the last loose ends. You'd be surprised how penetrating a bank committee's questions can be. I want to get this thing through without any hiccups.'

'Through?' His face brightened. 'You mean you will recommend proceeding with the plan? For White's, too?'

I allowed my smile to broaden. 'This is a good business,' I said. 'A very good business. All I have to do is to reassure myself that supply can keep up with demand. Once your plan has been launched. I cannot answer for White's; I simply report.'

'But your opinion must be influential.' He was getting his colour back by the sound. 'I have no doubt of that. This must be good news. At last, some good news.'

'Well—' I smoothed a modest crease in my trouser leg—
'I dare say I'll be closely questioned. But I think that the
facts must predominate.'

'Of course! Of course! *Bien sûr!* The facts. Please help
yourself. The door is open to you. And to Christian. As you
wish.'

'That's very kind.' I got up. He stared at me quite
brightly now, his eyes rekindled, a flush spreading into the
dark bristle of his chin as he looked up at me. I was having
the desired effect. 'There is some other material to absorb
before I'm finished, so I'll leave you to pick up the pieces
and get the business going again. *Courage!*'

He leapt to his feet. '*Courage* to you too, Tim! And, I
hope, to a long and beneficial collaboration between us! It
is still as I indicated to you: once the plan is adopted and
financed there are opportunities for all of us! You have my
assurance! Splendid opportunities; I am sure of that.'

I bet you are, I thought, as I left. I really bet you're
absolutely sure of that.

CHAPTER 20

The story of Kitty Newton is a sad one. She was born
Kathleen Kelly, the daughter of a major in the Indian
Army, in 1854. Her father became Governor of Alderney
at some point in his career but Kitty was brought up in a
convent until she was seventeen, then given in marriage to
a surgeon called Isaac Newton who worked in the Indian
Civil Service. On the way out to India to be married at
Hoshiarput in 1871 she fell during the long and doubtless
tedious voyage for an officer called Captain Palliser, also
travelling to India. It was her brother, Frederick Kelly,
who had arranged the marriage and Kitty separated from
Newton almost immediately after it, confessing to her
association with Palliser and her continuing preference for
him. Divorce proceedings on the grounds of adultery were

instituted in May 1871 and Captain Palliser's daughter, Muriel Mary Violet, was born at her grandfather's house in Yorkshire on 20th December 1871. The divorce came through in the following year.

No one knows much about Kitty Newton's next few years or how the impressionable girl, seduced on shipboard during her first excursion into the world, spent her time, but in March 1876 she registered the birth of another child, Cecil George, rather humorously giving the name of the father as Dr Isaac Newton. By that time she was living at the home of her elder sister Mary, who had married another Indian Army man, a colonel called Augustus Frederick Hervey, in St John's Wood. The house was not far from Tissot's house in Springfield Road. When or how she met him is not known and the child Cecil George does not seem to have been his, but Kitty Newton moved in to Tissot's house that year, 1876, and lived with him until she died six years later.

By extraordinary irony, the Oxford University Press, when they reproduced the Palliser novels by Trollope, used Tissot's pictures to illustrate the covers.

I was sitting in my hotel room quietly reading Sue's résumé of information about Tissot along with the books she'd recommended. One thing about Sue is that she knows that once I've got my teeth into a thing I won't let go of it. Sue, in turn, won't be left out. The net result is that we make rather a good push-me, pull-you sort of team, although in the past her reluctance to let me plunge into trouble has caused friction. Since marriage, however, her view seems to have been one of acceptance or, maybe, better a happy dead husband than a grumpy live one. The wives of racing-car drivers are perhaps a bit similar.

In Tissot's time it was quite the successful thing to keep a mistress in St John's Wood. Men might even leave dinner-parties in more respectable areas early in order to visit their mistresses, and although it was never acknowledged, it was understood. The ladies in question were kept hidden away discreetly and society was not offended. All this was part of the accepted pattern of successful, and hypocritical, Victorian life.

To Tissot's eternal credit, he never did this. He installed Mrs Newton openly, lived with her openly and obviously adored her. After her death his religious conversion was ascribed to his guilt at having treated her shamefully, of having engendered her suicide; this was disgracefully untrue. His open ménage with her meant that he had offended society's rules. For this transgression they were isolated; society withdrew from them with a shudder. Tissot, so often invited into fashionable society as an available and wealthy bachelor, was made unwelcome. He obviously didn't give a damn. It was the happiest period of his life. Kitty, with her two children, provided him with a ready-made family at home and a romantic partnership to give the dimension of love to excursions to the seaside—Ramsgate Harbour for instance—to travel, to public gardens and amusements. She changed his life completely.

It is a strange fact that from Tissot, who mixed with fashionable society and was present at many well-recorded dinners and social events until Kitty Newton's time, we have very few recorded conversations or sayings. Whistler, Sargent, de Goncourt, all of them mixed with him frequently, but little of what he said comes through. One thing de Goncourt says, however, is striking for an aspect of Tissot, generally depicted as a wooden, too-successful fashion painter, which tells us something of the more passionate side of him. He said, de Goncourt recorded, that 'he loved London, even the smell of coal in the air, because it smelt of the battle of life.' The smell of coal being like the smell of the battle of life is a vivid image, yet de Goncourt, who was very catty, described Tissot as an inconsequential, garrulous character, with a flood of tiring words among which an occasional painterly phrase attracted attention. This, while Tissot was illustrating de Goncourt's novel *Renée Mauperin*, was more illustrative of de Goncourt than anything else. Berthe Morisot, who visited London with her husband, saw Tissot's St John's Wood house in 1875 and remarked that he was successful, which he deserved, and 'very kind, a good chap, if a bit common'. There is the telling phrase: 'a bit common'. There has always been a hint that Tissot, the son of a successful linen-draper and a hat-maker, was not quite *comme il faut*. Extraordinary, the *snobbisme* of the French.

There might be a parallel with the Maucourts there, I thought, putting the information down for a moment. Or the Whites. They were both bankers derived from trade, just as Tissot was an artist derived from trade. Was that why old Charles was so enthusiastic? Some sort of self-identification? Why, with all the art of France available, had he seized this unfashionable, this 'London' painter to collect?

I shook my head at the wall. Not to collect: Charles Maucourt only had the *Graphic* prints and his excited knowledge, not a collection of paintings. It was a strange approach for a rich man's artistic involvement. Frowning, I picked up the story again.

After 1876 Tissot was happy, so happy and so blinded by love that it affected his painting. In picture after picture a rather characterless Kitty Newton stares out at us, or looks at children, or gazes oddly into space, her clean beauty dominating his work in almost waxen typification of the pretty lady in a pretty dress in pretty or social surroundings. There is a difference, though, in these social surroundings, from the paintings of the time before he met her. The big gatherings, *The Ball on Shipboard*, the large-scale works full of people, now make few appearances. It seems almost as if Kitty Newton was enough for him. They led, of course, a social life with intimate friends, but they were dependent on each other to an intense degree and this must have led to quarrels like those depicted in *A Passing Storm* and the tension of some of the portrayals of life in his garden.

Gradually, the backgrounds to his paintings of her drift away from domesticity to depictions of travel, of ships and departures. Not travel, ships and departures as a background to something else, as in his earlier work, but as subject-matter in themselves. Railway stations and docksides dominate the figures depicted, who tend to move to the edges of the canvas. Something is changing, there is a sense of things moving away, of flux. By the end of the 1870s it is clear that Kitty Newton's health is precarious.

To save Kitty's strength from the tiring business of posing for long periods Tissot began to paint from photographs of her more and more. We are lucky that many of these photographs have survived, preserved by Kitty's niece, Lilian Hervey. They are the raw material of several famous paintings. Tissot started to repeat certain backgrounds from photographs as well, perhaps unwilling to venture forth for long, to leave the now seriously-ill Kitty alone for lengthy periods.

Kitty Newton had consumption. Inexorably the paintings—and the photographs—trace her tragic decline. Tissot had to live with his adored partner knowing her to be under sentence of death. His reliance on photographs affected his work, some of it badly. In 1882, when de Goncourt was so unpleasant about him, he produced the illustrations for the writer's novel, *Renée Mauperin*, one of which depicts Renée and her father in the porch of the church at Morimond. It is derived from a devastating photograph of Tissot and Kitty sitting on a bench in his garden. Kitty is wrapped in shawls and blankets with her head covered, while Tissot, in an overcoat and wide-brimmed hat, holds her tenderly and protectively. She is, clearly, mortally ill.

She died in November 1882 at the age of twenty-eight. He never recovered. As soon as she was buried he left England, literally the day after, never to return, leaving the house and even several canvases uncompleted. He was forty-six years old. After this he painted the extraordinary *Femme à Paris* series, he produced acclaimed pastels—the *Princesse de Broglie* was one of them—he became deeply religious, travelled to the Holy Land, was duped and conned and made ridiculous by famous 'spiritualists' through whom he thought he had regained contact with his beloved Kitty beyond the grave. But he never came back to England. De Goncourt said that he was a cold fish, with eyes like a poached mackerel.

Kitty was buried in Kensal Rise. Rumours grew about her and his behaviour just as they had about his actions during the Prussian attack on Paris, on his reason for fleeing to England during the Commune. They were wrong.

Ironically his new devotion to the Catholic faith and his decade of illustrating a new edition of the Bible made him a fortune. Critics agree that his drawings, etchings and paintings of a religious character are pretty awful. Devout women knelt before them and behaved with hysterical piety at their exhibition.

It is strange that so many people, including James Laver, described Tissot in deprecatory terms, as a lightweight, a *coureur de dames*, a ladykiller, a *flâneur*, a lounger, a loiterer, a social dandy always dressed to kill, a painter of vulgar society, as though the paintings he painted, those detailed, obsessive, brilliantly-finished, hard-edged creations did not take ages of unremitting, bloody hard work and concentration, as though the effort and attention and shift after shift of lonely studio work did not count. The fact that he had an affair with a fallen woman with two illegitimate children, whom he treated excellently, and that he obviously loved her and watched her die slowly, day after day beside her, was taken to confirm that he was not serious, not like a married man. He is not noted for saying anything nasty about anyone, nor for drunken or violent behaviour, and he fought the Prussians valiantly with the *Tirailleurs de la Seine*, but his friend Manet never forgave him for leaving Paris during the Commune—Monet and Pissarro had already gone—and de Goncourt wrote despicable things about him, while Jacques-Emile Blanche quoted his own father as saying of Tissot, 'May God forgive him for his cowardice!'

This man, who was duped by the notorious 'medium' William Eglinton, a trickster who also duped Conan Doyle, believed that a seance engineered by Eglinton in Paris in

1885 he saw his beloved Kitty Newton once again reincarnated and that she kissed him before vanishing. The experience shattered and elevated him. He produced a celebrated mezzotint recording it. His emotions and his fervour were remarked upon even by de Goncourt and Daudet and his wife.

His biographers state that he exercised a laconic practicality in the pursuit of his life and career.

He returned to the peace and tranquillity of the Château de Buillon which his father had purchased with his successful earnings, moving back into the region from which the family had originally sprung.

I stared at the wallpaper on the hotel wall, frowning yet again.

The Tissots stem from the Italian family of Tizzoni or Tizzone who hailed from Vercelli. Vercelli is a town halfway between Milan and Turin noted in my memory for its rice puddings, but the Tizzones of Vercelli became the Tissots of Pontarlier and settled in what is now the Doubs, near the Swiss border. Tissot's father came from Trevillers, and he returned to the area when he bought the Château de Buillon; it was built on the site of an abbey and for this reason the story spread that in remorse over his treatment of Mrs Newton, Tissot had entered a monastic order and had become a religious recluse.

The story is entirely untrue.

The area round Trevillers was not known as the Doubs when the Tissots originally settled there. The departments of the Jura, the Doubs and Haute-Sâone were only formed after the French Revolution. Before that the region was known as the Franche-Comté. People in France still use the term, much as we might refer to Wessex, which cannot be found as a modern county.

I stared at the wallpaper even harder.

The Franche-Comté.

It was just one coincidence too many.

CHAPTER 21

I had a very bad morning. I went into Bellevie's and had to spend a lot of time with Tina Buisson, who was in very poor emotional shape. I remembered how she and Berthe Cauvinière had clung together at the news of Madame Delattre, the genuine bond in the moment of grief, and listened, I hoped, with sympathy.

'It's ghastly,' she gulped, over and over again, sitting in my little office where we wouldn't be disturbed. 'Terrible. Two deaths. Thierry won't miss Madame Delattre of course, that's well known. But he's devastated by Berthe's accident.'

'He does seem pretty upset,' I agreed. 'He and she worked well together, particularly on the famous plan. The market research was her major contribution.'

Tina Buisson gave me an old-fashioned look. 'A little more than that,' she murmured. '*Plus que ça.*'

'I beg your pardon?'

'Oh come on, *mon cher Anglais*, you're not as naïve as all that.' Her eyes fastened on my broken nose again. She moistened her lips a little. 'Berthe was my best friend here. She and Thierry were closer than mere statistics.'

'Closer?'

'Tim—' she gave me a tearful smile—'you don't mind me calling you Tim? You are one of us for the time being and very *sympathique*. I can confide in you, surely?'

'Of course. And Tim is fine.'

She smiled a little wider. 'You know I am Tina. Well, I think it was becoming clear to me that Berthe was working very closely with Thierry. Very closely. I mean, everybody likes Thierry, he is the new dynamic broom ready to sweep everything clean. Except for Madame Delattre, of course.'

'Of course.'

'Well, you know how it can happen.' She gave me a

significant, woman-of-the-world look from under damp, long-lashed eyes. 'When a man and a woman work closely together. To achieve harmony of work they often have to achieve another kind of harmony. You know? Poor Thierry; he must be shattered.'

'He's got a wife, hasn't he?'

She gave me another look, as though to say don't be so ingenuous and insensitive, then nodded. 'Of course. But Thierry had to work very late, such long hours, putting that famous plan together. He needed Berthe for a lot of the facts and figures, all the time. Since she was divorced . . .'

She let the sentence hang, as though that explained everything. I compressed my lips. We were talking of the man who had made such a to-do to me about Charles Maucourt and Madame Delattre, their effect on the business, while presumably conducting his own clandestine affair. Hypocrisy, it seemed, had never been confined just to Victorians and St John's Wood. A thought struck me.

'Since he had to work late, did he stay up here in town?'

Tina Buisson gave me another of her expressions and then a significant smile. 'Of course! Berthe lives much nearer than Thierry's house in the suburbs. I think he even had a key.'

'You mean he could have gained access to her apartment without anyone knowing?'

'Oh, Tim!' She looked quite shocked. 'What are you suggesting? He was absolutely potty about her! The plan was finished some time ago and he had no reason to stay on late. She had the habit, as you know, but he had gone home the other night, when she fell. My goodness, you have a suspicious mind.'

'Sorry,' I mumbled. 'Just thinking aloud. She had dined well, apparently, the night she fell. I wondered if she'd dined with someone, that's all.'

'She might have, but it wasn't Thierry. He went home. He phoned me from his house about a promotion in Grenoble and I had to phone him back. But I can tell you, Berthe was not a drinker. I'm shocked about what they are saying.'

'Oh dear.' We can all slip, I thought privately.

'Thierry will be all the more upset because he and Berthe were, how should I say, a bit estranged over something or another and hadn't had time to make it up.'

'Estranged? Why?'

'I don't know. But there was something. Some passing thing. I imagine.' She gave me another significant look. 'In affairs, these things are as much part of the frisson as the romance, after all. And the reconciliations, of course.'

'*A Passing Storm*,' I murmured.

'Pardon?'

'Nothing. Just an expression.'

'Well, anyway, I feel very sorry for Thierry. He must be feeling rotten and he can't show it too much.'

'Poor fellow,' I said, drily.

It took me much too long to disentangle her. She seemed reluctant to leave. I managed to get out of my office and get a quick look at the systems employed in the accounts department upstairs while most of the staff were out at lunch. There was no sign of Christian Maucourt yet and I began to get irritable. At the start of the afternoon I had located the suppliers' invoices and I also went back down to Berthe Cauvinière's office to go through her research files, particularly on market and product developments. By mid-afternoon I was simply confusing myself and I marched back, eventually, all the way to Maucourt's to find out what the hell was going on. It seemed to me that I wasn't getting much help.

'Your uncle,' I said crossly to Christian Maucourt, 'has been getting in the way again, hasn't he?'

He shook his head reproachfully.

'Tim, you must understand that he is a busy man. He runs the firm now. I'm sorry, he sends his apologies, but he needed help with an important submission for the Ministry of Finance. I had to delay my intended visit to Bellevie. It is not deliberate, you know.'

'Have you managed to do anything at all so far?' I didn't conceal my impatience.

He smiled knowingly and pulled open a drawer of his desk. Out of it came a thick computer print-out, a layered wodge of broad paper lined with typical faint green lines.

'Bomp,' he said, slapping it on the desk.

'Bomp? You mean a bill of materials processor?'

'Precisely, Tim. The factory has computerized stock and production control. I simply sent for a copy of last month's figures. Here it is; raw materials, packaging, etcetera, etcetera.'

'Brilliant! Well done! What have you gathered from it so far?'

He pulled a face. 'That is not so easy. There are a lot of things on it, after all. This is a huge business; I do not even know what some of the things are. Stearic acid? Pectin? Do you know what it is, pectin?'

'Pectin is a purified carbohydrate product obtained from the dilute acid extract of the inner portion of the rind of citrus fruit or apple pomade.' I grinned and held out my hand. 'I know all about pectin from my Brazilian days. Pectin consists chiefly of partially methoxylated polygalacturonic acids. You'd better let me have the print-out.'

'Swank. Swot. You are showing off to me. I bet you even know what it's used for, too.'

'It's an emulsifier. They use it for thickening and gelling.' I took the print-out from him. 'What we need to know is where all this stuff comes from. A look at the jolly old purchase ledger'll do that.'

'That should be computerized too. At least I think it is. What you are asking may be difficult to analyse.'

'I don't care if it's difficult. I don't care if you have to go inside the computer with a tin-opener or more simply just rifle the invoice files. I want you to get on with it. Urgently. Now.'

'Now?'

'Now.'

He looked at his watch. I knew what he meant. It was getting on towards late afternoon.

'I'm sorry, Christian, but there's no time to lose. We

have to move. I need you to help me with those accounts because I've got to finish off my plan presentation to White's and see your grandfather as well, right now.'

He smiled quietly, making me feel like a bully again. Christian Maucourt was intelligent, understanding, but he'd never be a bruiser. In later life, with experience, he'd get his way by his quiet firmness, by cunning—no, that wasn't fair—by intelligence and proper handling of people. His soft dark eyes, looking at me, must already be getting used to persuasion, to turning female heads, breaking hearts.

'I'll go,' he said. 'I'll go now. I promised to help you and I shall do just that. Will you be here for a while?'

'Yes. I'll come down to the shop as soon as I've finished.'

'OK.' He gave me a rather mocking look. 'You don't think that I should take my trusty Smith & Wesson revolver with me?'

'No, I don't. We're not playing cowboys.'

'A parachute?'

'That,' I said severely 'is in poor taste.'

He grinned at me and left. I felt disconcerted. I was behaving like a trampling old boar in a young gazelle's grassy coppice. I steadied myself, calmed down a bit, and marched along the passage to Charles Maucourt's office, where his secretary repeated her wait-here programme of the first time I'd visited, then ushered me into the presence.

'Mr Simpson!' Charles Maucourt came out from his desk with a smile of welcome. 'This is a pleasure. You have been to London, that I know, and you are very busy, Eugène tells me, quite apart from this second tragic accident, yet you have found time to come and lighten my day. How are you?'

'Well, thank you. And you?'

He smiled a slightly sadder smile and gestured to a chair as he returned to sit down himself. There was an air of *triste* resignation about him, the air of a man who has suffered an emotional loss, and is still convalescing from it, not sure if a complete cure can be found. He still looked stocky and strong, the grey hair *en brosse* bristling crisply, his elegant clothes fitting themselves to a powerful frame, but the snap and spring were subdued. 'I am all right,' he said. 'I think that I am all right. No better than that and no worse. I did enjoy your visit, though. It was good to talk art for a bit.'

'It certainly was. I think Tissot is a fascinating subject. I'm most grateful to you for drawing my attention to him.'

'Not at all. Not at all. I'm sure you would have come round to him in your own way eventually.'

'Probably. I don't think you told me how you started your interest in him, actually.'

'Oh.' He gave a shrug. 'I have always been interested in art. But Tissot I think I first came across in the journals of Edmond de Goncourt. Something roused my interest and although, of course, the Impressionists rather dominated my artistic attention, I saw one of Tissot's paintings— he gave me a wink—'it was the very sexy *Japonaise au Bain* which is in the museum at Dijon. Young men notice such things, eh? It is an attempt at *japonaiserie* which does not quite come off, the taste is a bit vulgar, and I thought, as well as admiring the charming characteristics of the girl, here is a man trying to get into the Japanese mode but in fact producing a voluptuous nude *au Courbet*. He was emulating Whistler's *Princesse de la Pays de Porcelaine*, which is far superior, but Whistler was a follower of Courbet as well, eh? Then afterwards I saw the Thames things which are again after Whistler but Tissot had much, much improved and they are technically wonderful. I like sailing, you see, and the rigging fascinated me because it was absolutely accurate.'

'Yes. He got that from his youth in Nantes, didn't he?'

'I believe so.'

I waited for a brief moment but no continuation was offered by him. If he thought of the Bellevie factory being at Nantes, or of any connection, he wasn't going to remark on it. Perhaps there was no significance to him.

'You share that hobby with Jeremy,' I said, filling in the silence.

'Hobby?'

'Sailing. Jeremy is a keen yachtsman.'

'Oh. I did not know that. Sir Richard, of course, was an oarsman—he rowed for Cambridge when they beat Oxford —but I do not think he is a sailor. It is interesting that Tissot's painting of Henley Regatta, now in your Leander Club, in the most Impressionistic of his work. Quite unlike the narratives. Richard once showed it to me during a visit to England. He is a member, you know, and we went to Henley together. It was a formidable experience.'

'I'm sure. Is he still here?'

'Here? Oh, in Paris, you mean. No, I believe he is in London and will not be back until tomorrow.'

'I haven't had a chance to congratulate him on joining your board.'

'Oh.' Charles Maucourt made a vague gesture. 'It is we who should be congratulated. On obtaining his services.' He gave me a shrewd glance. 'I hope it will be the start of an English invasion.'

He smiled meaningly.

'That's very kind. I am flattered. I'm sure you're aware that Eugène and I spoke yesterday?'

'Of course. And I hope you will consider us seriously. I do not wish to interfere in any way—Eugène is now our PDG and takes such decisions—but if things go well I would seriously like to start an Art Fund here. Or possibly to broaden White's Fund into a European Fund. Why not?'

'Why not indeed. It does seem that there are going to be a lot of changes.' I gave him a careful look. 'I haven't had the opportunity of discussing things with Sir Richard but I understand that these changes will be in place before the nineteen ninety-two kick off?'

He returned my look with an amused expression. 'There will be new orientations, certainly. I am afraid I cannot elaborate on what the present discussions cover but I'm sure that when the decisions have been taken you will be fully informed.'

I smiled back. 'Perhaps it will be like the old days you

and Sir Richard experienced in the *Franche-Comté*. The Maquis and SOE working together again.'

He grinned. 'Maybe. Maybe not. There was a lot of rivalry and jealousy, you know. Some of my countrymen who worked with SOE were shunned by the Maquis. Even, disgracefully, barred from receiving decorations and medals. Fortunately Sir Richard and I avoided such pettiness.'

'You're a Parisian, Mr Maucourt. How did you come to be active in such a distant place as the Franche-Comté?'

He made another dismissive gesture. 'I was first in Lyon to avoid the Boche. From there I moved to a group working along the Swiss border, smuggling people and things across. We worked along the line of the Doubs river and the Rhône–Rhine canal, even as far as Mulhouse, where the textile factories were.'

'Right to the end of the war?'

He nodded. 'As I told you, I missed the Vercors massacre. Agnès and I were in the area to the end.'

'Sir Richard too?'

He shook his head. 'Oh no. Sir Richard was blown, a bit like Harry Rée, the famous agent known as César, late in 1944. We got Rée out across the Swiss border. You should ask Richard about the SOE part. We were Maquis.'

'Fascinating. It must have been nerve-racking.'

'It was. Ah, but one was alive! I know we must forget such things, and it is better that we know, now, that they will never occur again. But it was vivid, every day was vivid, when it might be your last.'

I made a suitably agreeable noise of some sort to show my concurrence and stood up. 'It's been a great pleasure to see you. I'll let you know if we manage to find a suitable Tissot for the Fund. You'll have first view of it.'

He chuckled. 'Fine. Thank you. Don't go too far overboard for Tissot just because of me, though.'

'I won't.'

I went back to Christian Maucourt's office to scratch my head. Nothing made sense. Sir Richard was in England, presumably causing havoc at White's Bank in Gracechurch

Street. The patterns I was trying to form didn't fit. I got
the Bellevie plan prepared by Thierry Vauchamps, with
the assistance of his 'close' colleague Berthe Cauvinière,
now dead, out of my briefcase and stared at it. I thought
about Kitty Newton and *The Ball on Shipboard*, which was
before her time but certainly within that of the Jerome
sisters, and Reitlinger, and Charles Maucourt, but couldn't
cross-relate anything.

A lot of time went by; two or three hours. The computer
print-out was enough to make anyone's head ache. I left
components like jars and bottles and cartons alone, so that
I could concentrate on ingredients. There was no reason
for this except for Michel Bonnet's last notes, and the effort
was awful. There were placental extracts, lipids, and gly-
cols. There was allantoin and amino acids, paraffin, digly-
col laurate, hyaluronic acid, talc, caustic soda for soap,
triethanolamine stearate and aliphatic amines. Then there
were more recognizable, herbal, country-and-fruit type
things, ranging from apricot kernel oil, almond, aniseed
and aloe on through the alphabet via lavender, liquorice
and lemon to vanilla, verbena, walnut oil and yeast to witch
hazel. My head started to throb. How the hell could I
relate all this to the famous plan except by painstaking
product-by-product analysis? The plan was set out in
product groups, not ingredients. I'd have to go into much
more analytical detail to sort that out; had Michel Bonnet
really done that?

It was getting quite dark when the phone beside me
suddenly rang, startling me. It was Christian Maucourt.

'Tim? Are you still there?'

'Christian!' Remorse flooded through me; he was still
working. 'I'm awfully sorry; I got a bit involved. I'll come
down right away. Where are you?'

'Upstairs in accounts. Listen; there is something funny.
I may have found something.'

'What?'

'Tim.' His voice dropped. 'There have been two men
watching this place. One of them followed me here, I'm

almost certain I noticed him in the street. Every time I look out of the window there are the same two men across the street watching.'

'Do you know them?'

'No. But one followed me. Definitely.'

'Christ! You're not alone there, are you?'

'Oh yes. Everyone has left except me. The last one left about quarter of an hour ago.' There was a brief silence. 'Tim? I do not see the two men now.'

'Bloody hell! I'm coming. Right away.' Alarm bells started ringing in my head. 'Stay where you are. Don't let anyone in.'

'I'll meet you at the door.'

'No you won't! You jolly well stay where you are! If anyone comes into the building, hide. Hear me? Hide until I get there.'

'That's a bit dramatic. Surely—'

'Do as I jolly well tell you! Hide! That's a bloody order! Hide!'

I shot down the staircase of Maucourt's splendid eighteenth-century building and out into the street like a rocket. A short sprint took me into the Faubourg Saint-Honoré close to the Élysée Palace and then I was in full flight past the Embassy, beating all records to the crossing at the Rue Royale and on into the Saint-Honoré itself.

A soft boy, a dancer, a skier, a tennis-player; no violent, bone-cracking, personal-bodily-harm sports for him. And I had done it; sent him into this.

The Bellevie window was lit up with rather feeble lights emphasizing the dull discretion which Thierry Vauchamps had not yet had time to alter. The offices above were in darkness but, to my surprise, the street door at the side of the shop, giving access to them, was unlocked. I went in like a polecat to a rabbit's warren.

The entrance hall widened to the stairway, which had a wide circular well round which an elegant curved set of marble stairs with an elaborately-supported iron stair-rail spiralled its way upwards. On the first floor were Thierry

Vauchamps' and the executives' offices. On the second and higher up lived the accounts department, administration, minions of various sorts, those hewers of wood and drawers of water which any organization fits in where it can. As I started up at the bottom of the stairs, peering upwards into the gloom to see which floor Christian Maucourt might be on, three men came out on to the third-floor landing.

Two of them held the central one firmly grasped between them. A muffled sound came out of him, mainly because one of the other two men had a hand clamped over his mouth. As I started to run faster up the stairs this trio shuffled crabwise to the rail and the central one, with the hand clamped over his mouth, was positioned with his back against the stair-rail.

It was Christian Maucourt.

They were going to throw him over.

Another accident, I thought, as a twingeing knee and my tired legs protested at the pumping race up those bloody stairs, they've found him, wherever he hid, and they're going to throw him over for another accident, he must have been getting to something desperately important for them to be taking the risk of yet another improbable accident, my God I'm out of condition, this is killing me, surprise is essential but they've probably heard me clumping up in my stout Church's brogues like a rhino charging up a rocky slope.

One of the men bent down to grasp Christian's legs. The muffled, strained noise increased in intensity.

'Oy!'

I sprinted up the last flight of stairs letting out a great bellow. They'd have had him over before I could get there otherwise; I had to divert them, thus losing any element of surprise I might have had.

The one grasping his legs let go and turned to meet me at the top of the stairs. The great advantages of the situation for the man at the top in these circumstances are those of height and timing. As the bloke in my situation comes stumbling up the breathless stair you can pick when and how to kick him in the teeth or stomach with everything you've got. The stomach is nearer and safer, so that is what the leg-grasper went for. He was a slight, dark figure, lithe and quick, so that his foot came swinging in at what seemed terrific speed, straight towards my solar plexus.

Which was what I'd banked on, if you'll pardon the pun.

I sat down suddenly on one of the last steps, half-turning to take his shoe and ankle in both hands and give the heartiest heave I could, pivoting my weight round as I sat. It jerked him clean off the top step, past the side of me, and the combined propulsion of his own swinging kick and my leveraged heave made sure that he missed the top five steps completely, going high and over with all the impetus propelling him forward. His scream of fear choked off to a grunt as he struck the staircase wall; bounced off it, then went down the spiral in a smacking, grunting tangle of legs, arms, body and head on to the hard marble stairs, with their hard sharp edges, in bone-cracking impacts that stopped the grunts with whacking thumps and softer, deadlier noises.

'Tee—eem!'

Christian Maucourt had got his mouth free. I turned where I was sitting and saw him struggle with the burlier figure of the second man, who still held him.

'Tee—eem!'

The man's arm came free. As I sprang up on creaking legs I saw the flash of a knife-blade reflected in the dim staircase light.

'Tim!'

'Christian! Look out!'

I jumped forward, too late. The flash of blade buried itself somewhere inside Christian's jacket and came out fast, about to take another swift fatal stab as I hit the bigger man, not nearly hard enough, on the side of the head.

The man staggered back. Christian Maucourt grabbed his own chest with both hands, clasping the jacket to him in bundled folds, bent forward, and sank to his knees.

'Oh, Tim,' he said quietly, with an almost curious tone,

as though he had found something strange on his abdomen and was holding it.

'You bastard!'

I parried a thrust from the knife, trying to grab the man's wrist with my left hand and missing. With my right I hooked him to the jaw. It wasn't as hard as it should have been but a hook is the only thing at close quarters, and he staggered back to the stair-rail. Christian fell forward and rolled on to his side, still grasping himself, and let out a groan. Blood began to run over his fingers.

I stepped sideways to avoid him and jumped for another terrifying swipe of the knife to miss me. While the man's arm was still across I darted another blow at him, a straight left to his nose which jerked his head back so that I got my arm out before another knife-swipe sliced across. He took a step backwards to re-group himself, bringing his back to the rail. I crouched for a final close with him, baring my teeth. Christian let out another groan. Murder filled my heart, guilt and murder. The worst possible combination.

He must have seen my expression. As I moved towards him he lashed out, swinging his right foot upwards in a classic thug's drop-kick to the crutch, the one that stops the opposition dead and renders it out of action, ready for the final knife-thrust. I jumped, grabbed his foot and heaved it upwards in the standard unarmed-combat response, without thinking, wrenching it high upward and over before letting go.

His back was against the stair-rail. He went up and over, legs high in the air, one hand grabbing the rail, the other with the knife in it missing any grip completely. Then he was gone, head first.

He screamed all the way down. Just like they said Berthe Cauvinière did.

I can't describe the noise he made when he hit the floor three flights below. I was holding Christian Maucourt, turning him over, trying to see the damage.

'Tim,' he said weakly. He was starting to twitch, gone into shock, dead white.

'Don't talk! Don't say anything.'

'Laboratories,' he said, thickly. Then something else, something that sounded like jolly, as though mocking me.

'Shut up, Christian! I'm going to get help.'

I ran into the offices and found a telephone. I managed not to scream at the emergency services. Police, ambulance, everything, quick, quick; there was blood all over my hands.

I threw my jacket off, tore myself out of my cotton shirt and ran back to him. A pool of blood was spreading across the marble. I got the shirt to his chest, pushing his weakening hands away, and held it there, stanching the flow, stopping it, holding the pad of wet, red shirt tight with all the gentlest force I could muster.

'Jolly,' he gasped weakly, with a weak smile up at me. 'Jolly. Funny, Tim, I—'

'Don't talk! Don't say anything!'

It seemed like ages. Actually, it wasn't. They were there in about ten minutes. It just seemed like ages. The only thing that cheered me, as I shouted at them to leave the bundle of dead man at the bottom of the stairwell and the crumpled body on the stairs and to get up here, was that the flow of blood seemed to have stopped, even though I was sure, then, that he had lost pints of blood.

The hospital afterwards confirmed it to me, only they put it differently.

They used litres.

CHAPTER 22

The police interview room would have been quite like an English police interview room if the ceiling hadn't been so high and the furniture much more metallic. They had kindly lent me a shirt, which I had on under my jacket without my tie, which was somewhere in the Rue Saint-Honoré. My clothes, apart from the shirt, were bloodstained.

'Your position is anomalous,' Inspector Levroux said across the table. 'Very anomalous. The man you threw down the stairs has broken limbs and his skull is cracked in two places. He is in a coma and quite unlikely to survive. The one you threw down the central well is of course dead. The young man, Christian Maucourt, is also unconscious and may not be disturbed because his condition is critical. We have your version of events but no one available to corroborate it.'

Inspector Levroux was about thirty-five, plumpish, almost bald. He smoked a lot. So did his sergeant, sitting beside him. His sergeant, who wore a vast hairy jacket, was large and powerful. They were not hostile in any way, just cautious, and they regarded me owlishly. Put the way they put it, my throwing people down stairwells to their deaths made me sound very violent. Which, for a brief minute or two, I suppose I was.

'Well,' I said, 'I've told you. They were going to kill him, so it was, I suppose, a combination of first subject and then self-defence.'

Levroux puffed a puff of smoke. 'You are remarkably calm,' he stated, as though starting a psychological examination. 'Remarkably calm. Most men, having done what you have done, would be in a considerable state of emotion, even of shock. They would need tranquillizing.'

'Oh, you know how we English are,' I said, rather tersely. 'Cool to the very core.'

He smiled thinly. 'Perhaps this is not new to you. You have had this experience before?'

I shook my head. 'Can't say I've ever thrown anyone over a stairwell before, no.'

'It is extraordinary that since you appeared on the scene there has been a succession of deaths. All people involved with you or your work, however briefly. It forms a pattern.'

'Michel Bonnet wasn't involved with me.'

'With your work, he was. And you replaced him. Perhaps that was arranged by you too.'

'Oh dear. Then why didn't I run off and leave Christian Maucourt to die, I wonder?'

'Perhaps it would not have been to your advantage. For some reason we do not yet know.'

I sighed. This was getting nowhere. In life it is not what you know that matters, but who. I hate such clichés but there are times when they are needed, like my current need for credibility.

'Look,' I said. 'I know that the gendarmerie is very extensive but do you know of an inspector called Dagallier? Used to be in the Meudon area?'

Levroux's face changed a little. 'Why?' he demanded.

'He'll vouch for me if you ask him.'

Levroux frowned. 'As it happens, I know Dagallier. A successful policeman. Why would he vouch for you?'

'He and I got to know each other about three years ago. A rather violent affair then, too. I was on the right side, though.'*

Levroux groaned. 'Oh God,' he said bitterly, 'you're not a British policeman, are you? Some *sacré* CID man or Special Branch or something, poking where you have no business to be?'

'Good God, no! Me, a policeman? How dare you? I am a respectable citizen.'

His face went impassive. 'I do not find that droll, Mr Simpson, not at all droll. I will, as it happens, check with Dagallier. I was on a course with him recently. My sergeant will stay to look after your needs.'

He left, and the big sergeant regarded me steadily from the depths of his hairy jacket. Waiting in places like that seems eternal. The main consolation was that at least Christian was in the best hands possible. I had no doubt that the Maucourts would see to that. There was nothing to do but be patient. The funny thing was that it was still only just ten o'clock but it felt like after midnight; it had been a long day.

* *The Gwen John Sculpture*

Levroux was gone about fifteen minutes. When he came back he sat down, lit another cigarette and looked at me carefully, nodding a little. 'Dagallier vouches for you,' he said. 'From the last time, anyway. And there is a lawyer outside, a very senior *Maître* no less, who is the Maucourt bank's best brief, waiting in the ante-room. Under French law I am obliged to allow him all sorts of access and so on within a certain time-scale but since I do not propose to detain you he will simply check that you are quite happy when we leave this room in a few minutes' time.' He smiled cheerfully. 'Dagallier says you are a *brave gars* but he said to remind you that he told you, the last time, that your credit was exhausted, Mr Banker.'

'Oh dear, I'd forgotten that.'

'He also sent you his salutations, but bear it in mind. None of the *amateur detective anglais*. No initiatives from you. Got it?'

'Got it.'

'Good. This is our case now. Actually, the word of Dagallier is good enough for me but my sergeant here is likely to be even more positive.' He jerked a thumb towards the big, hairy-jacketed man.

'Oh? Why?'

The sergeant grinned. 'The dead one is called Morelli. A nasty Italian thug. The smashed one still hanging on is a Corsican called Favez. I rather hope he does not recover, but of course we need to question him about who they were working for. They are not those who take the initiative, they are hirelings, freelancers. You have done us a favour; we don't need them.'

'I see. At least, I don't. I can't think what they were after. I can't think why they went for Christian.'

'Nor can we just yet.' Levroux looked at me anxiously. 'I have your statement, which is fine and it is my belief, now, that those two engineered the fall of Madame Cauvinière from her apartment even though we cannot connect them yet. Forensic evidence is now suggesting that there was too much alcohol on her clothes for normal ingestion.

In other words, drink was forced into her and it spilled. There is also the question of Madame Delattre's fall in the Métro. We must re-examine that, now.'

'And Michel Bonnet?'

He raised his eyebrows. 'Who knows? That will be difficult. Now that there may be suspicious circumstances, though, the matter will be re-opened.'

'That's good.'

'Maybe.' He stood up and held out his hand to shake mine. 'Thank you. And my felicitations on your powers of defence and survival. You won't be leaving the country for a few days?'

'No, I won't.'

'If you think of anything at all you'll tell us, not go off on your own?'

'I will.'

He nodded, satisfied. I supposed he knew enough about me to get hold of me whenever he wanted, even from England, so he was quite safe in letting me go. Somehow I was sure I'd be seeing Levroux and his sergeant again, next time in an even more curious mood.

The Maucourts' lawyer was very serious, professional, and clucked over the blood on my clothes while I assured him it wasn't mine.

'It's Christian's,' I said. 'How is he?'

'I'll take you to the hospital.' The lawyer's eyes were troubled. 'It's a bad business. His father, Roland, is returning from the States on the first possible plane, with his mother. The condition is critical. The internal organs are damaged. He has the best medical attention available, though.'

'I'm sure he has.'

My visit to the hospital was pretty futile. I couldn't see Christian and there wasn't much point in waiting; they gave me a résumé of the situation and said it would be at least twenty-four hours before any change would be significant. I turned to go and found my way barred by the stocky figure of Charles Maucourt. There was no passing him by.

'I'm very sorry,' I said. 'I really am terribly sorry. It's all my fault.'

He shook his head. 'My dear fellow, you did your best to save his life. At least we can hope you have succeeded. He has had massive transfusions and is stable. I want you to know that the gratitude of my family will remain with you for ever.'

'Oh no. Look here, I sent him off to do a job I should have done myself. I never thought, never, that he would be in danger there in the Rue Saint-Honoré, but I shouldn't have sent a boy to do a man's job. It was unforgivable.'

'My dear Tim, no one can assume that the examination of prosaic accounting records could lead to a murderous attack. There is something terrible going on and I am afraid that the key to it lies in there.' He pointed at my head, jabbing a stubby forefinger in a sharp gesture. 'It is a nasty responsibility for you; it imposes upon you the requirement of solving the problem and it also puts you in danger. I am familiar with the situation from my own experiences. I do not envy you. What I want you to know is that my full resources, weak as they are, are at your disposal. The police, of course, will now pursue the matter actively but they do not have your knowledge, your start on the thing.'

'I'm afraid that's true.'

He put a hand on my shoulder. 'You look completely épuisé, my friend. Go and get some rest. We will wait here.'

'I hear his father is coming back from the States.'

'Oh yes. And his mother, of course.' He glanced back down the hospital corridor in the direction of the wards. 'Eugène is there, but— He broke off, as though I should understand.

I didn't understand. I gave him a quizzical look.

'Eugène is a cold fish,' he muttered. 'Always was. And Roland is a nice fellow but no genius. If it had not been for my problems, I would never have let Eugène into—He broke off again, avoiding my eye for a moment and looked at me again with a fierce glare. 'Christian is a bright boy, clever, disciplined, but sensitive to people, unlike Eugène.

All my hopes for the future centre on that boy. You blame yourself for sending him into danger, but it was we who pushed him to you, to work with you. We have as much responsibility as you. He has to learn, to experience life's dangers. You went to defend him regardless of your own safety; in war, one can ask no more than that. No matter what happens, we will always remember. Always.'

He turned abruptly on his heel and marched off, leaving me to stand alone in the reception area of the hospital, where people moved anxiously about and a telephone kept ringing. I walked slowly to the door and found a taxi.

What problems were they that made him let Eugène into what?

Control of the bank?

The taxi drew up at my hotel. I got out, paid him and went through reception to my room, ignoring the strange, fishlike eye of the late-night reception porter, who stared at me oddly. I assumed that it was my clothes that caused his strangely curious stare; bloodstains still patched my trousers with dark-brown blotches.

It wasn't that at all. Night porters have other preoccupations.

As I closed the door, the beside light went on and a tousled figure rose, clutching a sheet to what was obviously an otherwise undraped female body of considerable attraction.

'I thought,' Sue said, making a rather ambivalent gesture at herself and the bed, 'that I'd better come and occupy this myself before that blonde who is so conspicuous in your imagery got here first.'

I gaped. 'Sue? What are you doing here?'

She grinned alluringly. 'I'm playing truant, just like you did.' She rose a little further from the bedclothes. 'I didn't think I'd have to wait so long though. It's jolly late and— Tim! My God! You look *awful*! What on *earth* have you been doing?'

CHAPTER 23

In the morning, the maid served not one but two *café-complets*, leaving them on the side table, and left the room without so much as a blink or a raising of the eyebrow.

Sue rolled over and wrapped herself around me. 'It's very romantic,' she murmured, 'running away to Paris like this. Even if you have been misbehaving terribly.'

'There's not another woman in my life.'

'I should jolly well think not! You're quite enough of a problem without other women coming into it as well.'

'How did you manage to get away?'

'Edinburgh is having a cold spell. The exhibition arrangements are all under control. I don't need to be back there until tomorrow. I thought a quick trip to Paris, give Tim a fright, back tonight, would be fun. I got a cheap ticket; you said it was only like popping up to Manchester, remember?'

'So I did.'

'And you'd have been away those two or three days that you mentioned, so naturally I was starting to worry. You might be tearing the clothes off an encouraging French girl.'

'Rubbish. You never took that two or three days thing seriously, not for a moment.'

'Instead of which you were pursuing your more predictable hobby of murder, violence and mayhem.'

'Never was a man more innocently employed. But it might account for your presence. Your solicitous attention.' I smoothed her hair out of her eyes. 'Among other things.'

'What do you mean, other things?'

'Quite apart from your romantic inclinations—'I grasped her a little tighter—'I think there is something else. Something you have come to tell me personally.'

'Tim! How miserable of you. After all I've done for you by way of personal satisfaction.'

'And I for you. I'm right, obviously.'

She sighed. 'I think it's very annoying that your intuitions are so strong. That's supposed to be a woman's strength. I think we'd better have our coffee before it gets cold.'

'There I cannot quibble with you.'

We disentangled ourselves and, after suitable modesty was restored, sat at the little table to eat our breakfast. Sue crunched her croissant with satisfaction and downed a lot of thick *café au lait*. I phoned for some more. When everything solid was consumed I brushed crusty crumbs of bread and flakes of croissant off myself and sat back to look at her expectantly.

'Cough it up, Sue.'

She flicked a few crumbs away and blotted her lips carefully with a napkin. 'How strong are you feeling this morning, Tim?'

'Strong enough. Bad as that, is it?'

'Well—it's not that bad. But it's the end of an era.'

Her light flippancy now disappeared and she looked at me with what I knew was her serious look, the one she can't hide even when she tries to be amusing over it, or unconcerned, or some other disguise. The end of an era; eras always end when you don't want them to.

'Which one?'

She sighed. 'You and Jeremy, I think. That's the era I mean.'

'So you saw Mary?'

She nodded. 'I saw Mary. She sends you her very best love. She's always had a soft spot for you. That's what's upsetting her a bit but she says Jeremy can't help it.'

'He's being very furtive, whatever he can't help.'

She shook her head. 'It's not that, though in a way I think he's trying to shield you. Nothing is settled yet but Mary says there are terrific pressures to cut back on everything. I mean I do know, you know, even at the Tate, that things are in a dreadful state economically. Jeremy wants you to stay under his wing but he's pushed to justify it after all that decentralization. It seems you aren't fully occupied and the pressure is to cut costs.'

'Funny how one suddenly finds oneself becoming a cost instead of an asset. That bugger Peter Lewis is behind this.' I shook my head ruefully. 'So out goes Tim. That's the bad news, is it?'

'I did say it wasn't all that bad. Mary says you can move here to Paris at a much higher salary.' She gave me a speculative look. 'Did you know that?'

'The offer was made the day before yesterday.'

'And you turned down a job in New York.' It was a statement this time.

'I did. From Howarth, at the end of the Moreton Frewen thing. It was to run Christerby's over there. You knew about that.'

'Well, Howarth says, apparently, that he can't find anyone suitable at all. He says they're all poofs or crooks and he's just fired the last one. You can have the New York job any time you want it but, Howarth says, like now.'

I smiled reminiscently. 'Howarth's a proper Lancashire industrialist. Poofs or crooks, eh? That sounds like old down-to-earth, brass-tacks boiler-maker Howarth.'

'You liked him, I remember. So the feeling that Jeremy is having to deal with is that you can go to Paris or New York, where you will be far better off, and a large saving can be made in Jeremy's budget. He simply hasn't put you in the picture because he's been hoping, like Mr Micawber, that something else will turn up and that in any case you and he go together like Laurel and Hardy, or Fortnum and Mason, or something.'

'Not quite the similes I would have chosen, Sue.'

'Perhaps not, Tim dear. But you turned down New York, as I suppose you may well think of turning down Paris, for the reason that you and Jeremy have been loyal to each other quite apart from liking to work together. And for one other reason.'

'Another reason?'

'Yes. There was another reason why you turned down a job abroad.'

'Was there?'

'Yes.' She picked up the second coffee-pot and helped herself to some more. 'It was me, wasn't it?'

'You?'

'Yes, me. You know that very well and so do I. That's why I've come over. To talk to you about it properly. Tim, gallantry's nice but it gets you precious little these days. You turned down New York partly because of Jeremy but also because of me and my job at the Tate.' She gave me a wry, affectionate smile. 'I've often thought about it. You never said so, and you never even hinted. But I knew. And you can't go on turning things down just because of me.'

'Sue, it's not four days since you were offering to support me in idleness, presumably while I found another job in London. Your place at the Tate is very important.'

'Dear Tim. One day, not so far off, I—no, we—will start a family. What about my job then?'

'What about it? You'll take maternity leave and go back when you're ready, won't you?'

She smiled. 'I love the way you make it sound so simple. It isn't. I love my work but it doesn't weigh up against the needs of a family and you letting yourself go to waste as Jeremy's assistant instead of getting on. For a man, getting on is important. A woman weighs up what sacrifices getting on will demand and very often, because women are more sensible as well as more realistic, tells herself that the sacrifice isn't worth it.'

She picked up her coffee for a sip or two and gave me a significant look, as though to confirm this piece of irrefutable feminine philosophy.

'Damn it,' I said. 'God damn it. Damn the Bank. Damn Maucourt's. Damn Christerby's and Howarth. I don't want to face this now. Not now. The end of an era. Sod it, Not now. Damn. Damn. *Damn* . . .'

'That sounds much more like the man I married. When you've quite finished cursing, perhaps you'll hear that I'd be quite happy to live in Paris, or New York, particularly if we start a family. The break from the Tate and the change would be a good time to do it. And it's not as though Paris and New York are devoid of art, Tim. You know?' She cocked an eyebrow at me. 'I might just do better. Mightn't I?'

She calmly sat there, writing off something that I knew meant enormous things to her, just to help me. All right, change should be exciting, and people need change. But she had made her place in a famous institution, she was respected, she'd built up something of her own. I loved her and she loved me; she put that ahead of everything. Damn it. Damn it all.

'It's hard for you,' she said. 'You've got to make the decisions. I wanted you to know, while you're here and talking to these people. The telephone's no good for things like this. You can make your decision with what I've told you quite clear in your mind. All you have left to deal with is the problem of you and Jeremy.' She smiled again. 'That might be even harder. You go back together so far and through such very bonding events.'

'Is that why he's acting in such a repressed way?'

'Mary say's she thinks he's hoping you'll make the decision yourself quite independently. He warned you an offer would be made to prepare you. It would be much easier for him if you left of your own free will. Much better than him telling you what the choices are.'

I stared at her. In all of life there is always the first version, the story the first person tells you when the event has happened. Afterwards, if you are very lucky, you get the real story. Sue was giving me the real story, at least, the real story as far as it had got. I wondered if I'd ever get the real story at Bellevie, or that of Tissot.

'Don't look so glum, Tim,' Sue said. 'There are far worse choices to make in life. Cheer up. I'm here and we've got a day off together if you can take a day off, can you?'

'I can take a day off,' I said. 'For a wife like you I can take the whole year off.'

'Thank you, kind sir! I'm rather looking forward to whatever's going to happen. Once you get home I suppose I'll know?'

'You will. And thanks.' I got up, went round the table and kissed her tenderly. 'You can stay longer if you want.'

'No, I can't do that.' Sue smiled up at me and then, frowning, bit her lip.

'What's up?'

Her expression was serious again. 'I have a message for you,' she said reluctantly, 'from Charles Massenaux. I didn't want to deliver it but I promised. It's about some Tissots, I'm afraid.'

'Some Tissots? Plural? Good God, how many?'

'Three, he says. Coming up for auction, here in Paris.'

'Three? Who's selling them?'

'A lawyer. That's what Charles told me to tell you. It's a lawyer acting for someone who wishes to remain unknown. The lawyer says he has clean title for his client.'

'Three Tissots.' I sat down again, heavily. 'Jesus! Does Charles know what they are?'

'Oh yes. Charles knows all right.' Sue began to tick them off on her fingers. 'One: a later canvas from the *Femme à Paris* series. The stuff that no one seems to like very much, at least certainly not the French. It was too literary, too narrative for them, too English. Two: a picture of Kathleen Newton in the garden at St John's Wood. Hitherto unknown. And three—' she gave me a significant look—'a painting of the Thames somewhere below the Pool of London, with two girls in coloured dresses and a nautical man on a balcony overlooking steamships and sailing ships, and a meal on the table. Charles says it's a stunner. He said to tell you to shape up for a million quid. That is exactly what he said: the very words. A million quid.'

'Christ! Here in Paris?'

'Here in Paris. Not London. Here.'

'Wow.' I stared at the breakfast things on the table. Another still life, right in front of me. 'The muscular hare is finally within sight of the hound dog.'

'What?'

'Nothing. Just an expression.'

'That's what I feared. That's why I didn't want to give you the message.'

She looked harassed. I thought of her in the basement of the Tate Gallery, her own territory, and that wonderful painting with all those flags and those two young women, beautiful in their white Worth dresses with black piping all the way round, standing on a deck beribboned with colour. Sacheverell Sitwell got it all wrong, and so did James Laver. Despite what Sue said, for me those two ladies would always be the Jerome sisters, lovely Americans waiting for the cream of England's aristocracy to take them up, for Lord Randolph Churchill to be swept away in heart and head by Jennie, for Moreton Frewen, much later, to set his cap at Clara.

When you look at a painting, you see what you want to see; that's what art is for.

'It's all right, Sue. This time the art isn't a threat.' I stood up briskly. 'Come on, we've got a day off! Do you want to stay in Paris or should we go out of town, to Chantilly for lunch?'

'Chantilly?'

'Sure! We can take in the gardens, the art in the château, and then bet on the horses for the afternoon. There's a meeting on. What do you say? Shall we go out and back a few winners? Try our luck? See if it's in?'

She grinned at me, her eyes sparkling.

'Let's do that,' she said. 'Afterwards.'

CHAPTER 24

The Musée des Beaux-Arts is a large building in a side-street at the back of the cathedral in Nantes. I hadn't been into the centre of the city before and I had a bit of trouble parking my hired car. When Christian Maucourt and I had

visited Bellevie together we stayed outside, going to the
factory on a modern industrial estate not far from the high,
spidery road bridge which arches gracefully over the Loire
to the west of the city. For donkey's years Nantes was
famous for its girdered transporter at the centre, a construction much like the Runcorn–Widnes job, but they pulled
that down years ago, before they stopped building ships
along the river and while the biscuit factories were still
hammering out millions of *petits beurres*.

Sir Richard White was waiting for me in the great marble
entrance hall. He looked as neat and grey and well-kept as
ever, unruffled and unworried but cool as he clasped my
hand quite formally and gave me the ghost of a smile.

'I got the TGV down here,' he said. 'Very impressive.
You should try it sometime.'

'Ah,' I said. 'I needed the car. Planes and cars, that's
youth. We've just not got the train habit.'

'You should acquire it. In France and Germany it's quite
the thing.'

'Shall we go up?'

'Lead the way. It's your meeting.'

I bought two tickets at ten francs each and we climbed
up one of two long clean marble staircases. At the top the
attendants had no idea where the Tissots were, had never
heard of him. A prophet is not without honour and all that.
One of them phoned down to the foyer and then her face
cleared.

'*L'Enfant prodigue?*' she queried, looking at me.

'*C'est ça.*'

She waved us round a corner to the internal gallery set
round a vast central space like the balconies in a Spanish
courtyard but much, much bigger. The four paintings were
hung along the wall in a straight sequence, set in their
identical heavy gilded frames. They are the only Tissots in
the art museum of his handsome native city.

'The prodigal son,' I said to Sir Richard White, gesturing
at the four of them. 'They're a bit darker than I imagined
they would be. But let's have a butcher's before we talk.'

He nodded, less distantly than he usually did, and we studied them, one after another. Here upstairs the art museum was empty. Below us a classroom of school children was being ushered round the glories of the Impressionists or the sculpture of Rodin, but we were alone with the four paintings and a fine leather-buttoned bench, more like a settee than anything else. The great open galleries were clean and airy behind us.

In the first painting the prodigal son is about to depart. He sits on a dining-table in a room overlooking the Thames. His old bearded father talks to him, expostulating mildly. Through the windows, with their half-drawn blinds, you look out into the yellow smoky light of Victorian London, with a paddle-steamer and a tug puffing by. The elder brother stares out at this, elbow on the sill, and Kitty Newton, as his wife, sews next to the loaded tea-tray beside her.

Next, the prodigal is abroad, sowing his wild oats. He wears a neat suit with a trilby hat as he stares at a succession of well-dressed Japanese geishas who are too fixed in attitude and dress to be taken from anything except a photograph.

The third painting depicts the return. Barefoot, ragged, the prodigal son has been decanted from a cattle boat on to the wet cold planking of a lower London quayside. He is on his knees, clasped in his remorse by his loving father while the elder brother, heavily overcoated, looks on with Mrs Kathleen Newton, who is attired in an elegant fur coat. Cattle and pigs are being driven off the canvas to their fate.

Finally, the fatted calf. Beside an idyllic up-river Thames, deep in dreamy meadow and trees, the family are lunching off a table covered with white napery. A large silver meat-cover conceals the beef. From the river steps our hero, straight out of a healthy, hearty rowing boat crewed by men dressed, like himself, in whites. He and they wear a version of an I Zingari cricket cap which oarsmen never wore, but Tissot could hardly be expected to understand the niceties of English sporting club attire. At the table the elder brother carves. Mrs Newton is more relaxed, his father beams a welcome.

'The Prodigal Son in Modern Attire,' I said to Sir Richard White. 'Very improving. Less horrific than Hogarth and more understandable to the Victorian. Based on the Bible but absolutely British. Immensely popular, it was. As moral as Frith and Burne-Jones. Tissot himself thought they were pretty good; he left them to the nation. The French nation, actually to the Luxembourg. There were watercolour replicas and etchings. Definitely a success.'

'Extraordinary.' Sir Richard's tone was less formal.

'People have speculated on Tissot's self-identification with them. He had left his own father. In the first painting you see, there, on the mantelpiece, a large marine shell, a conch shell. Tissot's father was a keen conchologist. Biographers have said that his love of conchology diminished his regard for painting and robbed his son's artistic success of any value in his eyes. Tissot had journeyed abroad—to England—where he lived in sin. Just like painting number two. Not long after this set of four was exhibited at the Dudley Gallery, Tissot returned to France —painting number three, though Tissot was hardly in rags, except emotionally—and soon after, re-entered the religion he had neglected. Painting number four. Calm returns. End of story.'

'Remarkable.'

'It's a powerful one, of course. Tissot had used it before. He was feeling the effects of living as a Frenchman in London at the time he did these. His success was irritating the critics. Much as, later and ironically, he was regarded as an 'English' painter when back in France. It's quite a difficult matter, I suppose, that problem. One of national, as much as self, identification?'

Sir Richard White walked back from the last painting which he seemed to be examining closely, and sat down on the leather bench. His gaze ran along the wall, taking in the four large canvases.

'Tissot eventually went back to the Château de Buillon, in the Franche-Comté. You know? His father bought it after a long success with fashion goods. In the Franche-Comté. The Doubs was actually where the family came from. I'm sure you know it well.'

Sir Richard White's eyes, I now noticed, were not really blue. There was a shade of hazel to them which dimmed their tone. His pale skin was very clear and whatever diet it was that he lived on during his years in France, with the gastronomic delights of the Périgord on his doorstep and the wines of Bordeaux, Bergerac and Cahors to hand, he had not fattened or coarsened or slowed. He was either very lucky or very disciplined.

'You are very deceptive,' he said, looking straight at me with those eyes which, with their dimmed tone, made it difficult to see exactly what he was thinking, what was going on behind them. 'A very deceptive man indeed.'

'Ah. You said that to Christian Maucourt. I wonder why you say it. After all, I take it that it was really you who were responsible for my presence over here on this rather interesting sortie?'

He smiled, quite broadly. 'Well done. Although I suppose it must have become obvious to you by now.'

'Not that obvious. But I was at the races at Chantilly the day before yesterday, and I backed a couple of winners. Backing winners is something City moguls and, in the past, English landowners used to do, or try to do. Horses for courses and all that sort of stuff. This particular French course was one for which you could think of a horse. From past experience? An ugly brute with a vicious kick, but ideal for certain steeplechase courses with neck-breaking jumps. So you very gently arranged it. You even arranged it so that the people concerned would think it was their idea, particularly since it would be convenient in the difficult circumstances prevailing. You knew that, too. If you had suggested it outright yourself they'd probably have said no. It was very subtle. Masterly, in fact.'

He gave a sort of harrumph, looked at the first painting,

which was the nearest one to us, taking in the conch shell on the mantelpiece, then turned back to me.

'Mr Simpson—no, damn it.' He shook his head briefly. 'We can't go on like this.' The soft-coloured eyes caught mine magnetically, and held them. 'My family, and my friends, call me Richard.' Very deliberately, he held his right hand out towards me. 'Not Dick. I always hated that. Richard. I know your name well enough, I think. Don't I?'

'Tim.'

I took his right hand in mine and there, in that empty cream balustraded gallery, with Tissot's Prodigal looking down on us, we solemnly shook hands. It was a surprisingly warm hand he gave me this time. I clasped it firmly.

'Richard.'

'Tim.' He smiled again, and his hand and gaze released mine. 'I'm glad about this.' He paused, seeming to gather a thought that had occurred to him, before going on. 'I don't have to remind you of the past. When Jeremy and you saw me off, out of the Bank, three years or so ago, I loathed you both. Hated you. You entered my demonology, if you like. Not perhaps so much you, since you were Jeremy's instrument rather than the prime mover, but if it hadn't been for you, for your persistence and intelligence, it wouldn't have happened.'

'Look, I was sorry—'

He held up his hand to stop me, to allow himself to get it out. 'In fact, you did me an enormous favour.'

'What?'

'An enormous favour. I believe, in your subsequent, er. undertakings, for the Art Fund, you acquired a piece designed by the architect Richard Norman Shaw?'

'Yes, I did. A bureau bookcase.'

'Exactly. Well, I have always admired him as much as I know you do. In eighteen eighty-one, when Shaw was fifty, he was so ill with overwork that his wife took him to the Riviera. His friends never expected to see him again. For a while he was convinced that he was doomed to exile and slow decline. He came back to England briefly, then went

to Egypt but settled at Aix-les-Bains to take the cure.' Sir
Richard White's face lightened; he smiled reminiscently, as
though he'd been there himself. 'It completely revitalized
Shaw. From being convinced his life's work was over he
changed totally. He came back to England and went on to
do some of his finest architectural work. Well, I'm not fifty.
I'm seventy now, but my break did the trick for me.' He
gave me a smiling stare. 'After six months in the Dordogne
I came to see how stupid that project was, for me. The man
Dechavanne had duped me completely. You were young,
you were fresh, you trusted no one. I do not resent what
happened now, not at all. You—and Jeremy—prevented a
disastrous investment.'

'It was a good idea, Richard. Right in principle but con-
trolled by the wrong person.'

He retained the reminiscent smile. 'There's no need to
be kind. I was blinkered then, overtired, trying too hard. I
thought, when Jeremy first introduced you for that perfume
thing in Brazil, that you were a rugby-playing yahoo of the
type that Jeremy would like. I even thought, three years
ago, much the same thing. I underestimated you, of course.
The fate of the English. That's what I meant when I said
you are deceptive. You are very deceptive. You look like a
sporting, muscularly amiable, unintellectual Englishman.
You are a very dangerous man indeed.'

'Well. I'm not sure—'

He chuckled. 'Don't take it the wrong way. That's
enough about your character. The fact is that when Bonnet
had his crash I smelt a rat. Eugène Maucourt was going to
put another French fellow on the job, but I interfered. I
had come back, you see, to talk to Charles Maucourt about
business and to show that I was reinvigorated by my
enforced sabbatical. My mind is clear, rested, and I'm *not
going to sit and do nothing for the next ten years.*'

He said the last sentence with such emphasis and deter-
mination that I suddenly felt quite sorry for Jeremy, back
in London. Sir Richard White had returned: that there

could be no denying. He was a force that could not be discounted any more.

'So,' he went on, 'I simply told Eugène that I thought you, as an outsider, would be the best man for the job.'

'Forgive my interrupting—did you mention the Art Fund when you were talking to Eugène?'

He looked at me curiously. 'Yes, I expect I did. It would come up naturally in mentioning your CV, so to speak.'

'Did he react to it at all?'

'Er, well, now that you mention it, yes. He brightened a lot. He's not normally very demonstrative.'

'But it has always been his father, Charles, who's the enthusiast on Tissot? You even took him to see the *Henley Regatta* painting in the Leander Club once, I believe.'

He didn't reply. A cautious, thoughtful look had come to his face. I got up from the leather bench, walked up and down past the prodigal Tissots and went back to sit next to him.

'I was reading *The Times* obituary columns a few weeks ago. There was a big obit, with a photograph, of Harry Rée. Codename César. One of the most remarkable SOE operatives. When I read M.R.D. Foot's book, much further back, I always remembered Rée because he came from Manchester; his accent in French was so strong that the locals in the Franche-Comté had to pass him off as an Alsatian so that the Germans wouldn't be suspicious. It didn't mention that in *The Times* obituary.'

'No. It didn't.'

'Did you work with him at all?'

Sir Richard White nodded. 'Very briefly. I had that honour. He was a legend among the French. You must know how he invented blackmail sabotage. It saved thousands of French lives. His mother was French, you know, and one of his grandfathers originated in Germany. Yet he went to your college in Cambridge and was an Englishman, in the same way that in the first war Robert Graves was an Englishman. He had tremendous moral principles, had even been a pacifist. Why do you ask?'

'The Peugeot plant at Sochaux he sabotaged, which saved all those lives from RAF bombs, can't be more than twenty miles from Trevillers, where Tissot's father came from and not much more from Damprichard. You did say that Madame Delattre's maiden name was Damprichard? Same as the village in the Franche-Comté?'

'Oh yes. She identified with the area in more ways than one.' He shook his head. 'Very little escapes your attention, does it?'

'Three paintings by Tissot are coming up for auction in Paris very soon.'

He looked up sharply, his eyes focusing on mine keenly. 'What? When?'

'Soon. In Paris. Not London. They'll fetch a fortune. But the seller is using a lawyer to handle them.'

'A lawyer?'

'Yes, a lawyer. He's not the Maucourts' lawyer. I've checked.'

He frowned. 'Why would he be the Maucourts' lawyer?'

'Oh, please. I would appreciate your help. Even if it is difficult for you.'

He shook his head. 'I'm not sure what help it is you're asking me for.'

I bit my lip. 'This is difficult for me, too. Charles Maucourt and Madame Delattre were intensely active in the Resistance in the Franche-Comté. They were, indeed, the only survivors of their particular group. She was older than him, more mature, and a powerful character by everyone's account. She is dead now and of the dead *nil nisi* and all that. At the end of the war all sorts of looted goods were discarded by the Germans. The Château de Buillon had passed to Tissot's niece, who lived until about nineteen sixty-four. The estate and contents of the château were pretty derelict; she had preserved things as best she could but what was left was sold at auction after her death. I do not know what the château was used for during the war, who saw it, who was there, whether it was partly plundered, or not. After all, in the sixty years that passed after Tissot's death a great deal may have occurred. And at the end of a war chaos takes over.'

His eyes narrowed. 'I wasn't in the Franche-Comté at the end. Harry Rée's cover was blown, he was injured in a hand-to-hand struggle and the Maquis smuggled him over to Switzerland. I was there for a while after him. Things were certainly disintegrating. I went out by a different route and I missed the joys of the Armistice in France. I was back in London by then.'

'But you kept in contact with Charles Maucourt?'

'Of course. When you have hidden together, blown the enemy up together, shared your lives and—'

He broke off. And the same woman, I thought, was that what you couldn't say? Or knowledge best unknown? A moment passed silently beside the dark canvases and his eyes sought them, far away from mine. When he spoke again, he was brisk. 'Look, Tim, I'll tell you anything I'm free to tell you. Things said to me in confidence I can't repeat.'

'Of course.' I glanced at the stylized geishas waving themselves, supposedly seductively, in their flowered kimonos. 'How long has Charles Maucourt been in financial difficulties?'

'Good God!' He really looked shaken this time. 'How did you know that?'

'Just a guess, actually. Something he said at the hospital. I don't think he would have handed control over to Eugène if he'd still had his own fortune to deploy.'

He nodded slowly and put his hands up to rub his face, half covering it.

'Was it Madame Delattre and Bellevie that took his money? Blotted it up?'

'Yes.' His voice was muffled for a moment, then he took his hands away and looked up at me. 'It was. It was a bottomless pit. Not just because her nephews were profligate and so on, though that was the main cause. It was the running of the business. There were things she couldn't see or wouldn't see, wouldn't act on. Theoretically that is a hell of a good business. In practice, things were different. Do you know, I found your report on Brazil when I thought of you and you put your finger, then, right on the crux of the cosmetics business. It was extraordinary.'

'You mean the stock returns?'

'Precisely. In theory the cost is a low proportion of the retail price. In theory the margins are splendid. What everyone neglects is the amount of remaindered goods. You saw that straight away. So, apart from all the drawing of money to be squandered by the Delattre family, there wasn't a proper control of all those returned products.'

'And Charles Maucourt propped up the difference.'

'He did.'

'Why?'

Sir Richard White smiled. 'Come on, Tim. Don't pretend that you don't know.'

I looked again at the geishas in the scene of so-called dissipation in painting number two. The dissipation looked about as orgiastic as a Sunday afternoon tea-party at my old Aunt Evangeline's. Moral and sexual guilt, and obligations, are things which cannot be registered on scales of measurement. How long did it go on, I wondered, how justified was Thierry Vauchamps' indignation, how powerful was she? Very powerful, I expected. And when, at the end of the war, when France seemed to be in ruins, those paintings were acquired or captured or wrenched off whoever had them, was it Agnès Damprichard who had them put away for a rainy day, or Charles Maucourt, or both of them? And when, at the end of some financial tether, it was decided to sell them, to waft them under the nose of a visiting English art fund manager, did she object? Or did she insist on taking half the value realized? Even after taking all of Charles Maucourt's substance over so long a period?

'Eugène,' I said. 'You remarked that he hated Madame Delattre?'

'I did.'

'I suppose that was because of both the money and the infidelity?'

'The money.' He smiled quietly. 'A French son can forgive his father's infidelity.'

'The fact that these paintings are being sold in Paris, when London might fetch a better price, leads me to suspect the title. If they are sold here in auction *ouvert* and then they leave this country, it would be difficult for some long-lost owner to claim them back.'

He shrugged. 'Art is international. Bids will be international. Paris or London, the price will be good. I don't think title comes into it. I just think the owner doesn't want his name attached to the paintings for personal or family reasons. Or maybe, as in the case of a lot of rich men nowadays, to avoid spreading rumours that the owner might be in difficulties, thus affecting his credit. There could be a lot of reasons.'

'Richard, do the Maucourts' own any Tissots? Or did Madame Delattre?'

'I cannot answer that question.' He shook his head rather sadly. 'Please do not ask me again.'

In the fourth painting the smiling countryside and the sliding rippled river frame the happy family group, the elder son sharpens the carving knife behind the splendid silver dome of the meat cover, the old man beams at the healthy oarsman son, the wizened mother strokes the loyal collie dog. Two younger women, the brother's Kitty Newton wife, and another who is presumably a sister, look happily on. Below, with that famous perspective of Tissot's, the rest of the oarsmen in their I Zingari caps sit with oars shipped, having delivered the prodigal in time for lunch. But behind a trellis of climbing pink geraniums a figure in what looks like naval uniform calls or whispers from behind his hand. What is he doing? Who is he talking to, the crew or the prodigal? What is he saying? Words of temptation or of instruction? Who is he? A brother or an outsider? With Tissot, the trouble is that you never know.

'One last question,' I said. 'Then I'll drop all this.'

'I'll answer if I can.'

'You invested in Bellevie.'

'That's a statement, not a question.'

'Maucourt's have invested as a bank, quite apart from Charles's own personal support. If Agnès Delattre was still in the way and things might still be difficult despite the new plan, wasn't it a bit risky? I mean, it was perhaps a help in getting yourself on Maucourt's board, but all the same?'

He smiled. 'I knew you were coming.'

'Thanks. Flattery will get you a long way with me. But you hadn't had my report yet. You invested without that. And she still preserved that shop in aspic.'

He paused, then spoke carefully. 'There was an old obligation. Help was needed and it was called in.'

'An old obligation? Involving Madame Delattre?'

'Tim.' The voice was still courteous, friendly. 'You have asked me quite enough.'

'Sorry. I am extremely sorry. I'm being very intrusive. Forgive me.'

'That's what I expect you to be. You are forgiven. But I cannot help you any more.'

'Well,' I said, rubbing my hands together. 'That's all, then.'

'All? I go away for two days and when I get back I find that a woman has been thrown out of a window, Christian Maucourt knifed almost to death, you have killed one man and probably mortally wounded another, and you say that's all? All?'

'I meant about Tissot,' I said. 'For the moment, anyway. But while we're here in Nantes, I thought you might like to come and look at the company you've invested in?'

CHAPTER 25

Sir Richard White was impressed. He was impressed with the modern buildings, the gleaming stainless steel of the equipment, the shiny floors. He liked the computer terminals and the screens full of formulae that designated things with names like lauryl sulphate and isethionate. He listened carefully to everything Bastoni said and he smiled and shook hands with the heads of department to whom Bastoni introduced him, chatting to them amiably in his excellent French.

Bastoni was delighted. There wasn't a whisper from him about the British and the Common Market. Bastoni wore a much finer-woven Italian suit this time, one that gave elegant lines to his thin figure. He was visibly impressed with Sir Richard, with his air of authority, his disciplined grey manner, his title. It is odd that the Continentals, republicans who have executed and banished their aristocrats, show enormous deference to titled people whereas we British, who have learned to live with them, can take 'em or leave 'em. More than anything, though, Bastoni was delighted with Sir Richard's investment, his position on the board of Maucourt's, his obvious eminence as a leading member of White's Bank, or of its family, and hence his enormous influence and importance. To Sir Richard he showed tremendous respect and careful courtesy while retaining his own authority as head of the place, as an expert and a businessman.

To me, Bastoni was now openly friendly. It was as though we were old colleagues, longstanding associates of much shared experience. I assumed that Thierry Vauchamps had advised him of my positive reaction to the plan. The assumption that Bastoni would now make would be, presumably, that I had brought Sir Richard down for a formal tour of the Bellevie organization before everything was signed and sealed, with White's as much as Maucourt's. Money, regenerating money, would flow into the coffers of the Bellevie company and expansion would take place. Bastoni concentrated, followed every word of Sir Richard's, but made sure to include me in his remarks, smiled at me, took my arm on one occasion, laughed appreciatively at a remark of mine that was intended to be funny.

At the mention of the unhappy event in the Rue Saint-Honoré he became grave.

'Terrible,' he said. 'Horrible. I knew Berthe Cauvinière very well, of course. And young Christian, such a pleasant boy. One must pray that at least he does not follow the fate of the two murderous assassins.' His eyes fell on me. 'The whole organization is in your debt, Mr Simpson. We hope and pray your courage will be rewarded.'

'The fate of the two assassins? One of them is still in the balance, surely?'

'Ah no.' His face darkened. 'Have you not heard? I spoke to the Rue Saint-Honoré this morning. They got the news that the second man, the one who was still unconscious, died last night.' His face twitched for a moment, then corrected itself. 'It seems that it will be difficult to understand what this shocking attack was about. Incredible.'

He and Sir Richard both looked at me. It wasn't a comfortable experience.

'Well,' I said, to fill in the silence that had fallen and to divert my own sense of exposure to those calculating yet speculative pairs of eyes, 'we must hope that the police can find some other route to determine what they were about.'

'Indeed we must.' Bastoni's tone was not hopeful. 'If Christian Maucourt, as we all desperately hope, recovers, then perhaps some clue to this appalling affair can be gained. It seems incomprehensible; intruders frequently break into Paris offices of course, in the hope of finding cash. Or valuables, or equipment such as computer terminals and so on. Who knows?'

'Who knows indeed?' I echoed. 'We will have to wait

and see. I'm afraid modern life is all too full of these terrible examples. One never thinks they will occur so near home.'

Bastoni nodded, still grave in manner. I waited for the moment to pass, for the subject to die away, for my platitudes to wither on the air, then proceeded in a brisker vein. 'In the meantime we must get on. We cannot afford to lose the initiative.'

'Ah.' Bastoni brightened. 'You have news about the plan, perhaps?'

'I hope to have, shortly. There are just one or two matters of detail I wanted to clear up. I wondered if you could help me?'

'Of course. Anything I can do to assist, I will do.'

'Splendid.' I gave him and Sir Richard a brief smile. 'It's about the ingredients, you see. The ingredients in the products.'

'Oh yes?' Bastoni gave me a neutral look.

'The plan doesn't go down into that sort of detail. It's more concerned with product groups and market opportunities. Can you tell me: to what extent are the major products in the skincare range dependent on animal extracts?'

Bastoni's face didn't flicker. 'There are both animal and, er, vegetable extracts used in the products' he said. 'I think I gave you an example when you were last here.'

That's true, I thought, privately. Think of the list on the print-out: acacia, aloe, almond, aniseed, apricot, beeswax, berberis, camelia, hazel, ivy, juniper, jojoba.

'It is a careful balance we use. What kind of animal extracts are you asking about, Mr Simpson?'

'I was thinking of, say, placental lipids.'

Sir Richard White's face creased slightly. 'What are placental lipids?' he demanded.

'They are derived from the placenta,' I explained. 'The placenta is the nourishing lining of the womb. In certain cases I believe the human womb is used rather than a bovine one. The increase of abortions, particularly in, say, the Eastern European countries, has augmented the availability of such material. But the main source of placental lipids would be from cattle.'

'Good grief.' Sir Richard's voice was incredulous. 'What on earth are these extracts put in cosmetics for?'

'They are supposed to feed the skin. To eliminate wrinkles, for instance. Odd, when you think how wrinkled a baby is on its emergence.'

His face creased. 'Do women know about this?'

'Not directly, Sir Richard.' Bastoni's intervention was serious, unemotional. 'There is a lot of nonsense written by so-called ecological activists about such things. Most of the antipathy at present is directed towards animal testing. That is, testing of cosmetic materials on animals, causing some suffering. Fortunately our hands are clean in that direction. We oppose animal testing. Except in certain specific instances.' He gave me a careful look. 'The psychology of skincare treatments is a complex subject. The Japanese, for instance, use placenta extracts without the slightest sign of squeamishness. Here in Western Europe the trend is away from animal extracts.'

Lavender, I thought, lemon, linseed, liquorice, oat extract, olive oil. Alcohol, of course. In France that would come from sugar. Jojoba, I suppose that's Mexican.

'Does that answer your question?' Bastoni interrupted the sequence.

'Er, yes. Well, not quite. Take hyaluronic acid, for instance.'

'Hyaluronic acid?'

'Yes. It's one of the latest things in skincare technology. A biological polymer.'

'What on earth is it?' Into Sir Richard's voice came the faintly-testy note of a man who is beginning to realize that he has seen the impressive surface of something and knows nothing of what lies beneath.

'It is a water-retainer. It can retain up to six thousand times its own weight in water.'

'Good grief. Where does it come from?'

I grinned. 'A rooster's comb.'

'*What?*'

'The traditional source of hyaluronic acid is from the comb of a cock, Richard. There are new developments in biotechnology that may produce it from bacteria but right now that is where it comes from.'

He stared at me for a brief incredulous moment before speaking. 'Are you telling me, Tim, that this—this acid is obtained from the cranial gristle of barnyard fowls? Mashed up in some way?'

'That's it. Put into a cream, its purpose is to retain water at the surface of the human skin.'

'Good God.' His eyes were wide and he stared at a pot of white moisturizer on Bastoni's desk with visible distaste. 'How indescribably vulgar. Does everybody know about this?'

I shrugged and looked at Bastoni. His stare, resting on me, was unblinking as he spoke, almost sideways, to Sir Richard.

'The ingredients we use here, Sir Richard, are of the purest and the finest. We have to keep up with the latest laboratory developments. Our testing is perfect and unceasing. The products are impeccable. They compare absolutely with all those used by the most famous names in the business. The EEC has started a positive listing of cosmetic ingredients and we use them. It is true that they have only positive-listed two hundred or so out of the eight or ten thousand materials which are used in the industry, but that is not our fault. We do use hyaluronic acid and so do many others. The consumer, frankly, does not look very closely at the ingredients listed on the packaging and even if she, or he, does, there are very few with sufficient technical knowledge to understand what those ingredients are.'

'Amazing.' Sir Richard's tone had become thoughtful.

'We subscribe to all the profession's regulations. It would obviously not be in our interest to promote products that did not work or were damaging to the consumer.' Bastoni was still looking directly at me. 'I am not sure of the purpose, of the drift, of your questions and your, er, examples.'

'Oh.' I gave him a pleasant look, a purely non-aggressive one. 'You mustn't think that I'm some sort of animal-rights freak or anything like that. Nothing like that at all. What I'm trying to assess is the vulnerability of the plan to a major consumer-group attack on such products. The green movement is gathering pace. If we put a lot of money behind product launches that subsequently get hit by vegetarian, or bio-ecology, or anti-animal-extract movements, a lot of money could be lost.'

Palm oil, I thought, peanut oil, peach extract, parsley seed oil, rapeseed oil, raspberry leaf extract, rhododendron, rosemary, safflower, sandalwood, sage, sesame, vanilla, verbena, walnut, wheat germ, yeast, witch hazel; not all of this can possibly originate in France.

Bastoni's face had cleared. 'I understand. I understand your concern perfectly. It is true that a substantial portion of the skincare range at present is based on animal extracts and petroleum products. Ecology activists might well attack this product base. Thierry Vauchamps and I discussed the matter in great detail. It is for this reason that I have conducted an extensive programme of testing and research into what might be called more "natural" ingredients. Plants, herbs, trees and so on. Vegetables and fruit. In many cases we have already started to replace animal extracts with such ingredients. The future product launches will take such materials into them.' He was looking at me more positively now. 'We must not throw away the traditional Bellevie winners, though. Market opinions can change very easily. Lanolin and tallow are as "natural" as any herb. They have been used for many generations. But I think that your concern with that particular risk, quite right though you are to express it, is one which you need not allow to influence you unduly. We can cope with it. If the worst came to the worst, we could change to an all-plant range. But I do not believe that will happen. There will be a market for both types of product, you see. This is an enormous business and consumers are very different, one from another. Many market segments must be satisfied.'

He almost sat back, satisfied with himself. He had reason
to be. His little exposition had seen off any doubts on the
nature of the Bellevie ingredients. Ethnobotanists, vegans
and similarly afflicted persons need not be a problem. That
seemed to be it; I hadn't gone into the question of packaging
because there is more rubbish talked about packaging than
the rubbish caused by the packaging itself. Bonnet hadn't
been chasing after that. Bonnet had been chasing ingredients and I thought the content of them had been the
problem.

Bastoni and Sir Richard were looking at me.

'Well,' I said, closing the thing down, as it were, 'that's
most reassuring. Most reassuring. I think my mind is now
at rest on that score, thank you very much. There's no
difficulty in supply sources for all these—these herbal and
plant remedies, I assume?'

'Oh no' Bastoni said, still watching me. 'None at all.'

'Quite a lot of it, I imagine, is sourced here in France?'

'Quite a lot of it, Mr Simpson—quite a lot of it.'

'Unless, then, Sir Richard has any further queries, I think
we'll leave you in peace. Sir Richard?'

'Oh no,' he said. 'I have no more questions. I am most
impressed, Mr Bastoni.'

'You are very kind.' Bastoni gave him his most charming
smile. 'You are of course welcome here any time. And if
you have any further questions, you have my card.'

'Thank you.'

'May I take you to the station?'

'No, no. That's kind, but Tim here has a car.'

'Oh?' Bastoni looked at me. 'You are driving?'

'For the moment,' I said cheerfully.

'Ah.' He seemed to be about to ask a question, then
changed his mind, beaming at Sir Richard. 'Safe journey,
sir. And I look forward to our future collaboration.'

'Splendid. Thank you again.'

'Thank you, sir. Mr Simpson, thank you too.'

We shook hands with him carefully. I drove back towards
the city and on to the Malakoff station opposite the botan-

ical gardens. Sir Richard was thoughtful and silent for the whole way.

'Christian might not recover,' he said suddenly, as we stopped in the station forecourt.

'He must. For old Charles's sake as much as anything.'

'Life isn't always that kind. Life is a battle, with casualties. You know that.'

'It doesn't smell of coal any more, though.'

'What? What does that mean?'

'Nothing. Just an expression.' I looked out of the window. Not far away the Loire was flowing, wide and important for so long but now without its forests of masts, its cloth and slave trade, its launchings of submarines. Trains and cars and aeroplanes had ended all that.

He frowned. 'If he doesn't recover the only person who'll be able to shed any light on anything is you. The police will have no idea.'

'The police are brighter than we all think. They have methods we cannot use.'

'That's not the point I'm making. What I'm trying to tell you is to watch out.'

'Oh, I see. Thanks. I'll watch out.'

He held out his hand. 'Today has been an important day. Both at the museum and at the factory. I'm very grateful to you.'

I took the hand and shook it, finding it warm again. 'It's been important for me too.'

Under the car roof his eyes reflected dimmed light, quiet tone. 'We will meet again soon.'

'Yes. I hope that by then the two subjects of your visit today will have had much more light shed on them.'

He paused as he was getting out of the car. Behind him the TGV was sliding into the station, the long powerful angle of its sloping nose giving way to the high modern coaches with people looking down from the windows.

'Are you flying back now?' he asked, leaning in to look at me despite the fact that there was only a minute or two before he had to board.

'Not just yet,' I said.

He nodded, closed the door and strode off, a firm grey figure in the late afternoon light. As I put the car into gear I glanced after him and saw him wave, just once, to me.

CHAPTER 26

To take the N23 road out of Nantes towards Angers you drop off the approach to the A11 motorway around La Belle Etoile and make the conscious effort not to speed your way on through the tolls of the *Autoroute de L'Océane*. Coming up from the south of the river, as Michel Bonnet must have done, from the Rezé or St Sébastien side, it must have been a great temptation to accelerate away and off to the east, with Angers, Le Mans and Chartres up ahead. But something had made Michel Bonnet change his mind, drop down to a more humdrum speed, point the nose of his car towards Mauves-sur-Loire and follow the north bank of the river a bit closer than the autoroute does.

Closer, but not close. It's not a particularly scenic route just there. Occasional glimpses of the distant river come up, away to your right, but the road doesn't teeter along the north bank or anything picturesque like that. There are bridges across at Mauves and Oudon but they're little old things tucked away from the N23, which by-passes Oudon deliberately and then swoops in a bit closer to the river before it takes you through the back-centre of Ancenis, from which the D763 crosses the flow and goes back south-west towards Vallet. If you are driving, as you may have gathered that I was, with a map on your lap, one eye on the road and one eye watching the signposts, you tend to try and take in all these alternatives and think them through while not hitting an oncoming beetroot lorry or driving into the back of a tractor sporting a spiked hydraulic harrow at about chest level.

Out of Ancenis the road goes up and down a bit while

taking in a few bends. I stopped at the one Michel Bonnet had terminated at. Completely terminated at. There was no sign of the accident, none whatever, but then there rarely is. It was just a bend, a curve with a downhill angle away to the left, and he had gone off here, to my right, either driven off, or steered off, or forced off. If he had been forced off, there hadn't been any mention of that, nor of scrape marks on the side of the car, or the buckling of an impact. On the other hand since the car was burnt out and the accident itself must have caused scraping, no one much would have bothered about that.

Earlier in the year it must have been much darker in the evening, completely dark in fact, so that the affair would have been one of headlights flashing and smashing, shiny bursts of light if the road was wet—no, no one had said that it was wet. If Morelli and Favez chose their moment right they could have swiped him off the road, done the job in the dark, set fire to the car and been gone within minutes. Then away to have the marks taken off their own car or dump it, or have it processed by a wrecker.

Varades, the next signpost said, Varades and Angers, N23.

What the hell was there between here and Angers? The next big village after Varades is Ingrandes, then comes St Georges. After that, Angers. Why come this way? Why get killed here? Because he was doing something obviously wrong, something that made them suspicious, but what?

Not taking the A11. Taking the N23. As a route to where?

I drove past the fatal corner and came round the long right-hand bend just before Varades. It was an ordinary road, unexceptional. Nothing to get excited about. Nothing on it to catch the eye. I pulled into the side of the road and looked at the map.

At Varades there is a turn north where the D10/D57 goes up to Candé. South, the D752 crosses the river, over the Ile Batailleuse at St Florent and then snakes south to St Pierre Montlimart and Beaupréau, crossing the flat agricultural country to the ringed town of Cholet.

Cholet. Pronounced Cho-lay. Cholly. Jolly. I sat quite still, alone in the car.

Funny, Tim, Jolly—

No, don't speak, Christian! Don't say anything!

Jolly.

Christian said it gasping, trying to get it out. Try saying jolly with your breath rasping, catching at it, heaving, your guts sliced and blood running through your hands.

Laboratories, he'd said. Jolly, funny, Tim.

Cholet.

That was it!

Laboratories Herboristiques de Cholet. Cholet. I had even seen the invoices yesterday, and the name on the purchase ledger. Alcohol, acacia, aloe, almond, apricot, *anise*, berberis, *noisette*, hazel, smaller than *noix*, walnuts. *Huile de noix*, walnut oil.

Laboratories, Christian had said, then something I couldn't catch. Herboristiques? Was it that? The invoices had been there when he looked: ivy, juniper, jojoba, lavender—surely that came from Grasse or somewhere south? —lemon, liquorice, linseed—that's *lin* in French, *graine de lin*, but the oil from this particular lot wouldn't be used to lubricate cricket bats. Peaches, peanuts, parsley, rapeseed. They'd supplied it all. They don't grow peanuts much in France, do they?

We could change to an all-plant range, he'd said. Bastoni said that.

I bet you could.

But there'll be a market for both types of product, he'd said.

The invoices had included pectin and bay oil, keratin and embryo extract.

Not very *herboristique*, embryo extract, the oil-soluble extract of fetal calves. Nor is allantoin, obtained from the oxidation of uric acid. Natural perhaps, but not herbal. And why buy jojoba from a laboratory in Cholet?

Distribution, perhaps.

Alcohol? Surely you'd buy alcohol from a refiner, direct.

Very natural, alcohol, comes from starch and sugar. But not *herboristique*. And not the same sort of thing as all those plant extracts.

Someone must have got very greedy.

I put the car in gear and drove through Varades, out over the river, crossing south. It was getting dark now. The direct route to Cholet from Nantes is not along this route at all. You normally would head down the N149 from Rezé, got on to the N249 to pass Vallet and then straight to Cholet. It's the obvious way.

But if you'd said something, suspected something, maybe even let it slip, then decided to keep that to yourself, not let them know, you might just pretend that you were going back to Paris, cross north of the river heading for the A11 perhaps suspecting you might just be followed that far, then you'd slip off on to the N23 and go along to Varades, as I had, now, and take the D752 to Cholet. A typical French D-category road going cross-country, squeezing itself crankily through villages like St Pierre Montlimart and stopping dead as it wrestles with the streets of Beaupréau on the way.

The trouble is that Bonnet never even got as far as Varades. Once he'd avoided the autoroute and got on to the N23 they'd known, or guessed, from what he'd said, and cut him off before he got there.

I hit the ring road round Cholet and worked my way along it, looking for a Z.I.—a Zone Industriel. I found the one I wanted after twenty minutes frustrating circulation; it was new, typical of any new industrial development on the edge of any town anywhere. The Lab. Herb. de Cholet was signposted to where the building, white and modernistic, stood in a large plot which was already being filled with the framework and new construction materials of a large extension to the premises.

I actually swore out loud at myself.

After all my clever thinking, it had been a simple scam, a straightforward swindle.

I pulled the car up at the wire barrier fence of the property and stood looking in the gloom until Bastoni's 3-litre Alfa-Romeo pulled up alongside and he and another man got out.

I gestured at the extension as they walked a step or two from their car to stand close to me.

'You'll be pushed to fill that warehouse extension if the plan doesn't go through,' I said.

Bastoni was still in the finely-cut suit, straight from the office. The other man was bigger, rougher. He put both hands in his pockets, looked at me, then took them out.

'How much do you want?' Bastoni's voice was quiet, deliberate, like everything about him. Even the original remarks to me when we first met, the slighting reference about Britain and the EEC, must have been deliberate, a probe to find the emotional depth of Bonnet's replacement. And my reaction then had been instinctively right. This was typical, a slice-taking of someone else's money, quietly, clandestinely, and putting it away.

He must have been behind me at the station when the TGV pulled in, at the A11/N23 junctions, at Varades, all the way here, thinking it through with me as he was bound to do.

'How much?' he repeated.

'I beg your pardon?'

A flicker of irritation crossed his face. 'What, then, do you want? Money? Women? Directorships? What do you want?'

'I'm afraid I don't understand.'

'Of course you understand. You understand very well. If you have money you can have the women and the other things as well. You seem to like Tina Buisson. You can have her any time you want; I do not think that will be your requirement. You are a very experienced man, much more than you pretend. Tell me what it is you want.'

Across the road a shift started to come out of a factory and cars were started, revved up. A man shouted at another in a cheerful, valedictory way. A lorry rumbled past. I stared back at the laboratory and the looming skeleton of its new wing. Someone was very greedy. And lethal.

'You own this business, don't you? You sanction all the purchases from Bellevie. They've been growing steadily.' I gestured at the building. 'It's even conveniently close enough for you to visit and check it regularly.'

'You will not find my name among the shareholders of this business.'

'You and Thierry Vauchamps. I looked up your careers. You've worked together in the past. You've both got a stake in this.'

'Neither of us.'

'Nominees, it will be. It might never have been noticed if you hadn't started getting greedy. Alcohol and things like that.'

'Nothing of the sort. This company is competitive for alcohol supplies. From Italy.'

'It's a hell of a good idea. All those herbal things are going to be used a lot. Sources of supply are disparate. A central distributor as well as producer is a good idea. But you're the general manager of Bellevie's factory. You haven't disclosed your interest. Buying from your own company on behalf of Bellevie, lining your pocket at the expense of the Delattres and then the Maucourts, that's fraudulent. Corrupt.'

'You have no evidence of such a connection.'

I sighed. 'If Madame Delattre had not been so preoccupied with the profligacy of her nephews and—and with other matters, she might have noticed. The one person whose duty it was to notice was Thierry Vauchamps, the new general manager. I think he did, or at least his market research manager, who had access to all sorts of figures, did. You fixed him as an accomplice if you hadn't already arranged his appointment somehow. She was having an affair with him and kept quiet, temporarily, even though she must have suspected something. She didn't like it, though. When she let out that Christian was coming to see her and she would have to guide him, she was given an accident, like Bonnet. Bonnet was a real ferret, an accounts-rummager, he smelt something. So you fixed him.'

'Incredible. I could sue you. I have a witness here. All guesswork.'

'So why have you followed me here?'

'We came to see a supplier.'

'At this time of the evening?'

He let out a sort of wheezing breath and looked at the man next to him, then back to me. 'Mr Simpson, I think you are an intelligent man. I think that we are in business for money. All of us. Today I answered all your questions in front of your Sir Richard White satisfactorily, I think you will agree. Now you can recommend that the plan goes ahead.'

'Oh, can I?'

'Yes, you can. I think it would be intelligent to do that. For a start, you would have a position on the board of Bellevie here, then also on the UK company. Both positions would have substantial salaries. If you require your remuneration to be paid in Switzerland, we can arrange that. I cannot see why you should object to this simple and rewarding arrangement. We can discuss other benefits as well. Long-term benefits for all of us. Your future security would not be in doubt.'

'It's interesting that you are making these offers, not Thierry Vauchamps. I would have thought it was for him to decide on his board of directors.'

'He and I are agreed on this matter. We want you to join us. Please understand me, I do not want any more violence to occur. It is in our interest to make sure you are satisfied with the arrangements and that you remain in place while the plan is activated. It is worth a lot of money to us.'

'I'm sure it bloody well is.'

'Do not misunderstand what I am saying. You are obviously capable of taking care of yourself in certain situations but you cannot be ever-vigilant. We have considerable resources and it is, I, not Thierry, who controls them.'

Hackles began to prickle on the back of my neck. I've always responded badly to threats. The man next to Bastoni had his hands well in view, in front of him now, watching me, a dark threat in the half-gloom of industrial estate lamplight. The factory opposite had emptied and the cars driven away. We were alone beside the wire-mesh fence of the Laboratoires Herboristiques. I positioned myself carefully before replying.

'What do you think I will tell Christian Maucourt when he recovers? To forget the whole thing?'

'Christian Maucourt will possibly not recover. If he does, it will be for you to ensure that he does not carry out any more investigations before he leaves for his college in America. That will be part of the conditions of your remuneration. He will be debilitated for some time even in the event of recovery; he will accept your word. You will convince him that there is no impropriety in Laboratoires Herboristiques as a supplier to Bellevie. If, that is, you do not want another accident to occur.'

I hit him then. Just on the side of the jaw, with one of the best straight lefts my old school boxing instructor ever taught me. I should, of course, have hit the other man first, to put him out of action while I dealt faithfully with Bastoni, but I would have had to step across Bastoni and turn, which would lose the initiative and allow him too much warning.

Bastoni went down beside the car with a strange choking cry. The bigger, rougher man grabbed my arm and twisted it savagely back and up.

It was agony.

I've never dealt with a proper wrestler before. He had my arm in both hands, aiming to break it; the nearest thing like it that had ever happened to me was the odd occasion during a scrum, when both front rows are trying to break each other's necks, kicking each other hard, and the bloke opposite tries to wrench your arm out of its socket as well. I had just enough time to squirm round and jab my free thumb full into his eye.

He let out a great screech of pain and let go of my arm with one hand.

I didn't blame him; I've only had a full thumb in the

eye once myself and that was in a seven-a-side match in Northampton, when the opposing full-back stuck his muddy thumb under my left eyelid during an ill-advised ruck near the line. It was terrible. When he withdrew his thumb it seemed as though the whole squashy oyster was being scooped out with it, quite apart from the horror of feeling that half the turf in the county was stuck onto my retina. It finished the match for me; that eye has never been the same since.

I kept the thumb in there, driving his head back while I brought my right heel down on to his foot, pinning him. He grabbed my eye-probing hand in a knuckle-crushing grip and jerked it out with a hoarse cry. My other arm was still being bent back, so I brought my knee up into the place it hurts most, coming off his foot and letting him stagger back to the wire in a grunt of doubled-up pain.

I had him then. Space is necessary for a hitter and kicker like me, and two feet of space is more than enough. My twisted arm was sore but still usable and I hit him twice, once with the good arm and then a chop with the sore one. Then I got into hitting him and kicking him with the rage of repeated fury; the wire fence behind sang with the impacts.

Bastoni started to get up beside the car, pulling himself with his hands on the bonnet. I turned and hit him again, twice, in the stomach where it would hurt. Then I grabbed his jacket, thinking of Berthe Cauvinière, and Christian Maucourt whispering my name as he sank to the landing.

I was blind with rage and murderous in intention.

'That's enough! *Ça suffit!*'

The shout stopped me. There were lights, two or three cars, dark burly figures, people moving towards me.

'Enough,' the same voice said. '*Mon amateur detective anglais*, we do not want you to kill any more important witnesses and criminals. You must leave us someone to put up in court.'

'Inspector Levroux?' I stopped, out of breath, gasping. Bastoni slid to the ground.

'*Moi-même.*' He stood in front of me and tut-tutted

expressively. His hairy-jacketed subordinate watched me with amused interest, his big head cocked to one side.

'How—how on earth did you get here?'

'Oh! I am a French policeman, remember? Not a bobby, pounding the beat in London.' Levroux jerked his head at his big sergeant, who grinned and supervised other dark figures who took hold of the crumpled, stained figure of Bastoni. 'I am not a patient man. But I must congratulate you on your resistance. To bribery. You have refused quite a lot of money. Two salaries, after all; that wouldn't be bad, would it? And in Switzerland, too; tax free.' He made a reproachful wagging movement of his head. 'You have a shocking temper, though. You would never make a policeman. Never. I suspect, however, that it was not the bribe which made you so violent.'

'Eh? How the hell do you know what I refused?'

'I am a French police inspector, Mr Simpson! I have my methods.' He grinned at my bewilderment. '*Allez*, I am not being fair. Look.' He turned to Bastoni's car, felt under the front nearside wing and pulled out a small evidently magnetic object. '*Le petit bug francais! Voilà!* We are addicted to technology these days. This little devil will pick up any conversation within twenty metres with a clarity which is extraordinary. So while you and Sir Richard were talking to Bastoni in the factory we visited the car park.' He gave me a very direct, straight stare. 'There is one on your car as well.'

'Oh. Well, bugger you, too.'

'Oh, come! Do not take offence. You are so touchy. It was for your safety. We did not suspect you. Not after the confession of Thierry Vauchamps this morning. We just had to move fast, that's all, and gather what evidence we could.'

'What?'

He chuckled. 'Now you are allowing me to enjoy myself. Don't look so surprised. Routine police questioning of Vauchamps—all night, so I am very tired—led to his confession.'

'All night?' I was still out of breath, massaging my arm with a spare hand.

'Of course! What do you take us for? Vauchamps had an affair with the murdered woman, Cauvinière. The beautician supervisor—Mademoiselle Buisson—informed us of that. We established that Cauvinière's death was not an accident, or at least it was unlikely. We pulled him in and told him he was suspect number one. Absolutely at the top of the list. Jealousy, or fear of his wife, or both, and possibly a major fraud in the company, which Cauvinière was about to reveal. He cracked. Of course he cracked.' Levroux gestured expressively. 'The murder of Madame Cauvinière had already terrified him; he is not a Bastoni. It is almost impossible for anyone except a really hardened experienced criminal to resist the kind of pressure we can bring to bear. Vauchamps is just a seller of perfumes, a superficial, lightweight fellow incapable of contemplating the rest of his life in one of our more unpleasant prisons.' He smiled significantly.

My arm was returning to normal and I managed to smile back at him. 'An oubliette in the Bastille, I imagine?'

'No, no, my dear Mr Simpson, *vous plaisantez comme tous les anglais*, we do not have oubliettes in the Bastille any more than you have dungeons in the Tower. But we have some modern equivalents, full of very undesirable prisoners of all races with some excruciatingly horrible habits. Vauchamps found himself unable to contemplate such an existence. He told us a most interesting story. And signed it, in writing. My examining magistrate is very convinced.'

'Was I right? This was in Bastoni's control?' I waved towards the wire fence. 'This Laboratoires Herboristiques here?'

'Oh yes. We have details of the bank account of Vauchamps, of course, and Bastoni's, though those do not tell us very much. We also have the details of certain Swiss bank accounts, though, and a chain of share ownerships.' He gave me a calculating look. 'There are some very dangerous connections. From the Italian side. I think you are best advised to retire from the scene and leave the rest to the professionals.'

'I'm sure you're right.'

'Good! After all, you have done your job for your employers. Very well. They must be pleased with you.'

I watched his sergeant nod to the drivers of two cars, one containing Bastoni, the other the arm-twisting heavy. The cars started to move off and the sergeant came back to grin pleasantly at me from the depths of his hairy jacket.

'That was pretty good,' he said, patting my arm with a huge hand. 'The fellow you knocked to bits on the fence wire was supposed to be a real crusher. That thumb in the eye: *formidable*. I must remember that one. You're very dangerous when you're in a temper, aren't you?'

I looked at him and Levroux indignantly.

'Why didn't you just arrest Bastoni right out, instead of following him and me all the way here and letting me go through all this mullarkey? Eh?'

'You are so irritable.' Levroux shook his head sadly. 'You said that you English have such sang-froid; what has happened to you? You forgot your promise, *perfide anglais*; you remember your promise? No amateur detective work? You have been very *méchant*, even if you are scrupulously honest. But you must realize that for a policeman like me, the more we can hear and learn, the better our case will be. Bastoni will now say nothing. Absolutely nothing. But while he was still free and having to cope with you he could have let out all sorts of information. That he hired Morelli and Favez has been established; that he controls this swindle also. I was hoping for a little more, perhaps something about who controls him, in turn. Alas, that I did not get. Nor any confession about Madame Delattre. Vauchamps insists that must have been an accident. He denies anything to do with the death of the lady. I was hoping, but you extracted nothing on that.'

'I'm sorry.'

'It is not your fault. Without you, this whole thing might not have come to light at all.' A smile whitened his face in the half-light.' So now I have an offer to make to you. My sergeant and I are very tired. We are also very hungry. What I propose is that we go back to Nantes and I show you how a Frenchman dines when he wishes to impress a foreigner. Especially *un perfide anglais*. What do you say? Are you willing to be impressed As my guest?'

I wiped my hand on my handkerchief, finding all of a sudden that there was blood on it.

'I am willing,' I said, 'to be impressed.'

CHAPTER 27

'You look,' Sue said, as she put a plate of scrambled eggs on toast in front of me, 'very smart. Very polished. Quite the proper appearance for your meeting.'

I stared at the plate of scrambled eggs in surprise. Sue never normally makes breakfast. Usually I make tea for myself and coffee for her; toast or cereal gets made or appears on an as-and-when basis from either of us. This was something special; the dutiful wife was getting hubby out to work suitably braced for his day's encounters.

'The condemned man,' I said, picking up a knife and fork, 'ate a hearty breakfast.'

'Oh, Tim! Don't be such a gloomy old trout! Whether it's New York or Paris or London, at least you've got a choice! A lot of people haven't even got a choice.'

'True.' I forked up a mouthful of egg. The sun was shining brightly outside and light flooded our flat in Onslow Gardens. Our flat in Onslow Gardens; if we went abroad I supposed I'd have to sell it, or let it if the market stayed as it was: depressed. Letting it would probably be better. We might need somewhere to come back to, one day.

On the wall above the fireplace the man-o'-war beating its way to Clarkson Stanfield's Medway port had got no further. Spume and spray flew past its heaving timbers. I began to feel sympathy for it. The other paintings in the room, mostly Sue's, were of calmer scenes, things painted by ladies such as Sylvia Gosse and Laura Knight, Dod Proctor and Elizabeth Stanhope Forbes. Still lifes and circuses, with an interior by Ethel Walker. It was ridiculous; how could I just separate Sue from everything that made up the colour of her life?

'It'd be quite fun to go abroad for a bit,' Sue said brightly, spooning up some fibrous cereal of an improving character.

'A rolling stone gathers no moss,' I grunted, through the egg.

She compressed her lips. 'Nothing venture, nothing gain,' she retorted.

'There's an answer to that but I can't think of it.'

'Tim, what is the matter with you? It isn't just this meeting you've got. There's something else on your mind. What is it?'

I looked at her affectionately. There's little I can keep from Sue.

'Madame Delattre,' I said.

She put her spoon down. 'Madame Delattre? What about her?'

'They say—Bastoni and Vauchamps—that they had nothing to do with her death. She just fell, or was accidentally pushed, off the platform. And do you know, I think that they're probably speaking the truth. About that, anyway. There was no reason for them to kill her. Bonnet had told her nothing. When he phoned from Nantes, the evening of his death, Berthe Cauvinière asked if he wanted to speak to her. Vauchamps wasn't there. And Bonnet said no, it didn't concern Madame Delattre. Nothing to do with the shop. So she was no danger from that point of view. Why should they kill her? They've admitted to Bonnet and Berthe Cauvinière, but they absolutely deny killing Madame Delattre.'

'But Vauchamps wanted to re-vamp the shop. You said so. All that *crypte lugubre* stuff. She was in the way.'

'He had me to take care of that. He wouldn't have done

anything before I'd had a go at her. I was there to look after that problem.'

'That's true. She was obviously worried about you, you old pug-ugly. That's why she wanted to see you so quickly.'

'I don't think that it was about the shop at all.'

Sue stared at me, spoon still down. 'What was it, then?'

I had a mental image of Eugène Maucourt, cold and upright, gesticulating with the De Gaulle-like gesture in his office, wanting nothing to stop him. Then of Charles Maucourt, stocky and genial despite battles of life that would have destroyed so many weaker men. Nothing cold about Charles Maucourt; lots of life and fire and, presumably, love. Could he have done it? Was there a final point beyond which he could be pushed?

'I think it was about Tissots.'

Her face contracted. 'Oh, Tim! Oh please! No! Don't start! Please! Ever since you made me open up *The Ball on Shipboard* and those I've had a dread fear in my heart. Ever since then. Don't please tell me you're going to, that there's something else, that it isn't all over! Please! I beg you! Please! Don't go dredging up the past any more!'

She was white with anxiety. It pushed the Maucourts out of mind. One of them had done it, all my instincts told me, but I would never know which one. Bastoni had been just a simple crook, a fraudster, channelling business into his own pocket and killing those who threatened him. But the Maucourts had made sure I came to Paris, alerted me to Tissot then almost certainly found Madame Delattre across the path. Did she threaten? Had she been blackmailing old Charles, bleeding him white over wartime booty? Surely Charles's gallantry to an old flame did not demand that he ruin himself; there had to be some coercion. She was fit and active, even I'd seen that, and she was ready to talk to me. Not the sort of woman to fall under a train. Not with such extraordinary timing.

'Tim?'

There was nothing I could prove, no point in hopeless digging, making enemies close to home. What would I gain, now? I got up, went round to Sue, took her hand in mine, put my arm round her shoulder and squeezed her. 'Don't take on, Sue,' I said. 'There's nothing I'm going to do.'

'But I can see it in your face! I've seen that look before! Unfinished business, an unknown element, something you want to go after. It's there now.'

'I've promised you. I'm promising you now. It's all over.'

'How can it be over? With you?'

I let go of her and grinned. 'Why shouldn't it be?'

'Because it never has been in the past! That's why! Don't grin at me like that!'

My face returned to a serious expression. 'In the past, would it be fair to say that it was all over once I had the work or works of art concerned in my possession? Would that be fair to say?'

She hesitated. 'Well—yes—I suppose. Once the Fund got the piece.'

'Well, there you are, then.'

'There I am? Where? Where am I?'

'Exactly where I told you. It's all over and you've nothing to worry about.' I went back to my seat and finished polishing off the scrambled egg. 'I mustn't be late for an important meeting. The knives are out for the Art Fund. Once my position is established, I mean where I stand and what options I've got, I have to make an important decision affecting both our lives. I shall do the best I can.'

'You haven't answered my question!'

'Oh yes I have. I've promised you I shall do nothing about Madame Delattre. And I meant it. Although my mind may, from time to time, become preoccupied with thinking what the truth may be, about people who push Tissot and Reitlinger under my nose, there is little danger of my having the slightest chance of establishing it. And to reassure you, to convince you that there is no danger, I have made you the first to know that I have acquired the items for the Fund.'

'Items? You mean the Tissots?'

'Yes. All three of them.'

'All three of them?' She actually dropped her spoon into the improving cereal with a soft splash of skimmed milk.

'Yes.' I got up and wiped egg off my mouth. 'All three of them. You need have no fear about my pursuing matters any further.'

As I went round the table once again to give her another reassuring squeeze and an explanation, my eye fell on the Clarkson Stanfield and its sea-tossed man-o'-war.

'All that,' I said, 'has been just a passing storm.'

CHAPTER 28

Sir Richard White chaired the meeting. It wasn't in Jeremy's office. It was held in the main boardroom. Peter Lewis, bald and shiny, sat to his left. Geoffrey Price, our finance director, sat on his right. Jeremy White sat opposite me, next to Geoffrey. I sat next to Peter Lewis. We all said good morning to each other, very cautiously.

'Before we start,' Sir Richard said, evenly, 'I have a message for you, Tim.'

'Richard?'

Jeremy moved his head slightly at this exchange of familiarities, looked at me, frowned slightly, and cleared his face again.

'Christian Maucourt,' Sir Richard said to me, 'who is improving daily, asked me to reproach you for not visiting him before you left. His father and mother have returned to the United States. He is still very weak but he expects to see you shortly.'

'Thank you. Tell him I'll see him, for sure, next week.'

'Very good. I'll do that. There is a letter here for you, from his father.'

He passed it across and I put it carefully away in my folder, in front of me on the table. Now was not the time to bask in undeserved gratitude.

'To business,' Sir Richard said. 'The item on the agenda is the Art Fund.'

Jeremy's face flickered at me and Geoffrey. We tried to remain impassive.

'I much appreciate,' Sir Richard said, 'your agreement to discuss the Fund now, to make this, so to speak, your normal monthly meeting. Following the structural changes approved by the main board last week and my—return, so to speak, to active participation, it has been required that we should examine the question of the Art Fund and its resourcing from the Bank's personnel. I have read Geoffrey's admirable résumé and examined the accounts. I think I am quite clear in my mind what the state of the Fund now is. Has there been any further activity since your last monthly meeting? Any acquisitions or disposals?'

Jeremy looked at me. I couldn't help smiling slightly.

'Yes,' I said. 'I have acquired, on behalf of the Fund, three important paintings by James Tissot. The cost, to the Fund, is one million three hundred thousand pounds.'

Geoffrey Price's jaw dropped. Peter Lewis, beside me, stirred fitfully and let out a sharp cry. Jeremy, across the table, for the first time revealed a tiny sparkle in his eyes.

'Oh, well done, Tim.' he said. 'How frightfully exciting!'

Sir Richard White's eyes widened, then went back to their normal dim tone.

'I should explain,' I said, 'that the paintings were put in for auction to a firm in Paris—I was advised by Charles Massenaux of Christerby's—but, of course, on the Continent auctioneers act as agents and middlemen, as well as auctioneers in the sense that ours do. I made an offer before auction and it was accepted. The paintings were estimated, together, to be worth two million and the most important, a Thames scene, could certainly be valued at a million. The lawyer acting for the vendor obviously recommended that a bird in hand is worth two in the bush, especially in today's market. I believe that the paintings are an important acquisition for the Fund and certainly the price is fair to both parties.'

Sir Richard White cleared his throat. 'Surely,' he said, 'such an important acquisition requires clearance from the other trustees, not just by you alone?'

'Oh, of course,' I said. 'My offer is subject to approval by Jeremy and Geoffrey. Which approval I am now asking for.'

Jeremy smiled. 'I thoroughly approve. Providing, of course, there are no difficulties as to title? Who is the vendor? What provenance and so on?'

'Ah. There we do not know. The vendor wishes to remain anonymous. The lawyers acting for the vendor have offered a guarantee of clean title. They are one of the most respected firms in Paris. I have taken legal advice both here and in Paris. The subject is very complex but such a guarantee is virtually cast iron. If anything went wrong we could sue those lawyers.'

Jeremy shrugged. 'In that case I thoroughly approve. Pity not to have a provenance, though, Tim. You're sure they're genuine?'

'No doubt of it.'

'But no record of ownership?'

'I'm afraid not. You know how works of art can go missing.'

'Of course. Even Rembrandts appear from nowhere. Let alone Tissots. I approve. Geoffrey?'

Geoffrey Price nodded hastily. 'Oh yes. I mean, what's good enough for Tim is good enough for me. We have the cash in hand.'

'Passed, then. Next subject?'

Sir Richard White's eyes were directly on mine. For a moment we looked almost full into each other's minds. The Musée des Beaux-Arts at Nantes was what I thought of, and of him, sitting silent before the prodigal's Victorian return. Then Eugène, the son who hated Agnès Damprichard Delattre, and then old Charles, who had given her everything to the point of ruin, and the Franche-Comté, with Sir Richard and the two of them on the run, splitting up into different groups and combinations in danger, out on the mountains at night, huddling for warmth. The lawyer had said owner, not owners. My head said Charles, the money is going to Charles. The lawyer never indicated that the owner was deceased. What final claim, then, could she have made on him? Had she disputed the ownership? Was that what she was going to warn me about? Was she going to the lawyer to stake a claim? To foul up my clean purchase?

Eugène or Charles: either of them could have done it.

Or neither.

'The next subject,' Sir Richard White said, evenly, 'is the resourcing of the Fund. You meet once a month. Geoffrey has indicated that the accounting is not onerous but it has a requirement of man-hours as indicated in the accounts. Jeremy is effectively chairman and needs one meeting a month. The actual acquisition work lies with Tim. This requires monitoring of art sales statistics and an element of judgement, very important of course, but not always time-consuming. Do you agree?'

Jeremy grunted and gave me an appealing look.

'Not always time-consuming,' I agreed, 'but possibly because I am able from time to time to call on the resources and expertise of my wife at the Tate Gallery to assist me without cost to the Fund.'

There was silence. Jeremy smiled faintly at me and produced the ghost of a wink.

'I see.' Sir Richard nodded slowly. 'I see. The point is well made. And the point is taken.'

Peter Lewis stirred fitfully again and spoke for the first time. 'As an activity, though— his voice was harsh—'it's not exactly full-time, is it?'

'No one has ever pretended it has been.'

He frowned. 'It can hardly occupy you more than a day or two a month. And I hear you've turned down the offer to become managing director of Bellevie?'

'I have. Bellevie needs a proper marketer, not me. Someone from L'Oréal, or Revlon, or Unilever. Someone who'll modify Vauchamps' plan sensibly along the lines I've indicated in my report. In a couple of years Bellevie can be expanded further or sold at a good profit to one of the big five. I've no doubt of that. Any involvement of mine should only occur if I were to join Maucourt's and exercise a watching brief, a non-executive role, as I do for Christerby's. No more.'

'Well.' Lewis turned further towards me. 'In that case, I suggest you do just that. Or go off to join Howarth in New York. That would fit in well with your role with Christerby's. Or, since you're so bloody versatile, do both.'

Jeremy half-rose from behind his side of the table as he spat out words between his teeth. 'Now see here, Lewis—'

'Gentlemen!' Sir Richard's voice cut through sharply. 'Gentlemen! There must be no animosity! No vulgar factions, please! We are not here to push Tim into that decision today.' His look met mine once again, briefly, seeing deep as he spoke. 'Besides, there is an alternative.'

'An alternative?' Jeremy sank back into his chair, still glowering.

'Yes.' Sir Richard wasn't looking at me now. 'There is an alternative. I am, as as a result of the latest board decision, to divide my time between my duties at Maucourt's and here. I do not, however, propose to return to live full-time in England. One of the pleasures of old age is the relative freedom it brings, provided one's health is intact. For most people, however, lack of funds restricts that freedom. I am in the happy position of being able to come and go on genuine business activity. I shall travel between London and Paris. There is a need, however, for a proper co-ordination of activities in Europe and Britain as we and Maucourt's expand and diversify within the new structure. I need an anchor man and the two Banks need someone to make sure there are not conflicts of interest, clashes of activity. Such a person would need to enjoy the confidence of both banks, would need to be bilingual and could be stationed where convenient in view of both Banks' international activities. It could be London or Paris. I do not need to tell you, here, who could fill that role.'

Jeremy blinked. Lewis stirred again. Geoffrey goggled.

'Tim has the absolute confidence of the Maucourt family. Both in terms of his ability and, more importantly, in terms of tact and discretion. He could monitor the co-ordination of our combined activities excellently. They would accept him completely.'

As he said the words tact and discretion Sir Richard's eyes met mine once more, grey and expressionless. Charles, my head said, it has to be Charles Maucourt. He'll make a come-back, too. We live in the age of the older man. And woman.

'Monitor? Good God, Tim, he's turning you into another Jacques Delors!' Jeremy was boisterous. 'Who would this *éminence grise* report to?'

'I suggest,' Sir Richard replied, 'that it should be to me. For those co-ordinating activities. Since I shall only be in London virtually half-time or less, there would be no hindrance to his continuing with the Art Fund or for, for special projects to another director such as yourself. But make no mistake; he would have to be in Paris on regular visits, too. If, that is, he chose to base himself here.'

They all looked at me.

'My,' Lewis said, still harsh, 'what an *embarras de richesses* for you. Paris, or New York or London. Which is it to be?'

'I think,' I said slowly, 'I need two days' notice of that question. Then I can answer it.'

'Fair enough.' Sir Richard's voice went brisk. 'It is perfectly right that Tim should have two days in which to make his decision. I think that is all we need to discuss today. Any other business? No? Then the meeting is closed.'

He didn't actually bang down a gavel but he might just as well have. They all stood up. Shiny Peter Lewis turned sharply and was gone; Geoffrey Price nodded, winked, and left. Jeremy walked round the table and held out his hand.

'Uncle Richard,' he said. 'Welcome back.'

'Thank you, Jeremy.' The other took his hand. 'It's good to be back.'

They actually grinned at each other; families are unreadable to an outsider.

Then they both smiled at me.

In the painting called *The Fatted Calf* in Nantes there is still that extra man at the happy riverside table, the one with the naval-looking clothes, whispering something that may be directed at the prodigal son, but may be something else. Whether it is temptation or encouragement is very hard to tell. I shouldn't have let images like that prey on my mind, especially not at moments like this.

But you know me; I still believe those two beautiful young women in the centre of *The Ball on Shipboard*, down in the basement of the Tate, with their beautiful black and white Worth dresses, are the Jerome sisters, or at least were inspired by the Jerome sisters. It's too good a story not to think that there is Jennie, about to meet Lord Randolph Churchill, and there is Clara, who would one day become Mrs Moreton Frewen.

You see what you want to see, in any painting you look at.

The trouble is that, with Tissot, you never can tell. They said that he was a painter of vulgar society, a loafer, a ladykiller, served by mysticism and cunning, a shallow man, with eyes like a poached mackerel who found a new enthusiasm every few years so as to take out another little lease on existence, yet who exhibited a laconic practicality in the pursuit of his life and career.

You see what you want to see, in any artist you look at.